WIDOW'S WALK

A rooftop platform once used by sea captains
to survey the harbor.
Later haunted by their wives, watching the
waves for ships that never
returned.

For the girls they tried to tame.
And the boys who learned why that was a bad idea.

This is a DARK, fictional romance. Twisted, raw, and not for the faint of heart. For readers 18 and over. It contains mature and potentially triggering content. For a full list of trigger warnings, please visit the author's website.

They say she waits on the widow's walk.
Watching the sea.
Hoping for his return.
Cute. Love is a myth.
The bedtime story girls get before handing them a collar.
I was given threats and bruises.
Not lullabies.
I grew teeth where innocence should've bloomed.
I've heard the fairytales.
Read the poems.
Burned them all.
They raised me to kneel.
I learned to bare my teeth instead.
They tried to tame me.
I bit back. Hard.
Pain can be turned into power.
If you're twisted enough to use it.
I wear mine like eyeliner.
Sharp and black.
A monster in mascara.
I don't wait for ships.
I sink them.
If I'm on the widow's walk.
I'm not the woman searching the horizon.
I'm the widow with fangs.
And a silk web.

Joon kharâsh—Soul-scraper
Baba—father/dad
Maman—mother/mom
Zan-e sheytâne eslâh-nâpazir—The incorrigible she-devil
Kīram to khodam!—Fuck me!
(Literal meaning is, My dick in myself!)
Kīram to mādar-e kasi ke—Motherfucker
(Literal meaning, My dick in the mother of someone who...)
Kīram to in zendegi—Fuck everything
(Literal meaning, My dick to this life)
Goh khordam—I fucked up
(Literal meaning, I ate shit)
Dāram divoone misham—I'm fucking losing it
Che ghalati kardam?—What the fuck did I do?
Jāné del-am—The life of my heart
Haroomzāde-ye vasvasashi—Fucking seductress/That damned temptress
Lanati, kheili zibāyi—Fuck, you're so beautiful

PROLOGUE

I glance around at my family, cloaked in black, their faces taut with pretense as they gather around my sister's coffin.

All dry eyes. Not a tear in sight, except for my mother's. It's the first time I've ever seen her cry, but I know better than to mistake it for grief. That would require a heart, and I've finally determined she does not have one.

I used to believe otherwise. Used to beg for signs of softness. But hope is a fragile thing, and mine died the moment she forgot my thirteenth birthday.

And that was only months ago.

Since then, I've accepted the truth. I am nothing to her. I am nothing to any of them. My mother is no different than the men who torment me—my brothers, my father. Blood ties don't mean love in this family. They mean power, silence, and obedience.

When I let go of that last ember of hope, I felt...free. Liberated. As if the invisible tethers binding my heart to theirs finally snapped. I was no longer a prisoner to the idea of family. My heart now beats to a dark rhythm, one that doesn't belong to humanity. One that belongs to survival.

But even untethered, just as they are, I'm still an outcast.

So, my mother's tears aren't for my sister. They're for the idea of her. For losing the perfect daughter. The paragon of one. She was the oldest of us four siblings. Not only was the nine-year age gap a significant separation, but she and I could not be more different.

She was everything they wanted. Obedient, docile, blank. A vessel for legacy, for marriage contracts, for silence.

Gwendolyn was never my enemy, but she was never my shield either. And once upon a time, I was her shadow. Her wide-eyed little sister, trailing after her like she hung the stars. But that innocence quickly died.

She never joined in on the cruelty, but when the abuse escalated, I waited for her protection. It never came. She stood on the sidelines, quiet, composed, pretending not to see. Then later when the bruises bloomed and the blood dried, she'd patch my wounds in secret.

One month ago...

"When will you ever learn, Sinclair?" she muttered as she wiped the blood from my lip, a slight shake to her hand as she started in on my knuckles. "Keep your head down and stay out of their way. As soon as they get the smallest rise out of you, they become rabid. Like two dogs with a bone."

"I refuse to be submissive." I couldn't keep the accusation out of my tone.

Her eyes darted to the floor in shame, and I almost felt bad. "It's how you survive."

She didn't survive.

My sister's death doesn't bring me sorrow. It brings fire, an unforgiving blaze that's been smoldering in me for years, now erupting into something untamable. It doesn't destroy me, it reforges me into something sharp, unyielding, and nothing like what my family ever intended.

There are no warm memories here. Extended family and people I've never met approach me with their monotone condolences. None of them offered comfort or embraced me. It would almost be weird if anyone did. I'm not even sure if I ever remember being hugged.

After the funeral, we return to the estate to host the usual round of mourners and snakes in tailored suits. I want to disappear, to crawl into bed and vanish into silence. But voices from my father's office have me switching routes.

I turn toward the west wing instead, where I know I can eavesdrop. There's a vent in a bathroom directly above his office. I discovered it last year after watching a movie. Turns out, it actually works.

I enter the empty guest room and close the door behind me. Then, going into the bathroom, I lie down beside the vent and press my ear to the grate. Telling from the subject of discussion, it's the Golzars.

My stomach coils. My sister's death has obviously thrown a wrench in the arrangement with Blackwell Golzar, their oldest son. He was supposed to marry Gwen, sealed in blood and money.

My father's voice, that stings like a blade, cuts through the vent. "I still have another daughter."

My blood runs cold.

"No," another male's voice snaps. "I will not marry a child."

Blackwell Golzar, I presume. The voice didn't sound so cruel in nature, but disgusted. Furious even.

Though I am no child, I take no offense. I only feel relief.

Then one of my brothers opens his foul mouth. I brace for the usual toxic chorus, but something unexpected happens. Blackwell uses his booming voice to shut him down, and the room falls silent for a beat. I've never heard anyone talk to my brothers that way, and live to tell the tale.

I'm sure I will regret my choice later, but I have to see him. Blackwell. I've seen him only in passing, but I never really looked. He was just another man in a suit then. Another predator-in-waiting. But not now.

I bolt down the hallway, forcing myself to slow before I hit the stairs. I descend casually, trying not to look like my heart is hammering out of my chest.

I stop and post up outside of the office and begin to pace, pretending to be lost in thought. Despite every internal warning, I wait with anxiety and excitement.

The door swings open, and he comes rolling out like a storm. Shoulders tense, eyes ablaze. He stops the second he sees me. I stand there like a deer in headlights as he stares back.

My eyes break from his to study the rest of him, knowing I only have a second or two to do so. Dark eyes, nearly black, framed by thick lashes. His hair almost as dark, and rich skin from his Persian roots on his father's side.

He's handsome, objectively. But more than that. He's formidable. A grown man, and I'm barely a teenager.

His gaze rakes over me with something like contempt, or maybe horror, scowling before turning away without a word. Only a thunderous silence and the slam of the front door echoing in his wake.

But for a single second, he looked at me. Really looked at me as if I weren't invisible. And for the first time in my life, someone saw me.

I didn't mean to end up in the kitchen. I just needed to get away. From the murmuring guests, the cold stares. My feet carried me on autopilot until I found myself standing beneath the harsh fluorescent lights and the scent of roasting meat.

The clatter of pans and rhythmic shuffle of prep work came to a halt the moment they noticed me. They stopped and stared.

Then, like someone had hit the play button, they turned away. Back to their chopping and stirring, murmuring to each other in voices too low for me to hear. Pretending as if I weren't even there. Which I appreciate right now. I don't want eyes on me. It's why I wandered in here in the first place.

I drift further in, hands behind my back. I peek into a simmering pot, pass a tray of neatly cut vegetables. Floating through until I end up next to a man who drew me to him.

He's tall, but not like the men I'm used to seeing. Older than my father, but not yet greying. The only one who hadn't looked at me like the others when I entered the room. Not with suspicion, as if I were here to make trouble. Not with pity for the girl being raised by animals. He looked at me with calm, quiet curiosity.

I feel his eyes on me, and I learned long ago to never back down to a stare down. So, I meet his eyes with mine, unwavering. But I almost lose the contest when he gives me a small, but warm, smile. It's not something I'm used to.

"You hungry, little shadow?" he asks. Simply *asks*. Doesn't lash or bark.

My breath catches in my throat. I don't verbally respond. Only nod my head once.

"My name's Baxter."

CHAPTER ONE

T he Golzars are in my house.

I started drinking the moment I heard they were coming. Not sipping, but drinking. Not because I'm nervous because fuck that. I'd like to be in the right frame of mind when people start negotiating over my uterus.

Right now, I'm standing directly outside my father's office, leaning against the wall with a wine bottle in one hand and the stem of my patience snapping in the other. Two mob gnomes stand flanking the door like little lawn ornaments, trying to pretend like I'm not here. But the way their shoulders lock up when I shift tells me otherwise. They're skittish, and it puts a little smile on my face.

"The engagement will be announced next month. We'll host a party in honor of it," I hear my father say, I'm sure he's sitting behind his mahogany desk, trying to puff his chest out for the Golzars.

"Our family accepts," a deep, unfamiliar voice says.

A long pause follows it, and someone clears their throat. "Yes, we accept," another deep voice adds with a disgruntled manner like he's chewing on broken glass.

A dark chuckle happens, and the first unfamiliar voice speaks again. "I apologize for my son's surliness. He's still coming to terms with the arrangement."

Translation: He doesn't want to marry the psychopath you're offering.

My father's chortle makes my eye twitch. It's the kind of sound that makes you want to set something on fire.

"I'm sure the rumors about my daughter have something to do with it." He laughs again, and others join in this time. "I assure you, she only needs a firm hand, and she'll stay in line. But she's young and in good health. Should give you plenty of heirs."

My nostrils flare, and I white-knuckle the bottle in my hand. One of the gnomes scoots slightly like he's preparing for impact. I smirk at him, but he won't look at me. I lean in closer and imagine what it would be like to turn men to stone with a glance.

What Athena meant as punishment, Medusa turned into power.

"It's her sanity I'm uneasy about," comes a voice that has been living rent-free in my mind for years.

Blackwell. His voice, darker now. Sharper. Still low, still lethal. And still maddeningly disinterested.

"Oh, she's harmless," my father says dismissively, and I nearly burst into laughter.

The wine hits my throat against the giggles. *Harmless.* That's adorable. Pitiful, deluded man. The mob pups go rigid as if I'm about to do something to prove my father wrong.

"She's a fucking kook," Blackwell snaps. "I was promised your older daughter, not *her*."

The dead sister card. I roll my eyes so hard I nearly see God. Spinning around, I take another sip from the bottle. "At ease, boys," I say with a lazy salute.

I'm off to find some trouble.

I meander through the halls, barefoot and bottle dangling from my fingers. The house is always crawling with men. Testosterone around every corner. But they all avoid me like the plague.

I duck into one of the sitting rooms. Doesn't matter which one. Almost all of them have a mini bar. Some with bottles collecting dust, while others have hardly anything left.

I pluck a bottle from the cluster of wines and continue my tour of agonizing boredom.

They think I'm insane. But here's the thing no one tells you about going mad. It's not always a tragedy. Sometimes, it's evolution.

And they only have themselves to blame.

CHAPTER TWO

Blackwell

W hen I asked Anthony Ortiz if his daughter would be in attendance, the arrogant bastard nearly dismissed me with a scoff.

Apparently, he doesn't believe women warrant a seat at his table. Especially *that* daughter. But he must've sensed his mistake because immediately after we finalized the contract and raised glasses in that farce of a toast, he granted me permission to 'find her' as if she were a roaming cat.

I assume he thought the gesture was courteous. It was condescension, thinly veiled. Fine by me. I prefer handling things my own way anyways.

I haven't seen Sinclair Ortiz in years. Not since she was a pale little thing who hid behind her dyed hair and eyeliner like war paint. The whispers about her have only grown since her sister's death.

Madness. Violence. Isolation.

A girl better suited to an asylum than an estate.

The rumors about her and her state of mind had me conflicted with keeping the agreement between our families after the older daughter died. But I've put it off for as long as I could. Until my father finally gave me an ultimatum. Choose a daughter from one of three families, or he would.

I didn't choose *her*. I chose what was easy to manipulate. The Ortiz empire is valuable, but its owners are brittle. And should something unfortunate befall Anthony Ortiz, pushing out his two sons wouldn't require much force. With Sinclair, I can dismantle the remnants from within.

She is not my bride. She is my strategy.

"Where is Sinclair?" I ask the two guards loitering near the main corridor.

They exchange glances like startled prey. "She might be up in her room, sir," one says stiffly.

"Pacing her widow's walk," the other mumbles.

I turn to him slowly. "And where the fuck is that?" My tone is murderous.

His eyes slightly widen. "Upstairs, sir. Then left. There's a second staircase. Leads up to her quarters."

I blink. "In the attic?" They look like bobbleheads as they both nod in unison. "If you're fucking with me..." I warn.

"No, sir. She really lives up there."

Christ.

I leave them with a sharp glare, following their simple instructions, until I find the second staircase.

The steps groan beneath my weight. The higher I climb, the more I question my sanity. Maybe I should've waited. Set a meeting. Arrange a formal introduction on neutral ground. In daylight, with witnesses.

But something about catching her off guard appealed to me.

When I reach the top, I pause outside the door. Haunting and oddly soothing classical music seeps through the cracks. I try the knob, and find it unlocked.

Of course. No fear. No caution. Welcoming danger.

The door opens into a room belonging to a villainess from a different century. Black wallpaper shimmers faintly with baroque patterns under the flicker of dozens of lit candles. A maroon chaise lounge sits beneath the ceiling-high bookshelf, dozens of books cluttering it with worn spines. An open door reveals a black-tiled bathroom with a clawfoot tub that gleams under low light.

Heavy velvet drapes pool near the windows, and there's one thing that is out of place, like an angel in Hell. A grand piano. White. Pristine. Smooth.

I float past it, brushing the keys with a fingertip before reaching the oversized bed. The covers are askew, the scent lingering around it oddly sweet. Foliage drapes from a built-in canopy, vines curling down toward the large open window. A sheer curtain billows in the night breeze. And through it, her.

She stands barefoot on the rooftop platform, bottle of alcohol hanging from one hand, as her toes meet the edge. No barrier between her and the abyss. Black lace flutters around her like the wings of a mourning moth. Her bleached hair is messily tied, loose strands brushing the back of her neck. Her silhouette is all sharp lines and soft curves, ethereal and grotesquely beautiful beneath the moonlight. It's no wonder why men fear her. She is beauty, and she is chaos.

"Jesus Christ," I mutter. "What the fuck are you doing?" I say loud enough for her to hear. "You're going to fall and break your goddamn neck."

She doesn't flinch. Instead, she laughs, and it's light and eerie. "Oh, Blackwell," she sings, turning slowly. Her bow is theatrical and taunting. "My betrothed. I didn't expect you to enter my *kooky* lair so willingly." Her grin widens as her eyes glint, catching the word *kooky*—the one I had so graciously labeled her with earlier.

Good to know she listens.

She raises the bottle and takes a long drink, immediately wincing. "Ugh, I thought this was wine." She inspects the label with a crinkle of her nose, then shrugs it off and drinks again. "Tastes like varnish. Warms the belly though."

"Get your ass in here. Now," I demand, agitation rising. And we are *just* properly meeting. How will we make it to the altar?

She smiles lazily, and the moonlight catches on what looks like a diamond on her tooth. "Or what? You'll write me a stern letter? Call off the wedding?"

"You're deranged," I mutter.

Her smile widens. "And you're catching on." She looks away. "And it wouldn't just break my neck, I'd die," she quips, glancing over the edge. My heart jumps when she sways, and her laugh rings out like a dare. "The look on your face. Priceless."

"Sinclair—"

"Oh, come on. This would be perfect for you. No wedding. No mad wife. Just an unfortunate accident. Poor Sinclair, gone with the wind."

My fists curl at my sides, nails biting into my palms as I force myself to stay perfectly still. If I startle her, she might go toppling over and it'll look like I pushed the bitch, so I didn't have to marry her. And knowing the vulturous minds of her family, it wouldn't take much to spin.

She gasps after taking another swig and looks at the bottle in approval. "It gets better after a few sips."

She grins, then her eyes widen as she feigns another stumble. My heart seizes, but I keep my expression impassive this time.

"Oh, shit," she breathes, eyes still wide, hand splayed across her chest like she's just survived a thrill ride. She turns to me, laughing softly, her chest rising and falling with exhilaration. "Well, that was a rush."

I realize that one wasn't a game.

"You're only confirming everything I've heard." I take a measured breath and extend a hand toward her. "Now, come inside."

Her face softens, and she turns her back to me again. Sighing in contempt and cursing under my breath, I climb out onto the platform. The drop below is most definitely a death sentence.

We stand side by side in the moonlight. I keep my face forward, but I can see her in my peripheral staring blankly out into the darkness that surrounds the night. The silence we're engulfed in isn't at all uncomfortable.

"Do you know they call this your widow's walk?" I ask, unable to help myself.

She smiles faintly. "It is. In both definition and theory." She glances at me, gauging my reaction, then returns her gaze to the night. "It's a northern thing, dating back centuries or whatever. Rooftop platforms built on the homes of captains so they can overlook the ports."

"Why call it a widow's walk?"

She exhales a short, dry laugh. "Romantic folklore. The wives would climb up there, watching the sea for their husbands to return. Waiting. Hoping." She pauses for a breath. "But most of the time, the sea had already claimed them. The walk became a vigil. A place to mourn the lost before they were actually gone." Her voice drops as if she's reciting a ghost story she's told too many times.

"And the theory?" I ask even though I already know where this is going.

She turns to me, eyes gleaming with a sly smirk. My eyes flick to her teeth, and yes, there's a diamond embedded in each of her upper canines. And just behind her top lip, a golden hoop glints from a hidden piercing.

"The widow spider. The one who lures, mates, then kills. Unapologetic and efficient."

"And which do you prefer?"

She falters from my question but quickly recovers. "Well." She looks away from me again, leaving me to study her profile. "Either way, the male dies, and the woman lives." She lifts the bottle again. "Unrealistic but very romantic."

"You didn't answer my question."

She doesn't answer right away, but I can tell she doesn't need to think about it. "I don't pine. Nor do I have the privilege to kill without consequence."

We both let the silence settle between us, letting the night reclaim the space. I wonder if she was trying to warn me or dare me. And in that moment, I begin to understand something dangerous about her.

She's not looking for a rescue. She's already made peace with the edge.

"I'm sorry she died. I know she was the better choice," she says almost sincerely.

"None of this was a choice," I retort curtly, and I offer her my hand again. "Come inside."

"Why?" she lashes defiantly.

"Because this is foolish."

Her head whips around, eyes glowing like hot coals. "Foolish is letting assholes like you continue to decide the shape of my life. To pretend I have a say in any of this, when we both know I'm merely a transaction wrapped in lace. Accepting this fuckery is choosing a life of chains and quiet suffering. What kind of existence is that?"

I press my tongue to the roof of my mouth, trying to gain control over myself and the situation. If I want to get her off the ledge without incident, I need to stay rational.

"I won't ask you again," I say vehemently, failing miserably at the composure I know this moment requires.

She tilts her head, and something colder settles in her expression. "No. I choose the quicker death. Because at least that would be *my* choice."

Everything slows when I see her lift a foot with enough weight hovering over the edge to tell me she isn't bluffing. I move without thought as instinct takes the wheel. I lunge forward, wrapping my arms around her waist in one violent motion, jerking her body into my chest. Her head barely reaches my chin, and she grunts from the impact, the same time the bottle shatters to the ground.

With a snarl, I haul her through the open window, my grip crushing and unforgiving. Her spine arches at a painful angle with the pressure, but I don't ease up. I don't stop until I have her inside and spin us toward the bed. Her feet never touching the ground.

I throw her down and pin her with my body, pressing her into the mattress. Her robe opens beneath her like spread wings.

She screeches and bucks against me with a strength born of madness. "Why did you do that?" she screams through her teeth. "I die and you're free."

Her struggle dies out, and there's this deranged lucidity in her glassy eyes that rattles something I didn't know I had. The world goes mute.

Up close, stripped of all that dark armor, no makeup, or taunting smirk, I can see her. Pure raw skin, pink cheeks, and those uncanny eyes. Those brown laced eyes with gold and green that somehow look ancient yet young, all at once.

They paralyze me.

"We'd both be free," she whispers.

Something unkindly rips in my chest, burgeoning into something ugly. Something beyond madness that has me shutting down. Suddenly, everything stops meaning anything.

I lower my face until our noses touch, breath hot between us. "And what would people think? That I murdered you?" I snarl, now shaking with coiled fury. "You want to die? Do it on your own goddamn time. Not when I could be blamed for it."

Her nostrils flare as she glowers up at me. Her eyes suddenly dry. "Get the fuck off me or I will rip your face off with my teeth," she hisses, and I believe her. I'm almost moved by the power she exudes.

There's an intense moment when I hover over her, drinking her in. She's trembling but not with fear. It's electricity. I can feel it pulse between us. I remove myself from her, and she instantly scrambles up to her elbows, and I regret releasing her.

She's flushed in the face, chest rising and falling with labored breath, and only covered in small pieces of black silk under her black lace robe, still splayed open. Those wild eyes and messy hair. She looks freshly fucked and my cock responds to the beautiful sight of her like this.

My fists groan, and everything inside me urges me to break something. Or claim it. Instead, I say nothing and walk away. All the while, she's hurling curses at my back.

I should continue my leave and walk right through the exit, but her recklessness seems to be contagious, and in the worst way.

I go back to the office with new terms.

CHAPTER THREE

Sinclair

I am scathing mad as I'm tossed inside a large vehicle with my hands and feet bound.

How dare they snatch me from my own bed and try to haul me away with no answers to the questions I screamed at them?

They didn't want to give me answers, then I wasn't going to go quietly. So, I fought like a rabid dog. You're supposed to let sleeping dogs lie. Especially half-drunk ones having dreams that are more like fantasies of burning their home down with everyone in it.

It wasn't until I bit a chunk out of someone's neck and raked skin from at least two faces that they finally had the sense to bind my wrists and ankles and jam a gag between my teeth.

Didn't stop me.

I thrashed and roared against the fabric choking me, eyes brimming, limbs burning with the promise of more violence. When they dragged me out of the vehicle and to the private jet, I doubled down.

I screamed louder, kicked my bound legs harder, and thrashed my body with every ounce of strength I had. They tied me to a seat using a rope. Fucking rope. The kind you use for cattle.

"Fucking crazy bitch," one man muttered as he cinched the restraints tighter. I bared my teeth at him. "What are you going to do, huh?" he goaded, leaning in. Closely. Hot breath in my face. "Gagged and declawed, you're harmless."

I slammed my forehead into his nose. The crunch was music to my ears. His heckling turned into gurgling as blood gushed from his face. The others howled with laughter.

"You fucking whore," he seethed, and raised his hand. I was already prepared for it when his backhand cracked across my cheek, snapping my head sideways.

When I slowly turned back with a bloodied grin, their faces paled. They began calling me names like psycho, bitch, witch, and the classic whore, and I liked it. Laughed right through the gag as they all went to take their seats far away from me.

I knew I was helpless then, bound and in flight. So, I thought it would be best for me to take a short break to regain my strength. Save some energy for when we land and start in on my reign of terror all over again.

I allowed them to think I was spent when they hauled me off the plane to load me into another vehicle. Quiet. Recharging. I waited until we were on the move to lunge for the driver, turning the men into a frenzy as I went berserk on them. The van veered, men screamed, and by the time they regained control of me, they were breathless and sweating.

I fell limp again and have remained that way since. Even as we're rolling up to the estate and come to a stop, I'm docile. I wait until the door opens and someone goes to grab me, then I lift my bound feet and kick them square in the face, forcing him to stumble back. And I don't stop kicking. I start up my tantrum all over again.

Thrashing and screaming as I'm being dragged inside. Then I'm upright and there he is. Blackwall Golzar. A faint memory from last night. Or just hours ago, as the sun is only rising now.

Immaculate. Cold. Sculpted from wrath and indifference, standing in a stately office like it was a throne room. His father stands beside him, speaking lowly, then gives me a look of disappointment before leaving.

"Why is she bleeding?" Blackwell demands in a booming voice as he looks around.

My lungs burn with the effort of restraint, my muscles trembling from the fight they haven't stopped waging. My hair sticks to my face, skewing my vision, but it doesn't matter. I can still bare my teeth. Still resist. Still fight like hell.

"She fought us the whole time." Wrong answer. He's across the room in seconds, breathing down the neck of the man who spoke.

"I asked," Blackwell says, dangerously soft, "why's she bleeding?"

A hush falls over the room. The tension becomes suffocating. They all shrink back, and a few glance in the same direction. Likely toward the motherfucker who clocked me when I made him snap like a twig, losing control.

"It happened while detaining her," someone says with a brittle tone.

Blackwell doesn't move, but his stillness is no less volcanic.

"And you couldn't detain her without spilling blood?" His voice drips with hardly controlled fury.

"She went fucking crazy," the fool blurts out, sealing his fate.

Somehow, it gets even quieter. Blackwell turns his head slightly, his expression carved from ice. I should shiver, should cower at the sheer menace radiating from him. But instead, my breath shallows, and I think I might be a little turned on. Okay, so there's no doubt. I'm fucking turned on.

To make grown men tremble like cowards from one single look? That's the kind of power I crave.

"She killed Ian, sir," someone timidly mutters, hand still clenched too tightly on my arm. I grin viciously. "One of our men, sir," he reiterates.

The whole room holds its breath when Blackwell shifts. He stalks toward the speaker with the same quiet threat he used before. "So, it's not her blood?"

"Not all of it." His voice shakes.

"Then I will ask one final time, and you better have an answer for me." Blackwell's tone is flat, which is worse. It's the calm before the storm. "Why. The fuck. Is she bleeding?"

The little bitch doesn't answer fast enough. In a blink, Blackwell's hand is fisted in the man's collar, yanking him forward. The barrel of a gun is pressed to his temple before anyone can react.

The poor bastard is now shaking in his boots. "Because someone hit her!" he rushes out.

There it is.

A sudden trickle reaches my ears. Then the scent of urine hits my nose. My smile stretches as I glance down just in time to see it. Liquid spreading over the polished floor. The man is actually pissing himself.

I look up at Blackwell in envy. His lip curls up in disgust and he shoves the guy away. He looks down at the piss puddle like it's personally offended him and takes a sidestep to avoid it.

"Point him out," he says evenly.

It takes no more coercion for the little pisser to point out the guilty party. Blackwell swivels his head, eyes slicing through the room. Then his gaze cuts back to me. Holds it with dark intensity. For a long moment, we stare at each other. Unblinking.

Then, without breaking eye contact, he lifts his gun and pivots slightly. My grin twitches as if encouraging him to do it. He pulls the trigger. The sound is deafening, but Blackwell doesn't even flinch.

I turn slightly to see the body hit the floor like a sack of shit. *He just shot a man without looking, and didn't miss. Well, fuck me.* As soon as I'm satisfied, I dart my eyes back to Blackwell's.

"Leave us," he says with his eyes still on me as if they never left.

"Sir, do you—"

"I said leave us," he says with finality. No one dares to ignore him.

I hear the sound of the body being dragged away, then the door shuts with an ominous thud, sealing us in silence.

He leans back against the desk, untouched by the violence he enacted, his bespoke suit still pristine. Probably the same one from earlier.

The tension builds, and the only sound is my labored breathing. I shift, trying to keep my balance as my legs tremble and my wrists burn. But I stand tall when my instincts have me wanting to crouch in a defensive stance.

He watches me as if I'm a cornered animal. "I guess we should have tranqed you."

I show my teeth. The audacity. I mean, yes, I am feral, but how dare he even think of darting me like some kind of animal!

My resolve almost falters when I catch one corner of his mouth twitching. A flicker of amusement he's trying to suppress.

Fine. He wants a show?

He approaches me with confident, unhurried steps. Totally unaware he's stepping right into a lioness's den. A lioness who is thirsting for blood.

He stops, leaving a foot of air between us. Only my eyes move, locking with his. He remains tranquil and calm, and it makes me want to scream. How can he be so unshakable when I am boiling inside?

He reaches for the gag but pauses mid-air. "Do not bite me," he warns with a baritone that spears a chill right through me.

I narrow my eyes in response. He pries the soaked cloth from my mouth, lifting it up and over my head. I wipe the slobber from my chin on my shoulder, never taking my eyes off him.

I've never been one to shy away from a sudden urge, especially the self-destructive kind. So, when the image of spitting in Blackwell's maddeningly handsome face flashes across my mind, I don't hesitate or second-guess it. I gather a wad of saliva in my mouth, lean back, and hurl it.

Unfortunately, my aim is a little off, landing just south of glory. Hitting him in the chest.

His chin dips slowly and methodically. For a moment, nothing moves. Suddenly, I forgot how to breathe. And for the first time in years, fear curls cold and uninvited, trickling down my spine. I haven't felt fear in so long, so as it creeps in, I feel it everywhere. In my fingertips, in the tautness of my shoulders, in the thrum of blood rushing to my ears.

But it isn't a fear that weakens. It charges.

When he lifts his eyes again, they're endlessly black. Deeper. Bottomless. The kind of gaze that makes you forget where you are and who you are.

My heart slams against my ribs, and heat gathers between my thighs like an aftershock. My face feels feverish with shame and thrill, clashing beneath my skin.

With no warning at all, his fingers twist through my hair and wrench my head back. I hiss in pain when he yanks me against the hard line of his body. His face is inches from mine, all sharpened angles and fury. He snarls, practically foaming at the mouth. Even his perfect, dark hair is now undone.

His control is unraveling. His sanity is breaking.

And fuck me, it's beautiful.

"You have two choices here, little girl," he spits, spittle hitting my cheek. "Act like a proper human being and accept your place here, or you can tuck tail and run back home and do whatever the fuck you want to do with your life."

"That seems like a rather easy choice," I bite back.

His grip constricts, and my scalp stings with pain. "So, is that what you want? To crawl back to that hell just to kill yourself for nothing? No one will mourn you. No one will cry for you. No hearts will be broken. You will prove *nothing* with your death."

He speaks the truth I have always known, but to hear those words come from *him*, they feel heavier.

"At least I'll be free."

"Yeah? You think there's freedom in death? That there's some kind of paradise waiting for you on the other side?"

I don't respond because I have no idea what I believe in the afterlife. No idea of what happens once you die. Yes, there has to be some kind of higher power, but Heaven and Hell? Reincarnation? They sound too storybook.

"Your life here does not have to be imprisonment."

"Bullshit," I bite. "I was kidnapped, tied up, dragged to another state, and I'm forced to marry a stranger. That's not freedom. It's a sentence."

He cants his head to one side. "It depends on your perspective."

I glare at him. "How the fuck else am I supposed to see it?"

"You might not be free to choose everything, but you'll finally be free from your family."

"You don't know shit about me and what I want."

He seems like he's mulling over his next words as he stares down at me in a way that makes me feel stripped bare under a microscope. I usually thrive under a stare. Shock, fear, desire. But this feels different. This feels like exposure, and I hate it. It has my stomach in knots.

"I know you think your eccentricity shields you," he says softly but deadly. "But I see through it. I see *you*, little girl."

I give him a cunning smile. "Is that what you're into? Little girls?"

His nostrils flare, but he remains indifferent. "If I didn't have plans for that smart mouth of yours," he murmurs, "I'd rip your tongue out just to shut you up. Permanently."

Fuck, I love the way he talks.

He finally releases my hair and walks behind me with unnerving calm. When he cuts the zip-ties from my wrists, I almost moan in pleasure. My arms drop forward, and I bring them around to inspect the damage. I'm furious all over again. They're ghostly pallid, bruised, and swollen.

They will all pay for this.

He cuts the ties from my ankles next, then comes to stand in front of me again. His eyes drop down to the damage, but his face betrays nothing. No guilt or sympathy.

"Try anything, and you'll spend the next several days with your wrists and ankles bound." He reaches into his pocket and produces two small white pills, offering them in an open palm as if serving them on a platter. "Take these," he instructs blandly.

"What are they?"

"They'll help you sleep."

My eyes snap back to his. "You mean knock me into a comatose state," I accuse.

His little half smirk is confirmation. "Your father advised sedation before transport. I declined."

"Oh, how noble of you," I sass.

"I thought so," he muses, his levity maddening. "But I do see his reasoning now. You've made it very clear you cannot yet be trusted, and I'd like a good night of sleep." I don't move. "I will force them down your throat if it comes to it," he warns.

"I don't need to be sedated," I try saying as evenly as possible. "I'll..." I swallow hard. "Behave."

His lips curve into a grin that would chill anyone to the bones, but that fervent heat is back. I detest the way he's affecting me. "You'll now have to earn my trust back."

"Back?"

"I gave you the benefit of the doubt. You burned it to ash."

My breath comes out of my nose in smoke. "I didn't ask to be here."

"And here you are." He pauses. "So, what's it going to be? Take these of your own freewill, or choke them down with my assistance?"

I jut my chin out. "I would love to see you try."

His chin lowers with a dangerous gaze, an equal amount of delight in his amber eyes in the violence about to unfold. I should take the damn pills. But my fucking pride has always been louder than reason. Constantly in fight or flight mode.

So, I run.

He's on me within seconds, arms cinching around my waist like steel bands. I strain all my overexerted muscles to try and twist my way out, but the more I writhe, the more his arms lock down. He's over six feet tall with an athletic build but *fuck* he's strong as shit. Easily lifting my feet off the ground.

His breath is hot when he chuckles in my ear. "I figured you'd need coercion."

I scream through my teeth in frustration. "Fuck you!"

Next thing I know, I'm slammed to the ground, flat on my back, his body over mine in one fluid motion. I flail about, and he repositions so that he's kneeling on my arms. Just a few more inches and I can bite his dick off.

And I would...if I could move. The position he has me in is impossible to escape.

His smug grin is fucking infuriating as he gleams down at me in victory. "Open," he demands coolly.

I lock my jaw, and his pompous grin fades. *That's right* mother-fucker. *You will* not *be able to control me.*

He pinches my nose shut, predictably so. Thinking I'll eventually open my mouth to breathe. But I hunker down, ready to hold my breath for as long as I'm physically able to. I thrash my head in vain, trying to shake him off. I just need one breath to start this thing all over again.

But his grip tightens to the point of pain, until my eyes water and my head goes still in reaction. Giving him the chance to gain total and complete control. I'm feeling lightheaded, and my lungs are now panicking, screaming for air.

When my mouth pops open on reflex, he's ready. With his hand clamping my jaw, he shoves the pills in deep, snapping my mouth shut with bone-jarring force.

"Swallow." His voice is level as if there's no exertion at all.

I throw daggers at him, fuming, mouth tightly sealed. He pinches my nose again. This time, harder. My lungs stutter. My vision clouds. My limbs burn.

The pill goes down a throat that refuses to let me die. I try to fight it, to will my body into rejection, but instinct is stronger. Reflex kicks in, and my throat contracts. My body betrays me, moving on autopilot, doing what it was designed to do. Swallowing against my will.

He isn't sure if I've swallowed them yet, so he continues cutting off my air supply, and I keep resisting. But my fight is withering, my body starting to fail.

Spots dance in my vision. My limbs feel like wet sand. My chest is too tight to rise. I've been choked out before, so I know what comes next. The heaviness. The slow sinking detachment. Like my body's being dragged down while my mind scrambles to hold on.

Then—release.

He lets go of both my nose and mouth and I suck in air like breaking through the surface after nearly drowning. My chest lurches, the air burning as it's forced down. I blink through the tears, vision warped and wet, barely able to make out his face. His insufferably handsome face.

He's eerily calm as I cough hard, desperately wanting water but refusing to ask for it. "I'm going to kill you," I rasp, sending me into another coughing fit. Which is really hard to do when someone's big ass is practically sitting on your chest.

That earns me a dark chuckle. He opens his mouth to speak, and I hear his voice, but my mind is already muddled, and I'm feeling sluggish and dazed, so whatever is said doesn't quite reach me. His voice is already far away.

Then nothing.

CHAPTER FOUR

I t's been two dreary weeks of this tasteless mausoleum of a mansion.

After waking up that first morning, groggy, achy, and instantly peeved, I chose to play along. Temporarily, that is. Twenty-two years of captivity under my father's roof had me craving change, even if it came wrapped in more steel bars.

At least I won't have to pretend like I'm part of a family anymore. And there's a whole new crew to torment.

But it was only going from one hellhole to another. Told when to eat, shit, and speak. The henchmen tail me at a "respectful" distance, pretending they're subtle. And they're just as easy to ditch. Fucking bullets for brains.

I don't ditch them to escape. At least, not yet. I do it for the tiny thrill of it. That sliver of adrenaline as I watch the panic on their faces, frantically trying to locate me before someone finds out they failed their one and only job. To babysit the psycho. But that spark dies just as quickly as it flares.

The only thing keeping me from setting random fires just for the hell of it is studying this place. I roam the estate like a ghost with a vendetta, memorizing every hallway, every stairwell, every blind corner, and every damn nook and cranny.

This morning's stroll in particular brings me to the office where Dario Golzar and his charming son, my darling fiancé, like to hole up when they're actually here. Last time I tried to eavesdrop, one of their little rats manning the door snitched on me. They have yet to learn that this bitch *does* bite. But they'll learn. Especially when I can no longer tolerate the boredom. *Someone* will have to entertain me.

There are two mob pups on either side of the door. One is made of stone. Won't even give me a small glance or a muscle twitch. So, I focus on the one with the shifty eyes. Like a snare, I have his eyes locked with mine as soon as they make contact. I sway my hips the closer I get, and it must be too much for him. He darts his eyes away and swallows hard. But he's already shown me his weakness.

My arm brushes his as I press a finger to my lips with a quiet "*shh.*" He keeps his head turned, pretending not to see me, along with the garden gnome on the other side.

Good boys.

I lean in and press my ear to the seam of the door to listen in. Laughter filters through. Then an unfamiliar male's voice speaks up. "You need to sleep with one eye open around that one."

Could be vanity, but this conversation may be about little old me.

"I'm aware," Blackwell replies dryly.

"Tell me. What's she really like?" Silence. "I hear she's fucking wild. Ties men up, tortures them, then fucks them senseless." He pauses. "Some sinister shit."

"That's enough," Blackwell snaps without raising his voice.

"I mean no disrespect, Blackwell. I'm just saying—"

I burst into the room and saunter in as if I were to be expected. "Don't believe everything you hear in the girls' locker room, boys," I chirp with a cheeky smirk.

Blackwell's expression is smooth, sitting behind his father's desk, utterly unimpressed. The guest occupying a chair facing him is about mid-thirties and totally forgettable. His eyes balloon when he whips around and sees me.

"I'm sure you've been known to get a little *rough* in bed." Strutting through the room, I hop up, perching myself on the edge of the desk, and swing my heavy boots. "A man can gag a woman and bind her, and that's kinky. But when a woman takes control, suddenly it's sinister?"

He squirms in his seat, and Blackwell remains reticent behind me. He clears his throat to try and recover as he's quickly crumbling under my stare like a sandcastle. "I've heard it's a little more than rough play," he mutters.

"Oh? Pray tell." I cross my arms, grinning. "I do love a good story. Especially one about me."

He glances behind me at Blackwell, but he gets no help from him. A bead of sweat forms in his hairline, and it might as well be blood in the water. I hop down and close the distance slowly, savoring the way his posture stiffens. I plant my hands on the armrests of his chair and lean in, close enough to taste his panic.

"You know," I whisper, watching his pulse hammer at his throat, "I could show you sometime. Let you get a front seat to what my appetite really looks like." And because I have a thing for theatrics, I dart my tongue inside his ear. He jerks away as if it were a snake.

I giggle, delighted to see him visibly shaken.

"That's enough, Sinclair," Blackwell says from behind me. There's warning in his tone, but no real heat.

"Oh, come on," I coo. "I just want to play." I stroke a finger through his dark hair. He may be intimidated by me, but I bet if I cupped his crotch, his dick will be hard as shit.

"Clair!" Blackwell's voice cracks through the room like a whip.

I freeze. No one has *ever* called me that. Other than the names that were used to try and break me, I've only ever been *Sinclair*. And usually laced with venom and contempt. That single syllable hits harder than a slap.

I swallow down the ache and turn around with a plastic smile. His stare is sharp enough to cut. But I don't flinch under the blade. I twist it instead.

"We'll have to continue this meeting another time," Blackwell says, clipped and cold. His eyes never leaving mine.

Whatever the guy mutters behind me is drowned out. I'm anchored by my affliction. Caught on some invisible chain that's around my neck, pulling taut. Whatever it is tethering me to him right now, I don't know if I want to sever it or cling to it.

The sound of the door closing shakes me from the intrusive thoughts, and I fiddle with a pen on his desk as if unaffected. "Was it something I said?"

"You are promised to me." He chops up each word. "To me. Only." Good thing the goosebumps on my arms are concealed by my jacket sleeves. He cannot know what kind of effect his voice alone already has on me. "You will not disrespect me by touching another man."

I scoff, rolling my eyes as I round the desk and slide back onto the surface, closer now. Bolder in appearance. I won't let him see that he unsettles me, even if it hums beneath my skin. It's not fear. Not that. Fear requires something I don't have, and that's the will to live. The hope that tomorrow matters. And I stopped waking up wanting to be here a long time ago.

"I was only teasing him," I say, inspecting my nails, feigning indifference. "He wasn't my type. Too spineless. I like them a *little* resilient."

I meet him head-on when he languidly stands to his full height. With one step, he's in my space. His fingers are unforgiving as they dig into my thighs and wrench my knees apart to slot himself between them like he owns the right to do so.

I arch one eyebrow at him with a veneer of monotony, when in reality, my blood rushes to my cunt with lewd desire. He leans in, and I stand my ground, refusing to budge an inch. His proximity leaves my head hazy, and the intoxicating scent of him in waves has my cunt dripping with greed.

"I will only say this once, although I should not have to say it at all. But since you clearly need it spelled out for you, if I ever catch you with another man—or woman—I will fucking kill you."

A shiver coils down my spine, and all I want to do is kiss him until I taste blood from his pouty lips and ride his thigh like a bitch in heat.

"Funny," I say, toying with a button on his dress shirt. "I didn't take you for the jealous type."

My eyes open wide when his hand strikes out to grip around my throat. The tip of his nose almost kissing mine. "You belong to me, Sinclair," he seethes.

I am no longer bothered by men claiming ownership over me. I was born a possession, and I will die a possession. But only in flesh.

No one can own my mind. Nor can anyone ever tame it.

"Why the fuck are you smiling?" he snaps.

"How hard are you right now?" I ask, grinning, wide and wicked. His annoyingly handsome features don't budge an inch. "What are you waiting for, Blackwell? Take what's yours," I taunt. "Why abstain?" I drag a finger up and down his chest and tilt my head to brush my lips against his. "I am *yours,* after all."

He uses his iron grip on my neck to give me a little jerk to demand my attention. To demand control over the situation. "If I want you," he rasps, voice like steel, "I'll have you."

Something inside my chest stings from his blunt confession. It feels like...rejection. A mixture of emotions has me stupefied. I can't tell if I'm pissed or offended.

I hide the stab to my pride and swallow hard. Wrapping my legs around his waist, I yank my groin against him, and what do you know? There's a firm bulge there.

Confidence floods back, seductive and cruel. "Your cock says otherwise, Blacky," I purr. Then I grind against him slowly and brush my lips along the scruff on his chin. "You want to fuck me," I whisper.

He finally moves, grazing my ear with his mouth. "I have no desire to fuck you right now," he whispers back.

My whole body stills, and my teeth grind. He's lying. I know he is because I can feel his cock trying to burst through his pants. But it stings no less. To feel unwanted by *him.*

"Pity," I say smoothly. As if completely unaffected. Then I lean in as much as his hold on me will allow. "Because it would've been fucking wild."

I nip at his jawline, and his hand flexes around my neck. Then he lets go and takes a step back. Refusing to take the bait I'm offering him to on a silver fucking platter.

Unruffled, I hop down from the desk with lazy grace and saunter to the door. Leaving just as calming as I did crashing in.

He thinks he won. Let him.

The next one is mine.

CHAPTER FIVE

Blackwell

My patience is wearing paper-thin as I glance at my watch for the second time, waiting in the foyer for Sinclair.

It's the night of our engagement party. An obligation her family insisted on hosting at a venue closer to us. I doubt it'll remain a celebration by the end of the night. Not with Sinclair at my side. She might end up with my hands around her throat, squeezing the life out of her, by the time the last toast is made.

The intolerable fucking vamp.

I sigh and take a breath, preparing myself to go and fetch her. But just as I place one foot on the first stair, she appears at the top, looking like the angel of death, ready to descend back into the depths of Hell where she came from. And with the way she's been making my blood burn and my head pound, it feels like I'm already there. In constant hell, living and breathing it.

By the time I realize I've gone still, she's already halfway down the stairs. My eyes rake over the lace hugging her most prominent curves, the teasing slit that reveals her pale hip and opposite thigh.

The contrast of her pale skin under my calloused hands has my fists stretching at my sides to refrain from grabbing her as soon as she's within arm's reach.

I told her lies. Fed her venomous words about how little I desired her for the sole purpose of sparking a reaction. But I've wanted her since I had her pinned beneath me on her bed, snarling like a feral cat.

Her skin, as if untouched by the sun. A scent that is overpowering in the most exotic way. It's all maddening, and she knows it.

She stops one step above me, our eyes level. Her soulful gaze unreadable beneath shadowed makeup, and her body boldly close to mine. As if challenging me.

My eyes jump up to her hair, delicately tossed into something elegant with only a few pieces astray. "Purple," I grunt in disapproval.

Her plush lips curl into a vicious yet brilliant smile. "I was bored."

Purple, blonde, indigo. I've seen it all since she was a teenager. Another act of rebellion and a 'fuck you' to the world.

"Couldn't have waited until after tonight?" I mutter and head for the doors.

"Why?" she practically chirps as she catches up with me to walk at my side. "Wanted my hair to be perfect for tonight."

I take another soothing breath, steeling myself for what's to come.

We ride in silence, save for the hum of the tires and the occasional glance I steal in her direction. She stares out the window, aloof and distant, like she's already escaped. She looks poised. Elegant. Almost serene. A far cry from the chaos she brings with her.

She's a goddamn chameleon. A savage and a society girl stitched in one. Combat boots, dripping in venom. Then she's a poised debutante draped in pearls. It's unnerving how well she transforms, wearing both skins flawlessly. And somehow never losing that sharp edge underneath.

I'm so caught up watching her, trying to decipher which version I have of her tonight, that I nearly let it slip my mind. I reach into my jacket and pull out the small velvet box. "I almost forgot," I mutter.

Her eyes drift over, a tiny smile tugging at her lips. "What is it?"

"Your ring." I pop it open and keep my eyes on her face. Watching for something. A flicker of surprise. A twitch of genuine emotion. The slightest reaction. Anything.

She tilts her head, and her smile grows into something languid and sly. "Hmm," she hums, plucking the ring from the box and sliding it right on without hesitation. She holds it under the cabin light, examining the way it catches. "Cute," she says casually, flashing me a grin. The small diamonds in her teeth gleaming at me like a threat. The golden hoop barely peeking out from under her lip as if mocking me.

The one word is like a gut-punch.

Then she turns away like it's nothing. Like I didn't just put a goddamn engagement ring on her finger. A ring I spent too much time designing. Put entirely too much thought into, apparently. All for her to call it *cute*, drop her hand, and turn her head to look out the window like I'm not even here.

Does she even like it?

Does it even fit?

She gives me nothing, and it's infuriating. *She's* infuriating.

"I don't need to remind you of how important your conduct is tonight, do I?" I say with a little too much bite.

She lets out a low chuckle. "You mean my performance." She turns to me, smiling. "Don't worry, darling. I'll be on my best behavior."

My nostrils flare from her mocking tone. "I'm serious, Sinclair."

She gives me a theatrical frown, her eyebrows lowering. "You're always serious," she says, dropping her voice into a deep rasp.

"If you—"

"Here's something you should learn about me, and learn about me sooner to save yourself the trouble." I fall silent out of ire. "Telling me what to do is like issuing a challenge. A challenge I am more than willing to oblige. My entire life, I have been told to *behave*. I do not need to be *told* what exactly is expected of me. I know. Smile and only speak when spoken to, and men are superior and women are to be submissive and remain an object—"

"Are you finished?" I say dryly. I see that I've hit yet another button, as her face grows rigid and she goes silent. "Good. So, we're both on the same page."

I face forward, ignoring her attempt to burn holes into the side of my head with her gaze. I can almost hear her inner thoughts of violence and vengeance. For once in my life, I regret opening my mouth. I may have poked the fucking bear.

She's deathly silent the rest of the ride. And when the car rolls to a stop, she's out before the engine cuts. I step out after her, jaw ticking, a growl low in my throat. I yank at the lapels on my jacket and button it.

When she tries to storm ahead of me, I lunge forward and wrap my fingers around her lace-covered wrist, yanking her to a halt. She spins with the force, colliding with my chest. Her breath hitches, eyes burning as she fumes up at me.

I remain cool, when really, my heat matches hers. "I have let you rampage through the estate ever since you stepped foot in it like a hellhound off its leash, without a word," I grit out. "One night, Sinclair. One fucking night. Act like a goddamn lady." My jaw throbs by the time I finish.

She throws her head back and releases a dry, boisterous laugh that doesn't seem human. "A lady?" she echoes, incredulous.

"I'm warning you, Clair," I snap. The name slices through her smugness like a blade, and she falters ever so slightly. "You do not want to test me. I've let you run rampant to placate you, but tonight, I will have no tolerance for your games."

"And you wouldn't want them to think you don't have your bitch on a leash," she sneers.

"Is that what you need, *joon kharâsh*?" *Soul-scraper.*

She stares at me, eyes narrowed. Then she bares those glittering teeth in a grin that says she's about to set fire to something. The kind of grin so wicked it can peel flesh from bone. But it moves me in a different way.

"Shall we?" she says sweetly. But I know not to trust calm waters.

I guide her hand to the crook of my arm and lead us through the doors towards the ballroom. The air inside is dense, brimming with testosterone and veiled threats. My spine locks up like instinct, ready for impact as we enter. But Sinclair? Ever composed beside me like sin wrapped in obedience. But I know under all that polish is a fuse waiting to be lit.

We begin to circulate, playing our parts with rehearsed smiles and shallow conversation. I keep one eye on her the whole time, waiting for her to snap. To say something to get a rise out of me or do something to poke at me for sport. But she stays in character, smiling sweetly while she shakes hands and makes small talk like it's foreplay. I don't know if I'm proud or bracing myself for detonation.

Eventually, my parents make their approach. My mother beams. "Oh, Blackwell," she sighs, taking Sinclair's hands in both of hers. "You failed to mention how stunning Sinclair has become." I watch Sinclair in slight amusement. She tries to mask the flicker of unease, and when my mother leans in to plant a kiss on each cheek, I have to hide my smirk behind a cough. Especially when Sinclair's eyes widen in disbelief. "It is so nice to finally meet my soon-to-be daughter-in-law," my mother says, still clasping Sinclair's hands like she plans to keep her. She gives her an outward once over and adds, "You're radiant, darling. I don't think anyone else could pull off purple hair the way you do."

Sinclair recovers with the speed of someone used to being cornered. She plasters on a polite smile. "Thank you, Mrs. Golzar. It's nice to see you too," she says, only an octave over a robotic tone. Then she subtly pries her hands out of my mother's.

"Oh, please. Call me, Jaqueline." My mother doesn't skip a beat. She sidles up to my father, gazing up at him adoringly. "Don't they look wonderful together, Dario?"

My father offers a noncommittal nod. "They do." He couldn't care less how we look together. It's all about legacy, leverage, and gain. It isn't for the aesthetics.

It takes Sinclair less than a heartbeat to spot an exit. "Restroom," she says with a tight smile, already halfway across the room. Gone. Seeping through the cracks like smoke.

My mother steps into the space Sinclair left behind, chattering away as I offer the occasional nod, pretending to listen. But my focus is on the room.

My eyes sweep the area, finding all the usual suspects. Family, friends, frauds. I spot my uncle lingering in the back with a drink in hand, his family with him. I'll have to shake his hand and offer the proper pleasantries soon. But it's the trio across the room that tightens my focus. The beady stare from the Ortiz men. Sinclair's father, Anthony, and her two brothers, Lincoln and Royce.

They wear their suits like armor and their smug expressions like second skin. But there's no edge to them I haven't encountered before. They pose no threat. Not the kind that I fear, anyway.

I excuse myself from my parents and the vultures orbiting them. I cross the ballroom with measured strides. I shake hands with all three, my grip firm but restrained. Predictably, they all squeeze harder than necessary. Like boys trying to prove something. They fail to understand that brute strength does not equate to power.

It was my father who taught me that power does not shout, it whispers.

"I appreciate you hosting this," I say only to Anthony.

"It's the least we could do, getting Sinclair off our hands," he says with a hollow chuckle.

"You let her leave the house with that hair? Why didn't you tell us you were having such a difficult time controlling her?" Lincoln, the eldest, asks without a shred of interest. Only entitlement.

The ache in my jaw is back as I grit my molars and bite my tongue. I don't even want them looking at her. Don't want them speaking her name like it's theirs to use. I don't want them thinking they still have any kind of hold over her.

The surge of possession crashes over me. An onslaught of protectiveness. It's white-hot and unforgiving, nearly knocking the breath out of me. I have to pause to catch my breath. I can't let them see me unravel.

My gaze strays over to Royce briefly. Just enough to catch the glint in his eyes as he scans the room. There's something off about him. Not just cruel or corrupted but corroded. Something deeply rotten behind those eyes.

"I can certainly give you some tips." Royce's words are slightly slurred. Already intoxicated on dark liquor.

"I'm having no trouble at all with her. The color is hardly offensive," I say, thinking that I'm telling a little white lie when it isn't a lie at all. It's already grown on me. All of it has grown on me.

Her father starts prattling on again, Lincoln chiming in with overly practiced superiority. But I can't hear a word they say. I'm too focused on Royce and how his black eyes are sweeping the crowd like a predator sniffing out the prey.

Sinclair hasn't returned yet, and instinctively—no, absolutely—it's her he's searching for.

That primal protective instinct where Sinclair is concerned, bristles to life like a beast stirred from sleep. Death will be too good for Royce. He needs to suffer. I want his blood boiled, not just spilled. I will peel him apart, scream by scream.

Mercy won't even be a shadow in the room.

Royce slithers out of the room like an uncouth snake, and I give it all but two minutes to follow pursuit. Sinclair still hasn't resurfaced, and that creates an anxiety in me that wraps around my spine like a warning.

CHAPTER SIX

Blackwell

I don't waste any time with politeness.

I walk away from Sinclair's father and brother mid-conversation without a word. I've swallowed enough of their bile for one night.

As soon as I step outside of the main room, my senses take me opposite the restrooms. My gut tells me right away, something is wrong.

The further I venture down the hallway, the thicker the shadows become. The noise from the ballroom fades into a pulse behind me, and my alarm bells ring louder.

My strides lengthen, and my pace quickens. Then I hear it. Royce's voice, the wrong tone with Sinclair's name wrapped in it.

"I bet you're already spreading those legs for him, aren't you?" I hear him sneer with genuine vehemence. "Fucking whore."

Something in me quietly stirs. Like the click of a safety being switched off. But I remain rooted, even though it might kill me.

"I said fuck off, Royce," Sinclair snaps back with more emotion I've heard from her yet.

The joints in my hands are stiff with restraint when I register the sound of a scuffle. Everything inside me screams for me to intervene, but Sinclair remains such a mystery to me. I might learn more by watching what happens in the dark.

There's a maniacal cackle that I know belongs to Sinclair. "You're still obsessed with me. Still trying to convince yourself I ever wanted it," she spits. "Pathetic. You're just the sickness I survived."

Royce literally growls. "You only survived because I let you. But don't act like you've forgotten about me. That you'll ever forget about me."

"Oh, I haven't forgotten." She pauses, and I swear my stomach turns. "And when I think about you, it makes me *sick*. You have always made me *sick*. You're sick in the head. Always have been." The emotion leaks into her caustic words again, but there's something deeper behind them. I don't know how much longer I can stand here in silence.

His cackle sends a chill down my spine. "Oh, yeah?"

"I swear to God, I will fucking kill you! Get the fuck off me!" she screams, voice shaking with fury.

"Come on, Sinclair. For old time's sake," he muses through a strained voice.

One step is all I take before a guttural sound rips through the silence. Then the storm herself comes tearing around the corner, all fire and panic. She charges through the dark, so flustered she doesn't see me before it's too late.

Sinclair barrels right into me. She snaps her gaze up to mine, eyes wild and lip trembling. I can vividly see how terror and pure rage try to tear her in two. Then she stares up at me, silently asking if I'm her savior or if I'm the devil in the dark.

For her sake, I'm both.

"You fucking bitch!" Royce staggers into view, hunched over and clutching his side, voice shredded from whatever blow she landed.

I take Sinclair around the waist and draw her in beside me. Then I step forward, just enough to shield her. Her body turns to stone. She doesn't speak. She stays there, rigid against me. And I never, for a second, take my eyes off her brother.

His realization of my presence is delayed. His bloodshot eyes finally focus, and whatever fury he had before triples. He was not expecting to see me.

"Is there a problem here?" I ask evenly.

"None of your fucking business," he snaps. His gaze flicking between me and Sinclair, who has never been so quiet. "Family matters."

"When it comes to my fiancée, it is always my business."

Something I said lights a fuse, and he looks at me, the bloodthirst surfacing. I keep my feet planted when he advances, his posture coiled with intent, and I'm prepared to take him down. Begging for a reason. One excuse, and I will end him.

But I lose my moment because Sinclair is suddenly between us, with a flash of silver, and a knife pressed to his throat. He freezes. He might be drunk, but not enough to mistake the promise in her eyes.

"Walk away, Royce," she commands in an authoritative tone. Her voice low, sharp, and absolute, sending all the blood in my body to my cock. "Or I will slit you from ear to ear." I smile. Just a little, knowing without a doubt she'd do it.

My she-devil.

Royce's nostrils flare as he stares her down, and she matches his gaze with her fierce one. No words, only raw, unfiltered contempt crackling between them. Years of it built up and coming to a head.

Then Royce abruptly breaks away with a humorless, sharp snort. Like this is all some sort of sick inside joke only he gets. His step back is slow and deliberate, his eyes never leaving Sinclair's face. But something in his eyes shifts. Something colder and twisted.

And in that moment, I know. This isn't sibling rivalry. It's so much deeper than that. An unspoken history that has created a war and has been simmering for years.

"If you ever, and I mean *ever*, touch her, or look at her for too long, I won't come between you." I take a step forward. "I'll go right through you." My voice is smooth, like ice.

He gives no verbal response. His lip curls up as his eyes remain dark yet empty. He finally comes to his senses and realizes there will be no victory for him here, and he walks off.

"We should probably get back out there," she says as if nothing happened.

I stop her when she turns to leave, catching her arm firmly. That's all it takes for her to break. Spinning on me as if I had just let a storm loose. Fists flying, nails slashing through the air as I barely block the worst of it.

In the next breath, I have her confined against the wall with my body. Her chest is heaving, her hands are trembling, and when she looks up at me, I see it. Not only the fury burning in her eyes, but something older. Wounds that have never healed. Rage rooted in survival.

There's pain, and it runs deep.

"Get the fuck off me, Blackwell!" she screams, baring her diamond-crested teeth and thrashes.

"Calm the fuck down. I just want to talk," I say calmly.

"Fuck off," she spits.

I don't move and patiently watch as anger burns itself out until her breathing becomes somewhat normal. "Good." I loosen my hold on her arms, but I don't remove myself. "Why did he come after you?"

"It was nothing," she snaps. "Just stupid family drama."

"Tell me the truth."

"He's just a fucking prick, Blackwell. A drunk prick trying to start shit with me as usual." She seems to be having difficulty meeting my eye.

I study her closely, watching her struggle to keep the cracks from spreading. "Just say the word, and he's gone." I keep my voice low enough for only her to hear.

That hits her. She wasn't prepared for the offer, and it threw her off. She blinks once, twice. Swallows. Then, just like that, she makes another crack.

Her expression smooths over, sliding back into the version of her that never bleeds. She presses into me slowly, aligning her hips with mine, the curve of her body deliberate. Her dark painted lips tilt into a smirk when she feels how badly I've been affected.

She's fighting to bury whatever just surfaced beneath lust and control. And her weapon of choice—her body. She believes she's now in control, and I let her enjoy the illusion.

Only for a moment.

One hand slides to her jaw, holding it firm enough to still her. The other falls to her hip, locking her in place against me. The smirk falters, and her breath stutters. I lower my lips to hers, and her eyes flutter shut, but I don't connect.

"You think I don't see what you're doing?" I rasp, and her breathing picks back up. "You can only hide the truth beneath your seduction for so long." I smile when her nostrils twitch.

She licks her lips, and my hips jump forward involuntarily. Her eyes pop open. "I won't break for you, Blackwell," she whispers, but there's no venom in it.

I drag my thumb along her jaw, gentle in a way that makes her freeze more than any threat. "I know, *joon-kharâsh*. But eventually, you will bend."

I fist the frail fabric of her dress and yank it up until I gain access underneath. I stifle a groan when I'm immediately met with moist flesh at the apex of her thighs. No panties and fucking wet.

She mewls with closed eyes, and her head falls back against the wall as I run my fingers against her sensitive bud, stroking back and forth. Her lips are so inviting as they part, and it nearly undoes me.

It's beyond tempting. Whether she means it or not, it's a fucking trap. Because one kiss, I won't just lose control. She'll take it completely. It's not pride I'm concerned about, it's survival. Giving Sinclair the upper hand could mean losing everything.

She moans, rocking forward to add more friction, and I pin her to the wall with my hips. She growls in frustration, squeezing her eyes shut. Applying more pressure to her sopping cunt with two fingers, I tease her entrance, dipping only a fingertip in with each stroke.

Her fists curl around the fabric of my jacket, knuckles turning white. Her jaw slackens with her shallow pants, laced with the sweetness of red wine. As if she has forgotten every reason to hold back.

When I slide two fingers inside of her, she cranks her head back to taunt me with the slender column on her neck. The milky-white skin almost glowing like a beacon, causing my mouth to water.

It drives me to put more effort into getting her off, needing to feel her explode and watch her come undone. Cupping the back of one thigh, I crank it up over my hip to open her. I use my fingers to fuck her, slapping my palm against her pussy. Her juices stick to my hand, and I can smell the sweet aroma spiraling up between us.

Gritting my teeth, I thrust another finger inside of her, and my hips jerk on instinct. My cock is begging for her cunt. To feel it wrapped around me from tip to hilt.

My eyes won't stop stealing glances at her lips. Not yet. Not until the thrill of newness wears off. Where I am in complete control.

She chomps down on her bottom lip and whines. Her muscles coil, and her back bows. Then, like a rubber band, she snaps.

I watch with intrigue as she soars, head back like she had a shot of heroin. My lips brush against her plump bottom lip, and I barely move mine, but enough to have me mad with desire for her kiss. So fucking close. I almost did it. But I keep my head on straight.

Sluggishly, I lean back as I retract my hold on her cunt and let the fabric of her dress fall. She's listless, coming to and fluttering her eyes open. It takes a few heavy blinks, but she yanks herself out of the trance and morphs back into her caustic and arrant self with that sharp grin of hers that can carve bone.

I give her space and continue watching her. She fixes her dress, ironing it down with her hands, then checks her hair. "Well, that was fun. Thanks for the orgasm." She grins brightly, and the gold hoop behind her top lip catches the light. "See you back in there."

I'm momentarily stunned, watching her walk away with a sway she didn't have before. And I know without a doubt that it has everything to do with the vulgarity I gifted her.

I shake myself out of it and follow in the same direction. She snatches a champagne flute off a tray without pause and disappears into the crowd.

I have to stifle my chuckle as I grab a drink for myself from the bar, but when I bring the glass up to my lips and catch her scent on my fingers mixed with the aroma of whiskey, I wish I could throw all caution out the window, track her down, and throw her over my shoulder as I take us out of the room.

CHAPTER SEVEN

Sinclair

I t's late as I aimlessly sail.

Restless, bored, and in need of some kind of entertainment. Someone to play with. So far, no one has piqued my interest. But that all changes as I walk by one of the house's many pointless sitting rooms and find Harlan tucked away.

Harlan is the youngest brother, married with two kids, and so deep in the closet he should be choking on mothballs. I've only had a handful of short conversations with him, but I've seen enough to see what he's hiding. And I always find what's hidden.

He's alone, sitting too upright in a leather chair, one leg crossed over the other, and pretending to read a book. But he hasn't turned the page in too long.

I'm already close enough to pounce when he finally notices me. "Hello, Harlan," I say cheerfully.

He glances up enough to acknowledge me, then returns to his book like I'm a passing inconvenience. "Hello, Sinclair. Hunting for another victim to drag back to your lair?" he murmurs dryly.

I smile as I trail a finger along the edge of a credenza, and I circle his backside like a lion sizing up its prey before it realizes they've been spotted. "I have no idea what you're talking about," I say innocently, and I lift the decanter with a flick of the wrist, popping the crystal topper. "I've been an angel since I got here." After topping off his glass without asking, I give myself a modest pour and sink into the velvet chair across from him.

He snorts, flipping the page without looking at me. "Right," he murmurs.

I vigilantly watch as he stiffly holds the spine of his book with one hand, and his other hand twitches as if eager to fidget with something. Immediate regret burns my stomach when I take a sip of the bourbon and manage not to grimace. "So." I lean back and casually cross my legs as I begin swirling the glass in my hand lazily. "Why are you here at one in the morning instead of your picture-perfect home life?"

He's hardly amused as he arches one eyebrow at me. "Needed some peace and quiet."

"Mhmm," I hum, lips brushing the rim of my glass before tilting it for another punishing sip. I don't think I'll ever like the taste, no matter how many times I try.

He eyes me again with more focus. "Something on your mind?"

I hold his gaze, weighing my approach. "Does anyone know?"

He blinks. "Know? Know what?"

I roll my eyes and set my glass down with a soft clink. "Let's not play games, Harlan. I know what it is you are hiding." The color drains from his face, and his fingers flex on the hardback still in his hands. But there's no change in his face. "There's no need to lie to me."

I watch him patiently as he tries to calm the growing storm behind his eyes. "Mind cluing me in on whatever it is I am hiding? Because I'm a member of a crime family. I have many secrets."

"You know which secret I mean. One you may have never said out loud. One that has never made it past your teeth," I drawl.

He slams the book shut with a little too much force. "I'm not here for your entertainment, Sinclair."

"Everyone is here for my entertainment." I grin. "It's the only thing that makes any of this tolerable."

"Well, I am not interested." He gets to his feet as if to leave.

"Hiding it won't make it untrue," I sing out, striking a nerve that stops him cold. I lift the glass to drain the bitter contents that cause my nostrils to flare. "Always tie up your loose ends, Harlan. Especially if it's something you wouldn't ever want to get out. More than it already has."

He's abruptly in front of me, looming, shoulders tense, eyes mad. "If you think you can blackmail me some bullshit—"

A real, genuine giggle comes out of my throat, which seems to shock him in outrage. "Relax, Harlan," I say, still smiling. "I'm not laughing at you, I swear. I'm just surprised I could crack you so easily."

He stares at me, a flare of disbelief in his eyes. *God, I love it.* "Watch your mouth, Sinclair," he growls.

"Oh," I purr, shimmying my shoulders as if ice just skated up my spine. "This alpha man side of you is kinda hot. Effective too." I tilt my head playfully, teasing the edge of his control. "I almost believed you might hurt me." His eyes burn, and it faintly jabs at me from the inside, so I soften a little. "Look, your secret is safe with me." I pretend to lock my lips and throw away the key. "I won't tell a soul."

"You can't if you don't have a tongue," he threatens, voice low and lethal. The second time someone has threatened to remove my tongue since I've been here. Not bad.

My natural reaction would be to match his threat with one of my own, but I stop myself. "Harlan, I'm serious. It's insane that you have to hide who you are, building a life around pretending to be someone else. But I get it." I glance down at my empty glass. "We don't exactly coexist in the real world. We're born in cages. Some gilded, some rusted, but all inescapable. Legacy. Duty. Reputation. It's all bullshit, but we can't escape it." I shrug one shoulder. "We all have a part to play."

His throat bobs with a swallow, but he doesn't say anything. Just lets the silence hang between us, but it's fine. I've always had a talent for making people squirm in it. "I hate whiskey." The words feel weightless as they fall out. "Not quite as life-altering," I add, lips twitching with a crooked smirk. "But it's something I pretend to like to—I don't know."

I let my words linger for a moment before looking at him. I find him still watching me, but his face finally shows something. Humor. His face cracks into a smile as his shoulders relax and he backs away until he plops back down in the chair, melting into it. "That does not at all make us even."

I giggle softly. "Okay..." I skim through the catalog of sins in my head. "Uh, I hate chocolate. Actually, I hate anything sweet." Except for red wine, but I keep that to myself. He narrows his eyes at me. "What?" I chuckle. "Secrets don't have to be explosive," I murmur, finding it hard to keep eye contact. This could be the realest conversation I've had with anyone in...I can't even remember. "They just have to be yours." I steal a glance up at him, and I find his energy suddenly so comforting. As if I could sit here for hours divulging secret after secret, peeling back those layers I've spent my entire life wrapping myself in.

"True." He drains his glass and rises to make another trip to the minibar. "But you can do better than that." He glances over her shoulder with a boyish smirk.

I roll my eyes and sigh. "Fine. What would you like to know?"

He turns around with a glass in each hand. When I eye the one holding the stemmed glass with red wine in it, I fidget a little in my seat, but I don't let it show on my face how much I hate that he knows a damn thing about me. When he offers me the red wine, I raise an eyebrow and take it, careful to look unimpressed.

"Here's something better to help loosen those lips of yours." He pauses. "Don't worry, *joon-kharâsh*," the words roll off his tongue so practiced and perfect. There's a twinkle in his eyes, looking at me over the rim of his glass as he takes back his seat. "It'll be our little secret," he adds with a wink.

I'll bet no one knows how clairvoyant Harlan is. I hate how I couldn't see how he's been watching me like I've been studying him.

"Tell me what that means, and I promise to give you a good secret."

He laughs, and for the first time, I see dimples crease in his cheeks. "I don't know if I should." He's teasing me.

"Then I'm not exchanging any more secrets with you," I quip.

He gives a long pause for theatrics. "Soul-scraper."

I almost choke on my wine. "What?" He grins and joins me in laughter. "Soul-scraper?" I echo, still laughing. "What does that even mean?"

He shakes his head, still chuckling. "Meaning you get under his skin."

I laugh a little more because not only is it too accurate, it's dark and poetic. "I'm pretty sure I get under everyone's skin. In fact, I make it my life's mission."

"Well, mission accomplished. Now, give me something good." He gets right back to it. "Tell me about that guy you killed."

I shoot him a cheeky smirk. "Which one?"

"You know exactly which one I am referring to."

Yes, I do. The one everyone thinks I killed while fucking. But I actually killed him *after*. I'm not *that* sick.

"That's not exactly a secret."

"No, but the truth behind it is."

"There's not much truth behind it," I say a little too defensively. My mask fraying at the edges.

He leans forward slightly. "Humor me."

"How will you know if I'm being truthful or not?" I challenge.

His smirk is slow. "Try me," he says smugly.

"It's not a very interesting story." He sips his drink, his gaze unwavering. "Fine." I heavily sigh and drink half the glass of the most delicious red wine.

Harlan doesn't speak, doesn't push. Only waits.

"He was one of our mob pups," I begin. "We were fucking in secret." I pause and mull over my words, deciding on how much truth to give him. Something inside shoves at me, forcing me to give more than I have ever been willing to give. "He got a little too close—too comfortable." He was supposed to be my entertainment. Until he wasn't. "He began saying things, making promises, and assumptions. Yet, when my brothers would use me for their own sick entertainment, he'd stand there silently. As if he were a piece of furniture."

I grow quiet, finding it more difficult to look at him. So, I fidget with my ring. The most gorgeous piece of jewelry I have or will ever own. And it's odd because the large diamond is blue. A dark blue, but still blue. Yet I happen to love it. There's something so uniquely captivating about it.

"I realized he'll always be like the rest of them. Thinks he can own me, manipulate me, and use me. So, I let him think he did that night. Pretended to eat up every sweet word he whispered in the dark. Melted into every kiss, every touch."

When I glance up at Harlan, the sincerity in his face has me buckling down again. My slow grin is controlled, unshakable. "So, when I reached for the blade, he never saw it coming."

He lifts his glass to his lips, and his eyes twitch with disappointment. With the anticlimactic ending or the short version of the story, I don't know what he expected out of me.

"Sorry it wasn't the story you were hoping for." I keep my tone playful. "I didn't end a man mid-orgasm or torture him while pleasuring myself. Everyone prefers the messier version, but it's not the truth. The truth is quieter and cleaner."

"More dangerous," he quickly adds, then he full-on grins. "Like the widow spider."

My cheeks heat, and I find myself bashful. They've called me that as if it were a curse. But I have always worn it like a title.

"He thought he'd be the man you won't bite. But you're a woman who lures, traps, and consumes. Seduction with teeth."

I bite down on my bottom lip, still smiling. "I think those are the most romantic words anyone has ever said to me."

He chuckles, dimples popping. "I'm sure." He sips from his glass.

"Glad you bought it." I revert back into my preferred persona.

"You could have told me any version of the story, truth or not, and I would have gotten exactly what I was looking for."

I stare at him, tongue dried up. "Am I so transparent?" I sass.

"No, I'm just that good."

I roll my eyes. "Yeah, okay."

"You have no idea how much it drives Blackwell mad." My eyes jump up to lock with his. "He hates that he still doesn't have you figured out yet."

I want to laugh it off. I want to flash teeth and roll my eyes and toss out some biting remark, but instead, my fingers tighten around the stem of my glass. Just enough to betray something.

He watches me for a drawn-out moment. Not in a daunting way. Observant. Then his head tilts to one side, eyes narrowed like he's seeing something in me I didn't mean to show. "You ever feel like you've played so many versions of yourself, you're not even sure which one was real to begin with?"

His unexpected question rattles me, but I cover it up with a laugh, bringing the glass up to my lips and taking a sip before responding. "Every version is real," I say. "In the moment."

I don't elaborate, and he doesn't press.

CHAPTER EIGHT

Blackwell

"**B**lackwell," my father's firm tone cuts through the room.

"Yes?" I look up and realize he's now standing in front of his desk rather than sitting behind it like he was before.

"I asked how the estate is coming along?"

"Oh." I clear my throat. "It's nearly done. Possibly a few more months before we can furnish it and move in."

The words may come out easily enough, but the thought of sharing a home with Sinclair is an idea that still sits strangely in my mind. Like trying to keep a live wire in my pocket, thinking it won't burn me.

She's been complacent on the surface, playing along, but I don't trust it for a second. She's trying to disarm me like she has done with her security detail.

Every damn day she ditches them, just long enough to stir panic, then resurfaces without apology as if nothing happened. Wearing the same damn expression—boredom mixed with defiance.

She's not looking for an escape, she's testing the boundaries. Testing *me*. It's all one big game to her. Even if the gate was left wide open, she'd probably stay just to keep everyone trying to figure her out.

It drives me mental never knowing if she's reaching for her lipstick or a knife.

My father looks down and nods. "Something wrong?" I ask.

He sighs, eyes drifting towards the window. "I have to tell you something." He pauses and turns his face to me. "It's about my health." A knock on the door cuts through the moment. "We can talk about this later."

"No," I snap. "Fuck whoever knocked. I want to finish this conversation now."

He gives a soft laugh as if trying to diffuse the tension. "It's not that bad. Just some concerns that might have me stepping back more." The knock persists. "Enter!" I'm left balking at my father as the door opens behind me.

Scout, our head of security, pokes his head inside. "Apologies, sir, but could I have a private word with you, Blackwell?"

My father chuckles as I sigh, dragging a hand down my face. We both know what—or rather, *who*—this is about. "Excuse me," I mutter, rising. "I'll be back later to finish our conversation."

"Good luck," my father calls out after me, far too amused.

The woman may not have killed anyone, or made an escape—yet. But the woman has been a goddamn headache since she step foot through the gates. Any sane man would have shoved her into the back of a car, sending her right back to where she came from, but I'm a little unhinged myself. I crave the chaos and what may rise from it.

I join Scout outside of the room, and we put some distance between us and my father's office before speaking freely. "I hate to bother you with this, again, but it's become more of a problem," he says lowly as we walk towards the surveillance room.

I pinch the throbbing at the bridge of my nose, the ache already building. "Just show me."

It's no surprise when he leads us to the control room and starts showing me some recent footage of Sinclair in the gym sparring. I've already warned her not to turn our men into her chew toys. Clearly, she took that as a challenge.

"And this was yesterday," Scout says before queuing another clip.

The resentment and anger roll off her in waves. Even through the screen, it's so palpable and thick enough to taste. Her jaw is locked, her teeth clenched like she's biting back a scream. Her nostrils flare with every breath, every strike laced with something further than aggression.

She doesn't spar. She vents. She bleeds through every hit, every kick, every merciless takedown. It's not discipline. It's a purge.

Sinclair is undoubtedly lethal. If she weren't so hell-bent on being a goddamn menace, provoking anyone within a hundred-yard radius, she could channel all that raw skill into something useful. But that would require control, and control is not her style.

The video ends with Sinclair pinning a man to the mat, arm wrenched at an unnatural angle, before snapping it without hesitation. His scream is muted by the recording, but I feel it in my molars.

Then she grins. Fucking grins. Flashing those diamond-dusted canines like a trophy.

I swing my gaze to the live feed. There she is, pummeling a punching bag as if it were trying to assault her. Sweat gleaming across her milky skin, tracing the line of her throat down to her chest, glistening as her body moves with fluid, violent rhythm.

"I'll take care of it," I mutter and leave.

I make a quick trip to my room to change into some joggers and a T-shirt before heading to our gym. As I enter, there are a few men scattered around the equipment.

"Everyone out," I say loud enough for everyone to hear without having to yell.

Sinclair pretends not to hear me, her fists still flying as she continues to beat the shit out of the bag as if I'm not even there. I watch as bead after bead of sweat drips down into her skin-tight top, and my jaw clenches.

Her sweat, her fury, her audacity.

It's maddening.

I'm locked on her as the room clears and I prowl forward, my steps slow and deliberate. Every soft grunt that escapes her each time her fist makes contact ignites something primal in me.

She still refuses to acknowledge me, and it pisses me the fuck off. I want her attention the second I enter the room.

"From now on, when you want to spar, it's with me."

"Why?" she says, breathless, unrelenting.

"You know why. We already had this conversation, and you decided to do the exact opposite of what I said."

She finally drops her arms and turns to me with that signature smile, but I can't stop watching the sweat trickle down her chest, disappearing between her breasts. Her body isn't only fit, it's a masterpiece of muscle and temptation.

She's built like danger, but disguised as desire.

"How is it my fault your men take it easy on me? If they made it a fair fight, they wouldn't be walking away bleeding." She fidgets with her gloves and tape.

"You broke someone's arm."

"Shit happens," she mutters dryly, again avoiding my eyes.

"You bit a chunk out of someone's chest."

"I fight dirty."

"Sinclair," I say her name sharply, and her eyes slowly roll up to meet mine in defiance. There she is. "From now on, it's me you spar with."

One side of her plush lips curls up, and her eyes sparkle in delight. "You want to get in the ring with me, Blackwell?"

"If you want to fight, you fight me," I repeat.

"Come on," she purrs. "You've been dying to hit me."

I don't take the bait. "Not now."

She frowns. "Why not?"

"You've been going at this for a while. You're drained, and I won't go easy on you. I want you at one hundred percent."

The look in her eyes turns razor-sharp. "I want to spar *now*."

I fight the smile itching my lips. "You sure, *joon-kharâsh?*"

Her nostrils twitch. The endearment I've claimed for her hits a nerve. Which is all the reason to keep using it.

She steps inside the ring as if it belongs to her, and I follow suit. We begin the dance, circling each other.

It's she who strikes first, her flurry too rapid for how long she'd been burning through her stamina. Every movement is crisp and calculated.

A fist lands and blood blooms at the corner of my mouth. I grin through the sting, knowing she wouldn't hold back. But I underestimated her, and she's wearing a grin like she knew I would.

"Sorry," she pants, eyes glittering as she watches me wipe away the blood with the back of my hand. "Am I supposed to be going easy on the mafia prince?"

My grin is slow as I mentally remove the gloves.

I lunge, and even though I said I wouldn't be easy on her, I still refuse to hit her. So, my strategy is simple: wear her down and wrestle her into submission.

Our arms end up locked, and her sweat is slick against my skin. There's a static jolting between us with the proximity. She gracefully maneuvers out of our entanglement, and I grunt from the shot she took at my ribs. Not from pain, but shock.

We continue for only a little while, and as soon as I see the steam leaving her, I take that moment to take her down. We hit the mat hard, in a tangle of limbs and sweat. She tries to scramble away, but I'm faster.

Grabbing her thighs, I drag her delicate body underneath me and use mine to weigh her down. When I catch her wrists to crank them over her head and slam them to the mat, there's a sickening and subtle crunch under my grip.

I pause, but she doesn't. She uses my hesitation to her advantage and wiggles an arm free to jab me in the chest with her elbow, knocking the wind out of me. But not enough to disarm me.

I recover quickly, regaining control and locking her down again. I bare my teeth with frustration simmering under my skin. "Are you done?" I snip vehemently, panting hard.

She's grinning up at me, taking in shallow breaths. "Now, that was fucking fun." There's a sheen of sweat over her face, and blood trickles out of her nose and into her mouth. I gawk at it in fascination, wanting to follow the trail with my tongue. "Not bad for a mafia prince."

She darts her tongue out to lap up the blood painting her upper lip, and that's it for me. I crush my mouth over hers and kiss the fuck out of her. Her blood is as sweet as I imagined it would be, yet it leaves a sizzle on my tongue as I inhale her.

It isn't tenderness. It's another battle for the upper hand. Our tongues thrashing with dominance and our bodies undulating with sexual frustration as if I were already deeply rooted inside of her.

As if we've done this before.

Made to do this.

Made to fight.

Made to fuck.

The kiss deepens, and finally, the line between battle and surrender disappears entirely.

I can't get her tight shorts down fast enough and she's just as eager to hold my heavy cock in her hand as she's pushing my pants down. I hiss when she wraps her small fingers around my length and gives it a firm pull. Just one touch and I'm throbbing.

Her hands snake under my shirt to roam over my torso. I whip my shirt up over my head and practically fumble with my cock to spear her. I've never felt so flustered in my life. Never. It's beginning to fuck with my head, which in turn enrages me.

Growling through gritted teeth, I grip her dainty wrists in my hands and slam them back above her head as my hips meet her thighs when I bottom out. It's like I can suddenly breathe, and the fog recedes a little so I can take back control of my own body and take ownership of hers.

She stills for a moment, but when the moment becomes too much, she snaps her head up, seizing my mouth like she's starving for something only I can give her. My body reacts on primal instinct. My hips take over and piston forward, hard and rough. I kiss her with equal brutality.

The heat her pussy wraps my cock with, it's a burn I feel all the way up my spine. There's no moaning or groaning. Only grunting and heavy breathing, as we both refuse to submit to whatever it is trying to dominate us both.

My skin is so hot, I wish I could jump out of it. But it doesn't stop me from punishing her cunt with violent thrusts. She doesn't let up with her mouth. She grapples my tongue with more effort, hikes her knees up higher, and her pussy gets tighter.

Her breath is shallow, panting out of her parted lips. Her body locks up under me. Knowing Sinclair is about to come all over my cock, has my blood rushing. That tingle at my spine bursts through my tightening balls, and the moment the muscles in her cunt squeezes, I fucking explode inside of her.

I'm slightly trembling with every last thrust, every spurt like another climax in itself. Fucking hell. Every single thing about this woman is already destroying me.

I feel like I've already given up some of my dominance to her, but I think she has too.

The air is thick with the heat we burned through. Our clothing still tangled at our feet, and the sweat cooling on our skin. I can't move. The sex was hard and fast, but I expended every ounce of energy I had left into it.

"Do you mind letting go of my wrists?" The meekness in her tone has me snapping back in.

I blink down at her, and I'm thrown off guard to see how small she suddenly seems. Her face is blank, but I can see something she's trying to mask behind her eyes. My mind finally catches up, and I realize I'm still tightly grasping her wrists. And one of those hands is swollen, the skin already red and angry-looking.

I let go immediately, and she brings her arms in protectively. "Let me see," I say lowly.

She hesitates but doesn't stop me when I gently cradle her hand in mine and rotate her wrist. The wince she tries to hide stabs at me. I knew I felt a crack in her hand when we were wrestling. It's much worse than I thought.

"Motherfucker," I mutter and force her up to her feet with me. "We need to get that looked at."

"I just need to put some ice on it, it's no big deal," she tries playing it off, but I'm beginning to see under the ruse of her hardened exterior. She might actually be human, with a heartbeat and everything.

"We're having the doctor take a look at it," I say with no room for argument.

CHAPTER NINE

Blackwell

After a call with our doctor, he insisted that I bring her into his office for X-rays, claiming it sounded like a fracture.

The moment we arrived, I got pulled into a call that couldn't wait, so I begrudgingly sent her in without me. They're closed inside the room longer than I like. My phone call was ten minutes long, and I feel like I've been waiting even longer.

They finally emerge, and Sinclair is moving slowly with this hazy, dazed grin. "Doc gave me the good stuff," she lazily drawls.

I snort despite myself, then turn my attention to the doctor. "Ms. Ortiz has a significant fracture. It'll require surgery for it to heal correctly." His eyes linger on Sinclair with a sympathetic look that puts me on edge. My fingers flex at my sides. "May I have a private word with you?" he asks cautiously.

I glance back down at Sinclair as she sits there, eyes glazed and smiling at nothing in particular. With a sign, I nod and signal to Hawk to stay with her. He, like Scout—sharp, loyal, unshakable—is one of the only ones I would trust with keeping an eye on her while off the estate.

The doctor takes us to his office down the hall and shuts us inside. I drop into a chair as he takes his seat behind the desk with a large manila envelope. "Do you have access to Ms. Ortiz's medical history?"

"I haven't gotten to that yet."

He looks hesitant before sliding the folder towards me. I pick it up and open it to several radiographs of what I assume is Sinclair's. He's quiet as I flip through them one by one. Rods, pins, scar tissue, and abnormalities in the bone. Arms, legs, ribs. Most aren't fully healed, and hardly anything is untouched.

My face scorches with anger, and my hands begin to shake by the time I'm finished. Slamming the folder shut, the edges crumble under my coiled fists. "Did you ask her about any of this?" I grind out the words.

He rigorously shakes his head with wide eyes. "No, sir. I know it isn't my place. But it would help if I could have some insight into her past surgeries."

"Help with what, exactly?" I ask defensively.

"Well, for one, the surgery on her hand," he explains carefully. "But beyond that, it's clear several of these injuries were either ignored or handled by someone who did not know what they were doing. It's not just damage. It's damage layered over damage." He pauses and lowers his voice. "This is evidence of long-term trauma. She's likely been living with chronic pain for years."

I study him hard, searching for any sign of deception, but I see none. Only concern. "When does she need the surgery?"

"Once the swelling goes down some, I can fit her in."

"I'll get what I can on her medical history and let you know when we're ready for surgery."

I stand with the folder, the weight of it heavier than I expected. It begins to burn my hand as if I can feel every break, every tear through it.

I haven't said a word since we left the office, but Sinclair easily fills the silence on the car ride. She's humming some aimless tune, and drums her fingers on her thigh as if there's a song playing only she can hear. Her body is slouched against the window, and all I can think is how human she seems right now.

"Blackwell?" she says my name on a long, contented sigh.

"Yes?"

"Do you love me?"

My head snaps to the side to gawk at her as she rolls her head in my direction, eyes barely focused. "What?" I practically splutter.

She sleepily grins. "Just checking." I narrow my eyes on her wondering what the fuck she's going on about when she bursts out in giggles like it's the funniest thing. "The look on your face," she mutters, then starts messing with the hem of her shirt, so easily distracted.

The heaviness of the folder in my lap is too much to bear. I put it in the space between us and run my hand down my face with a sigh.

She gasps, causing me to jolt upright, searching for the danger. "Can we stop there?" she asks with childlike enthusiasm, her face nearly smashed against the glass.

Once my heart jumps back down from my throat, I frown and look around. "Where?"

"There!" she points to some fast-food joint now behind us.

"For what?"

She looks at me and tries to roll her eyes, but they only flutter. "For food, *duh*." I let out yet another sigh. "I've never had fast food before," she pouts.

I frown at her. "You're serious?"

"Deadly." She giggles at her own joke, making me snort under my breath. "I wasn't allowed," she says lightly.

With that small confession, I can't say no to her. I tell Hawk to turn us around and take us to the fast-food place. "You sure about this?" I mutter.

"I heard it tastes like shame and regret. I want it."

I stare at her, and a part of me needs to know what it was that I saw in her folder. Demand to know about every single scar on her. But the other part of me knows to stay quiet. She's so stupidly soft and innocent right now, I need to let her bleed herself all over the car.

We pull up to the window, and I ask her what she wants. Her reply, "Everything."

"You're going to throw up."

"Worth it," she responds with a full-on grin.

My head is pounding by the time we walk through the front doors. But Sinclair is still high on painkillers and sugar, floating on whatever is keeping her like this.

The second she spots my brothers, she gasps and makes a beeline for them. "Oh my God, Harlan!" He raises an amused brow and lets her throw herself on him as if they've been friends for years. "I had a cheeseburger!" she proudly announces, slightly swaying on her feet. "From a fast-food place."

He helps keep her steady while adoringly smiling down at her. I clench my jaw so tight I can feel it in my ears. I know their friendship is innocent, at least on his end, but when she grabs hold of his biceps and grins up at him, their proximity and familiarity with one another has me wanting to put them both through a damn wall.

Harlan shoots me a look, silently begging for help. "And how was it? Everything you hoped and dreamed?" He plays along, voice and demeanor light.

She shakes her head like a child, and I can imagine the way her petite nose is scrunched up like she did when she took her first bite of the cheap food. "That was *not* meat. But the French fries were okay." She shrugs, then whips around to face me. "Can we have tacos for dinner?" she asks, completely unaware of how both my brothers are desperately trying not to laugh.

I rub my aching forehead. "Sure," I mutter to appease her. "Harlan, will you escort Sinclair to her room?"

"But I'm not tired," she pouts, bottom lip jutting out.

"You will be." The meds will have her on her ass soon. "Meet me when you're done," I say to Harlan.

I throw myself down onto one of the sitting chairs in an unoccupied room and slap the thick folder down on the coffee table. I feel like I've been dragged through hell, blindfolded and barefoot, with that woman lighting a match at every turn.

Dane joins me only a moment later. "What's going on?" He takes a seat across from me with a curious look.

"She broke her hand. Going to need surgery." He doesn't say anything, but I can feel him watching me. "We were sparring."

"Shit happens," he says casually and unconcerned.

If only it were that simple.

"Pour us a drink, will you?" I utter under my breath.

Dane rises with a grunt and goes to pour for two. We sit silently with our drinks while he scrolls through his phone, and I stare at the envelope like it's a loaded weapon sitting between us.

My mind continues to picture every pin, every break, every internal scar in print.

Just as Dane grumbles something about going to find Harlan, he steps into the room. "Sorry. Thought it best to remove the alcohol from her room. Had to wait until she was distracted."

"What was she doing when you left?" I ask.

He chuckles and steals Dane's drink. "Talking nonsense, high as a kite. Got her into bed, though. Probably passed out by now."

"So?" Dane starts. "What's going on?"

I nod at the envelope. "I want the Ortizs gone."

Dane reaches for the folder and flips it open. His expression shifts instantly as he starts leafing through the scans.

"What's that?" Harlan asks.

"Radiographs," Dane mutters, and his eyes cut to me. "These Sinclair's?"

I nod once. It has Harlan's curiosity piqued and on his feet. Dane takes a seat as Harlan peers over his shoulder, watching him flip through one after another. The look on his face has me insane.

"Was she in an accident or something?" Harlan asks with genuine concern.

"I don't know," I murmur.

Dane's eyes widen. "You don't know? What did she tell you?" With Dane distracted, Harlan steals the folder from his hands and takes it with him to sit down.

"I haven't asked her about it yet," I say lowly. Harlan only glances up at me, but Dane looks at me as if I've lost my mind. If only they knew. "You saw the state she was in," I snap. "Who knows what kind of bullshit she'd come up with?"

The lie is for myself. The truth is, I didn't trust myself to open that box quite yet. I'm not sure if her lies would infuriate me more than the truth or not. Either answer would have me uncontrollable.

I avoid their stares and sip my drink while the room grows deathly silent.

"Does *Baba* know?" Dane finally asks.

"Not yet. I wanted to talk with you both first."

As they flip through the pages of her past, I feel her presence in the back of my mind like a brand. Right now, she's upstairs, drugged, listless. But all I can think about is her bones snapping and pieced back together, over and over again.

The drinks do nothing for the pressure behind my eyes. Not enough to help dull the weight of what I saw in those scans. The sound of her laughter from earlier—light and drug-laced like it belonged to someone else entirely—still echoes.

Eventually, I leave my brothers behind as I go and take the stairs two at a time. I hesitate for only a second before turning the knob and entering her bedroom without knocking.

I'm instantly overwhelmed by the smell of her. The only light comes from the dim-lit lamp on her side table, like I've noticed a few other times. It solidifies my belief that she doesn't like the dark. She pretends to come from it, but in reality, she hates it. Possibly even afraid of it.

Her limbs are tangled in the sheets as if she tried to fight sleep but lost. My eyes stray down to her bandaged hand clutched to her chest as if even in her sleep, she knows it needs protection.

It almost feels wrong to see her like this. There's something cruel about the way she looks when she's unconscious. To witness her so exposed. No armor. No sharp comebacks. No harrowing smirk present. She's unguarded and peaceful.

She's simply Sinclair.

And it wrecks me.

I sit on the edge of the bed, elbows on my knees, watching the steady rise and fall of her chest. As I continue to watch her, my blood continues to boil.

What did they do to you?

How the fuck do I decode every lie and every scar like it's a goddamn blueprint?

CHAPTER TEN

Blackwell

I sit there, jaw tight, nerves fraying, while stewing in silence, waiting for her to come around.

Two goddamn days since the doctor gave me that folder full of her past no one has had the decency to care about. For two days, the questions have been rotting me from the inside like poison.

She begins to stir, her lashes fluttering as her face softens, dazed and delicate. I move to alert the nurse. She and the doctor sweep in to check her vitals, murmuring updates, and making notes. I step back, out of their way, but not out of reach. Keeping a close eye on everything they do. Every beep from the monitors, every flick of their pen, every touch to Sinclair.

I've sat in silence. Bit my tongue. Swallowed my questions like broken glass. But time has not dulled the fury. And I won't know peace until I get some answers. She's out of surgery and lucid enough. And I am done waiting.

As soon as the room is once again cleared, I take the chair next to her, and we're both quiet.

I clear my throat. "How are you feeling?"

She turns her head with this dreamy look on her face as if she had no idea I was here. "Hi," she whispers with a slow grin.

My eyebrows twitch. "How are you feeling?" I repeat.

"Oh, I'm good." Her speech is slowed. "Like *real* good."

My lips twitch. "Well, surgery went well." She giggles in response. "But I'm sure you're used to this," I say, unable to keep the edge out of my voice.

Her smile remains as she faces forward and shrugs her shoulders. "Had a few."

I lean forward. There's a part of me that wants to leave her be. That maybe I should give her some more time, but perhaps this is the *only* time. Now, when she's too raw to perform, too tired to lie through her teeth.

"Tell me about them."

"Which one?" Her head lolls to the side, eyes heavy-lidded as they find mine. She's still groggy, but so effortlessly beautiful that the steam inside me slightly cools.

"Start with the rod in your arm."

She squints with a distant look. "I can't remember. They kind of all blend together."

My jaw flexes. "Then tell me who caused it."

She lets out a quiet yet bitter laugh, staring off at nothing. "They all blend together, too."

Her aloofness, her indifference, it grates against my skin like razors. But she's talking, so I push forward. "Fine. Then tell me what you do remember. Who hurt you?"

She chuckles, and I can't understand it. "Everyone has hurt me," she says softly.

"Who, Sinclair? Your brothers? Your father?"

"It was nice not being on the receiving end for once. To be the one spilling blood."

I frown. "Who?"

"Your goons," she exacerbates. "Your beefy goons that were too scared to hit back. It wasn't exactly a fair fight, but it felt good pounding on someone," she mutters.

"Is that how it happened? The break?"

"How *what* happened?" she yawns dramatically.

"Your injuries," I drag out through my teeth.

"Sparring," she trails off as if she's fading on me.

"Sinclair," I say, demanding her attention.

She looks at me once again and smiles. A real smile. One where there's warmth in her eyes and no malice in her grin. "You're cute when you're mad."

I try to hide the heat in my face and wipe away my smile with a hand. "You're pretty cute like this," I mutter.

"Like what?"

"Vulnerable. Sweet."

Her eyes widen like I slapped her. "Sweet? I don't think anyone has ever called me *sweet*."

"Well, no one has ever called me *cute*."

She giggles and fuck me if it doesn't jab at something in my chest. "It's fun pressing your buttons."

I shake my head. "And you have quickly adapted to them."

"I learned from the best."

The levity drains from the room, and I inch closer. "Tell me," I say as gently as I'm capable of.

"It was only a small fracture," she shrugs with glazed eyes and a smile on her porcelain face. "I should've stayed out of their way." She flops her head side to side. "But I'm a glutton for punishment."

Her deluded answer has me reeling with frustration. "What was only a fracture?"

"My arm, *duh*." She sighs.

"Okay, so how did you end up needing a rod in your arm?"

She groans like a child not getting their way. "I told you," she whines. "I had a broken arm and didn't stay out of their way. I still fought them."

"They let you fight with a broken arm."

She snorts, looking away again. "*Let* me? They were chomping at the bit, seeing any weakness from me, and they went rabid." She flexes her hand on the topic of conversation—her arm. "They made sure to turn that fracture into mutilation."

I hold my breath. "Your brothers." She doesn't answer, but she doesn't deny it. "And your father. He let them?"

"*Let* them," she echoes, her voice trailing off. "He encouraged them."

"What about your sister?"

She stares up at the ceiling. "She *kept her head down. Stayed out of their way*," she says as if mocking someone. I'm guessing her sister. "She took everything."

I frown. "Took what?"

"Anything. Everything. She just...took it. I thought she liked it." Her blinks are too long as she's quickly fading now. "Guess not."

She's struggling to remain conscious, but I need more. "Tell me about Royce."

She doesn't respond at first, but when she does, the chill in her voice is worse than her silence. "Someone should really put that dog down. He's sick."

I lean in even closer, my tone careful. "What did he do to you, Sinclair?"

The light in her eyes flickers as she yawns again, slow and heavy. Her eyelids droop, and I know my time with this docile version of Sinclair has ended. "Rest, Clair. We'll talk more later."

She flutters her lashes at me, and I can make out all the colors that make up her hazel eyes. "No one has ever called me *Clair* before."

That hits hard, and I suddenly feel uncomfortable. I squeeze at the back of my neck where the tension is building. "I don't know where it came from," I murmur.

"You have to have friends to have a nickname. I wasn't allowed friends. Only a list of approved acquaintances. I hated all of them." Her words are meant to be sharp, but they come out slurred.

I snort. "Yeah, I heard how you scared them all off."

"It was certainly entertaining. Until it wasn't." She sighs. "I met your cousin Kamea once before our engagement party. Don't tell her this, but I didn't hate her." Her lips are slightly curved, but her blinks grow slower.

"Wouldn't want anyone to know there's a heart in there."

She stares back at me. "I could say the same for you. You don't have to be here."

"You're my fiancée and my responsibility," I say robotically.

She gives up the last of her energy to smile. "I fucking love your lies," she slurs.

"Why?" I ask instead of what.

"Because it's easy to see the truth beneath them."

I'm silent as her eyes finally succumb to the fatigue, and her breathing has already evened out. But as soon as it's quiet, I go back to plotting.

The only other thing I can seem to think about other than Sinclair lately is the sweet revenge I will have on her family. Plotting, fantasizing, mapping out their extermination.

CHAPTER ELEVEN

I conceal the cans, the bowl, and bottled water beneath my jacket like I'm smuggling drugs.

The hedge maze has become my refuge. I spent an entire day mapping it out. Now, it's where I go to ditch my stalkers Blackwell still assigns to tail me most days. Dumbasses with pecs for brains. I'd hide behind hedges and watch in amusement as they wandered like overgrown toddlers.

Today, for whatever reason, I don't have anyone following me. No shadows. No footsteps behind me. No one to lose as I breeze through the maze like I've done it a thousand times. There's a bench deep inside, tucked in the heart of the greenery. It's where the world feels far away, and I can pretend for five minutes I'm free.

It's also where I met Blender. A cat who looks like she got tossed into a blender and barely survived. She's mangy and may have the appearance only a mother could love, but she's sweet and friendly, despite whatever she's been through.

I say *her* because I get a survivor vibe from her. Not a masochistic entitled asshole one.

She's living proof of what people are capable of when there are no consequences. No accident could've carved wounds like hers. I would know. Her scars are forged with malice and intention.

Clicking my tongue and whistling softly, I call her name. She appears only seconds later, leaping from the undergrowth like a purring phantom. Hopping right up onto the bench, and to me, rubbing her dirty, skeletal body all over my legs.

I smile and hide the cringe when I run my hand along her spine, where I can feel every vertebra. "Hey, Blender," I say softly. She keeps rubbing against me aggressively, purring. "Got a surprise for you."

I pull out a can of wet food and she loses her shit. Circling, meowing, tripping over herself, trying to climb into my lap. I peel the can open and she barely lets me set the can down before diving in face-first.

"Whoa, whoa—slow down," I say gently, trying to ease the can back. I did some research and learned that I shouldn't feed her too much too soon. To give her a little at a time.

I vigilantly watch her as I open the bottle of water and pour some into a bowl. Once she devours half of the can, I take it away and try to slide the water to her. She protests immediately, clawing at my jacket sleeve, trying to scale me like a tree. "I know, Blender. I'd be pissed too. Go ahead and claw my eyes out." She continues her tantrum. "I'm sorry, but no," I say firmly, and raise the can over my head.

She doesn't give up, and for the first time in my life, I do. "Jesus, alright!" I set the can back down. "Have at it. Eat yourself into a coma. Just trying to help," I mutter. She attaches herself to it instantly. I tuck her with the food, and the bowl of water under the bench.

"Enjoy. I'll be back tomorrow." I pet down her bony back. "Try not to die on me, okay?"

I stash the extra food cans and bottled waters in the shrubbery before rising. Then I whip around when I feel the shift in the air. Like I'm not alone. There's no sign of anyone, but it doesn't mean there aren't eyes on me. Just to be safe, I take the long way out of the maze. At a swift pace, no one would be able to keep up *and* remain unobscured.

I can make out the house up ahead as I near the exit. I throw a glance over my shoulder to confirm I'm not being followed when—"Sinclair." Blackwell's voice, though familiar, still has my heart lurching. He's standing just outside the hedges, smooth and collected. "I didn't mean to startle you."

"You didn't," I say defensively.

"Of course not," he says dryly, unimpressed. "We're going out tonight."

I blink. "Out where?"

"Dinner. Then the casino. Be ready by eight."

"Got it. I'll see you then."

I brush past him and head right upstairs, pretending I don't feel him behind me, watching. As soon as the pressure of his eyes fades, the nerves begin souring my stomach. There's an anxious twist in my gut I cannot rationalize.

Why does he affect me like this?

Yes, it's dinner, but it's not like a real date. It's a staged outing. A PR campaign for our alignment. I'm just there as a prop. Not his fiancée or lover. His chess piece on display.

Still, I don't stall. I don't drag my feet to needle him like I usually do. I can't sit still long enough to kill time anyway. I'm spiraling, and I fucking hate it.

I refuse to spend any special time on getting ready. I don't fuss over my hair. I let the purple fade, and I part the platinum down the middle, sleek and cold. But my makeup is all bite. Sharp wings, smoke-smudged lids, lips painted in a bruised wine.

And just to be petty, I wear something that is a middle finger to every mob wife aesthetic they expect of me. A relaxed fit animal print skirt starting from high up on my waist down to my calves and exposing one leg. Black leather stiletto boots come up past my knees. And over my patterned black sheer top covering my arms and up to my throat, I have a black leather top that is a cross between a corset and a moto jacket.

Before I can talk myself into changing, I grab a coat and leave the room in hopes of grabbing a drink before it's time to leave.

My legs slightly quake as I hit the top of the stairs. I don't want to do this. I should refuse. Cause a scene. Become insufferable so he gives up and goes alone.

No. I have never shied from anything that rattles me. Fear is a dare. And I'm the kind of girl that bares her teeth and runs headfirst into the fire.

As soon as I hit the landing, I find him coming from around the corner, head down, focused on his phone. I cross my arms, trying to remain stolid when I'm still shaking inside.

He takes notice of my punctual arrival and stops cold. His eyes rake me from head to toe, most likely inwardly insulting my appearance.

Okay, maybe I did dress for *him*. For him to *hate* it. For him to be so vexed by my attire, he demands that I go back upstairs and change. Any second now, he'll tell me I look like hell on heels.

In three, two...

"You're on time," he states blandly, pocketing his phone. The handsome devil is in one of his bespoke suits—all black, sharp, and lethal.

"I'm hungry," I give him the lame excuse for not making him wait.

His eyes roam the length of my body again, and I don't flinch. "Good. Shall we?"

I'm a little disappointed when he doesn't verbalize his disdain for my outfit. Either he's becoming more tolerant of me, or I am becoming less intolerable.

I almost laugh at that thought.

On the drive, I cross one leg over the other, letting my foot lazily sway while I pretend to be engrossed in my phone. He's glued to his own phone, the silence thick and humming with consuming thoughts.

Usually, I thrive in silence, but tonight, it claws at me. I feel like every breath I take is rehearsed. Every inch of my posture is calculated. And I catch myself wondering if he's stealing glances at me.

It's not until the car slows that I look up. I see the glowing letters of the restaurant's name. *Piccionini.* I know the place, and I'm even more uncomfortable since he told me we were going to dinner. It's intimate, elegant, and romantic.

Without waiting, I open my own door and step out, not missing the subtle, vexed exhale behind me. Chauvinist ass. His need to open my door isn't out of chivalry, it's out of pompous superiority.

I meet him around on the other side of the vehicle, ignoring the heat of his gaze as he buttons his jacket. His hand finds the small of my back as if it has a right to be there, and we move together.

Flanked by two meat suits behind and one in front of us, we walk into the most old-money Italian restaurant in the state. The owner greets us personally and escorts us to a secluded table in the back. The lights dim with every step we take, the air heavy with wine and pleasant aromas. It's a setup for lovers, not for power plays.

Blackwell exchanges pleasantries with the owner in perfect Italian, and I swear I'm not impressed. I'm not. In addition to English and Farsi, he also speaks Italian. It's just useful information to me.

He pulls out my chair for me, and I resist the urge to roll my eyes before sinking into it. I look around and it's exactly as I remember it, though wrapped in an uglier lie. Feels a lot like my old bedroom. Dark and deceptively safe.

Red wine is poured, and I don't hesitate to reach for the glass. Anything to avoid speaking. I lean back and sip, trying to let the sweetness of the wine give me the ease I'm becoming desperate for.

"So, who are you meeting with at the casino?" I ask, finally making eye contact with him, and I find him already staring at me.

He takes a drawn-out moment before answering me. "No one from the inner circle, but those close to it," he murmurs.

"Will your father or your brothers be there?"

"Dane will."

"Not your father?" I raise the wine glass to my lips to drain the rest of what's left.

His eyes flick away for half a beat, and I find it very telling. "He won't be there tonight."

"Is he out of town?"

That earns me a sharp look. "My father doesn't always need to be present at every meeting."

I frown. "Why not? He's still the head of the family, is he not?"

It's obvious the question hits, and just like that, he smooths his expression. "He is, but he trusts me to fill in for him when needed."

"And it's needed?" I press, arching a brow. "Is he gone, or just..."

He sighs as the tension in his jaw builds. It only provokes me more. But before he can give me his rebuttal, the owner comes back. They talk quietly, keeping it in Italian, then after he pours me another glass of red wine, he disappears again.

I squint at him over the rim of my glass. "Did you just order for me?"

He quirks a brow. "You speak Italian?"

"No, but I'm not daft."

One side of his mouth tilts and goddamn he wears a smirk well. "Just hush and drink your wine."

My mouth pops open in indignance, but before I can fire back, something unexpected happens. My head falls back as I burst into laughter. I laugh harder than I have in so long. I can't even remember the last time I genuinely laughed.

It hits me so fast, I barely register the shocked look on his face. It has me sobering, and I bring the glass to my lips to try and hide the leftover giggles.

There's a charge sparking between us. The heated glare taking over his handsome face is so familiar I can feel it move through me like molten lava, heating me to the point of melting me.

His unabashed look says we'll be fucking in the car on the way to the casino.

He doesn't ask me about dessert, not that I would eat any anyway. And when we walk out of the restaurant, he walks with urgency.

The closer we get to our blacked-out getaway, my skin dances with exhilaration, and my nipples are tightening. I have the strongest urge to cross my legs to stave off the desire burning between them.

I've grown silent as he opens the car door, and I slip inside first. Those fucking unwarranted nerves are back. This time, it has everything to do with what we're about to do. Fuck. I haven't been nervous about sex since I found out how much I liked it. Since I knew exactly how to weaponize it.

"Drive around back," Blackwell says to our driver, then pulls me into his lap with one smooth motion.

I'm stiff against him, but I keep my face relaxed. He stares at me, and I brace myself when he raises a hand. I swallow, and his fingers make a gentle trail down the side of my face and neck.

The car stops again. "Out." One singular word, low but audible, and the two men up front exit the vehicle without a glance back.

The doors seal shut, and we're surrounded in silence.

Okay, breathe. Get your shit together, bitch. When it comes to seduction, you got this.

I'm bold and make the first move. I use his shoulders to steady myself as I swivel in his lap so that my knees are on either side of his hips, straddling him. My skirt naturally hitches itself up. We're both wearing that knowing smirk.

"Are you going to fuck me or what?" I say lightly, even though I'm about to come undone. From desire or trepidation, or a bit of both.

His hands slide onto my thighs, his calloused skin against the smoothness of mine. A titillating contrast. I get comfortable, slinging my arms over his shoulders. Our faces so close, exchanging a breath.

My pussy pulsates when his hands begin inching up my legs, disappearing under the silky fabric of my skirt. The muscles in my core jump when he makes contact, but I keep a straight face.

His eyes skitter all over as his thumb begins to make languid, small circles. Our heads gravitate, creeping closer. I don't know who makes the first move this time, but our mouths suddenly fuse, and his efforts with his hand double. Rubbing my pussy, making my hips rock on reflex. Our tongues wrestle and our bodies come together.

A moan spills from me, and I can't take it anymore. But before I can shove his hand away to tear his cock out and impale myself, he sinks two fingers inside of me, curling them. My hands fist the back of the seat, nails stabbing into the leather. My muscles freeze up, and my mouth goes slack, but he doesn't stop his tongue from lavishing every inch of it.

My forehead bumps into his, and I squeeze my eyes shut from the onslaught of ecstasy. A silent scream flows out, bleeding into his tongue, and I convulse on his hand.

I'm dazed and confused when I begin to descend, and shame paints my cheeks. I don't give him the chance to catch it, though. I go for his belt with shaky fingers, but I manage to get the task done.

I have his cock out and I point it up and sit down on it. As soon as my ass meets his lap, he grabs me by the back of my hair and crushes my mouth with his. I let his bodily responses decide on the pace. When he grunts, it's frustration, so I go faster. When he wilts and his kisses turn sloppy, I slow it down. I'm not ready for it to end just yet.

It's not until our skin becomes slick, and the air turns too thick to breathe in, that I take us both to the peak. I hit mine first, and he grabs hold of my ass to slap me up and down on him when I no longer can until I feel his cock swell and thump inside of me, and he goes still.

It was only our second time fucking, but somehow, we're so in sync, it feels like we've already done this hundreds of times before.

Yet it's still mind-blowing.

67

CHAPTER TWELVE

Blackwell

I bring my finger to my upper lip to feign an itch just to catch another whiff of Sinclair.

The wicked sweetness of her.

We walk through the private entrance of the casino, and she strolls beside me as if she didn't just wreck me in the backseat only minutes ago.

I was buried inside her, spiraling into madness, and somehow, it's not enough. It's never enough.

My fingers flex at my sides, dying to touch her. To drag her off somewhere dark and private to lose myself all over her body again. No woman has ever done this to me. To have me starving for more when I've just been so thoroughly satiated.

But here I am, hungering for her. Still haunted by the way she feels clenching around me. The way her mouth steals my breath. The way I feel bereft when I'm not rooted inside her.

When we walk out to the main room, I spot the women of the men I'm here to meet, clustered with cocktails in one of the private lounges.

"I need to meet with them privately," I tell her low under my breath. "You can join later. I'll introduce you."

"No, thank you," she quips, mischief in her tone. "I'd rather spend your money on playing Blackjack."

Before giving me the chance to argue, she's already walking away, hips swaying in deliberate, taunting arcs. Knowing her reclusive behavior, I assumed she wouldn't want to socialize. Not after a life of being ordered to smile at whom and forced to consort with a revised list of debs.

I wipe the stupid smirk off my face and head to the private room where I'm expected. This deal is critical and high stakes. And I am to conduct it without my father.

My father's absence speaks volumes. He told me about his heart condition weeks ago, downplaying it with his usual professionalism. Sometimes forgetting that I'm not only a business partner or employee. I'm his son. His family. I deserve more than diluted truths. And the fact that he let my mother intervene and insist he stay home tonight confirms the actual severity of it. It isn't just stress. It's far more serious than he's letting on.

My brothers are already there, working the room in their distinct ways. Harlan, with that effortless charm and charisma, can emulate like turning on a switch. And Dane, the taciturn one, laconic by nature. He's a man of very few words, but when he speaks, you listen. Every word carries weight.

I find myself more aligned with Dane. I've never been one for idle talk. I'm deliberate and reserved; I don't waste my words on men who would sooner stab me in the back as soon as I turn it.

The air is always taut with tension in a room full of men in power. But tonight, it hums with something more palpable, more visceral. The kind of pressure that settles hard in your gut. Everyone is thoroughly searched before entering, but the precaution does little to soothe the unease coiling inside me.

It could be because my mind is not entirely here. My mind keeps drifting to Sinclair, knowing she's out there exposed.

I want nothing more than to snag Sinclair and get us the fuck out of here. However, walking out before the deal is sealed would be seen as a slight. A personal insult no one here would forget and never forgive.

Thankfully, it unfolds without friction and as planned. Smooth, at least on the outside.

Still, my hackles are raised as we wrap it up. And I won't exhale until she's beside me again.

I glance across the room at Scout, and there's a subtle crease between his brows as he surveils the room. His eyes scan every person in it and every single move they make. Something's wrong. I can feel it. I've felt it the moment I stepped foot in the room.

I signal one of my men with a look and a nod toward the back. "Retrieve the women."

A few minutes pass before the doors open, and they file in, drinks in hand and laughter circling. I pay them no attention as introductions are being made, my eyes keep straying to the threshold.

Too many seconds crawl by, and of course, no Sinclair.

I grunt, trying not to visibly shift as my pulse kicks up. Just as I decide to go tearing through the casino myself, she strides in. Head held high and eyes gleaming with mischief. Every step she takes is designed to test my restraint as she approaches me.

I manage to stay put despite the internal war within myself. "Did you enjoy spending my money?" I murmur as she plants herself at my side.

"Sure did." She grins, unrepentant.

"Any luck?"

"A little." She shrugs while glancing around. "So, how long are you going to make me suffer through this?"

My lips fight against the humor threatening them. "Not long."

I've been nursing the same drink since I got here, pretending to be present. But my attention sharpens when I spot two men having what appears to be a heated conversation. Voices are raised, hands are waving, violence crackling through the room.

I snap a look to Hawk, and he's already headed my way. "Get her out of here," I order sharply.

"And miss all the fun?" Sinclair teases, the rebellion in her already sparked.

"Sinclair," I growl in warning, but her eyes are laser-focused on something else. Something that has her lit up. Before I can grab her, she sprints off, and my heart jumps. "Clair!"

The room explodes into chaos. The sounds of chairs scraping, voices raising, and glass shattering have my gut turning as I keep my focus on Sinclair. She is my sole priority.

I'm fucking seething with dread as I push by anyone in my way to find my batshit fiancée, whom I have not let out of my sight since she twisted from my grasp.

Her tiny figure has a man pinned beneath her like a true conqueror. She's feral as she beats his face to a pulp with this giddy, demented grin, blood splattering all over her, most likely rebreaking her fucking hand.

My men are moving in fast now, pulling bodies apart and restoring order. I surge forward and wrap my arms around Sinclair's waist, setting her upright. Relieved she's unharmed. She's breathless and wild-eyed, but she doesn't turn on me.

"Get her the fuck out of here!" I bark at Hawk, who's already on it.

"He's coming with us," she states in a surprisingly equable tone despite the carnage still scorching her gaze.

Something about the authority in her demeanor has me rooted, and I stare back at her with morbid curiosity, wondering what her play is here. Then I glance down at her bloodied victim, hardly breathing. He's nobody and won't be missed, so I humor her and grab Scout's attention as Hawk hauls her away.

After I'm certain Scout has everything under control, I leave. The disrespect given on our territory will not go unpunished. But I need to get Sinclair away from it all and then speak with my father first.

I am beyond reasoning when I get into the vehicle, joining Sinclair. As soon as the door shuts, we take off, and I grasp her left wrist. I'm not so gentle as I pull her hand up to inspect it. "It's fine, Blackwell," she says in a curt tone as if I have offended her.

The fire in my eyes matches hers as I snap my glare up. "Do not speak right now," I sneer. Her mouth bobs open to argue, but I'm faster. I seize her jaw in my hand with a little too much pressure and thumb her bloodied bottom lip.

Something breaks inside me. I am now shaking when I pull her in closer, where our noses touch. Fire and brimstone swirl between us as I try to breathe through the onslaught of emotions. Like a dark tide trying to pull me under. "I am warning you." My voice is so low it's almost inhuman. "Not. A. Word."

Her nostrils flare, and I know she's fighting the urge to be combative, but she's prudent to heed my warning, and we ride the rest of the way in strained silence.

The second we reach the estate, I throw the car door open, grab her right hand, and yank her out after me to drag swiftly inside. My vision tunnels, I'm so blind with rage. I breeze past everyone without a word, or registering anything they're saying, gripping Sinclair's hand so tightly my knuckles turn white.

We head straight for my bedroom, the only place where I can afford to lose control.

The door slams shut, and I finally release her hand and practically stumble forward. I suddenly feel like I'm suffocating and tear at the collar of my shirt as if it's choking me. The room tilts. The walls close in.

I peel my clothes off, but I feel no less trapped. A sheen of sweat forms on my naked torso, and my heart hammers inside my tightening chest.

Fuck.

Fuck.

I pace, flexing my hands as they go numb, tingling at the fingertips. It's getting harder to breathe. The air won't reach my lungs fast enough. I'm dying. Or am I having a heart attack?

"Are...you okay?" Sinclair's disinterested tone somehow breaks through the haze.

"Don't." My voice is raw, torn from somewhere deep.

"You're kind of freaking me out here," she mutters.

Stop fucking talking.

Stop fucking talking.

Okay, breathe.

Breathe.

"Blackwell?" Her voice is closer, but I have my eyes trained on the floor, willing my body to obey me. "Whoa, Blackwell," she rasps softly.

Her hand rests on my shoulder, and like a fucking shock, everything stops. The pounding. The shaking. The suffocating noose around my neck. Her simple touch brings me serenity. Stilling the storm inside me, extinguishing it entirely.

As the tightness in my chest slowly releases, I lift my head to meet her angelic face. She tilts it with something that looks like concern written all over it. She's never looked so exposed. So innocent and youthful. All those years of hell she was put through, stripped away, if only momentarily.

She stares back at me like I'm something fragile. Then she lifts her hand just as cautiously to cradle my face gently. All I can do is stare back and swallow down the thick lump rising in my throat.

Neither of us can move as the pressure between us begins to build. The hairs on the back of my neck stand, and I watch as her poreless skin pebbles with tiny bumps. The air crackles, and our breathing kicks up in tandem.

As time slows, we finally combust.

CHAPTER THIRTEEN

Sinclair

Our bodies come together like it's unnatural for them ever to be pulled apart.

His lips are controlling, and he kisses me in a way that is going to have me fucked up forever. My entire existence was for the sole purpose of a toy for my brothers and father to try and break. Torture, abuse, humiliation, depravity, my body used for whatever fed their evil minds.

But this. This right here. This kiss. It fucking ruins me. My bastioned heart tearing open and letting him in. And I can't stop it. I'm not even sure if I want to. My brain screams for me to shut it down, to run. But my heart keeps filleting, willingly bleeding for him.

The little bit of his clothing is gone, and mine quickly comes off. His body is already slightly slick with sweat, sliding against my skin.

He sits on the edge of the bed when the backs of his legs hit it. Our mouths still fused, I climb on top of him, ready to impale myself. But he has other plans with me.

I'm flipped on my back, breaking the kiss. He grins, and I can't help but grin back. His eyes crinkle at the corners, and the brown in them almost sparkles. I want to stroke his face and tell him how handsome he is. But I'm me, so I don't.

But right now, I feel so...light. So carefree, but not in the usual detached way. Nothing outside of this room matters. Only our bodies and our pleasure.

He gives me soft, chaste kisses to my lips. Just enough to pull me in, then remove himself, over and over. It's somehow more sensual than when we devour each other. His hands sliding down then up my body, yet keeping it somewhat wholesome.

But we are not wholesome human beings. I want him inside me. I want more.

Just as I grow fervid with frustration, he starts to trail his lips and tongue down my body. Briefly stopping at my breasts to toy with my nipples. Teasing them just enough to give me pleasure and leave me begging for more.

My lips thin when he gives my nipple a bite. A zap right to my pussy. I arch my back and thread my fingers through his soft locks to hold him there. It's all the provocation he needs to rise to the challenge. He tongues the same nipple before chomping down on it, this time harder.

My back bows and my head snaps back as I open my mouth with an audible gasp. My thighs clench around him, and my hips buck, dying for some friction where the apex of my thighs throb with desire.

He releases my nipple, and I whine as my face tilts down at him. His dark gaze locks eyes with me, a smirk teasing his lips. He makes a wet trail down to where I swear has its own heart now, and it's beating with a thumping rhythm.

It's been so long since I've let anyone go down on me. There's usually no foreplay. When I'm feeling sexually deprived, I go out to one our clubs, find an attractive enough man, and fuck him in the VIP or the bathroom. Just sex.

And with the way he's taunting me, licking me, and kissing me everywhere but where I need it, he knows how badly I want it. I'm so fucking pent up, I don't even care. Fuck my pride.

When my nostrils flare in warning, he gives me a smirk right before he lowers his mouth right to my center, and I flinch in reaction. I feel it everywhere, from my fingertips to the tips of my toes. Everything reacts, burning and yearning for him to fuck my pussy with his mouth.

And he delivers.

He oscillates between long and languid swipes with his tongue, to quick, rapid ones with the tip of it. I'm panting, my muscles straining. My body pathetically desperate for him to send me over that edge.

He stabs his tongue inside me, nuzzling his nose against me. It's all too much. It feels so fucking good, and he keeps me on that fucking edge. I want to scream. I want to fuck his face. I want to put a stop to this.

As if he can read my mind, he takes my entire pussy into his mouth with a strong suction, then releases a little pressure to tongue me over that edge and to my death. My whole body coils, my back coming off the mattress, my head snapped back, my jaw unhinged on a silent scream.

It's fucking beautiful.

I stare up at the ceiling, smiling. My muscles now so relaxed they've gone limp.

"*Joon-kharâsh*," he rumbles against my sensitive flesh. Then chuckles when I quiver uncontrollably. I know my cheeks are glowing when I gather the courage to face him. "I could eat you for hours, but my cock might punch a hole through the mattress if I don't fuck you," he murmurs after placing a gentle kiss on my hipbone. But I don't miss the way he almost cringes looking at the nasty scar on my other one.

My reddened cheeks heat with a grin, swallowing down a girlish giggle. He looks at me, grinning back like the devil. His body climbs up mine lazily. My breathing picks back up to a pant, and I can feel my heart trying to pound out of my chest as he gets closer.

His face hovers over mine, and we just stare at each other. What the fuck is he doing to me? Why the fuck am I letting him? But I can't stop. I don't want to stop.

I can smell myself on his breath as it dances across my face. It has my pussy throbbing all over again. And when his hard cock butts against me, sticking to me, my knees fall to the mattress. My core a votive offering, a desperate plea.

Everything stops when he softly brushes some hair off my face with such gentle fingers. The world is silent. My mind clears, empties of all thoughts. All I can see is him.

He must sense the panic beginning to rise within me because he releases me from his stare and reaches a hand between us. His knuckles grazing that wickedly sensitive cluster of nerves, causing my eyes to practically roll to the back of my skull.

He gives it a few feather-light strokes just to torment me, then puts me out of my misery to press the tip of his cock to me, and pushes his way inside, knocking the air out of me.

It's pure torture how slowly he makes his way in, all the way to the hilt. On reflex, I squeeze his hips with my thighs and wrap my arms around his shoulders to yank him down. I kiss him with desperation, pouring things I can't explain into him. He returns the same ardent lust, kissing me deeply and pulling his cock out to the tip to slam back in, jolting my body with the brutal force.

My hands begin to roam around his taut body. His skin is firm yet soft as my fingers glide along his bronzed skin. I love the contrast between us. His dark and my light.

My hands find their way to his solid ass to grab on, demanding he fuck me harder. A growl rumbles low in his chest, and he thrusts into me with more speed and violence.

Yes.

I break from the kiss to gasp for air and crane my neck back. He nips at my throat, and it has me spiraling upwards. Up and up until I'm seeing fucking stars. I whine and circle my arms around his neck to keep him close as I hit that wall and begin to descend. The fall is just as glorious as the rise.

I close my eyes to savor the moment, and he spills into me. His pace slowed, and an uncontrollable twitch here and there. I grin against his shoulder to feel his composure waver. To know I can do that to him.

This was far from the kinkiest sex I've ever had. It wasn't even that long or raunchy. But it was...*something*. Something about this was so much more satisfying than anything I've experienced.

And it terrifies me.

eHe see

CHAPTER FOURTEEN

Blackwell

The first rays of sunlight filter through the shades, cutting faint lines across the room.

I lie there, watching Sinclair sleep. I hardly slept at all. I couldn't, not after last night. After seeing her body so overtly displayed for me, illuminating every mark on her porcelain skin, every story her scars tell, it's haunting me. Consuming me.

I can't stop my mind from obsessing over it. Over *her*. I have so many pressing matters, but she seems to be all I can think about. About the life she had to simply survive, and about the vengeance I will carve into the bones of the people who made her, piece by bloody piece.

My brothers and I didn't grow up in a warm family environment, but we were cared for. Protected and treated with respect. Our world was brutal, but *Baba* never used that brutality against us. He was hard on us, yet with reason.

And *Maman*—she was direct and maybe even cold at times, but never cruel. She knew the life we had to prepare for. She warmed up more as we grew older and passed the age of being coddled.

Of course, I fight with Dane and Harlan, and there will always be some competition there, but we would sooner catch a bullet for each other than to spill each other's blood. We value family, not for the sake of alliance and power, but for the sake of being family. Uncles, aunts, and cousins included.

Who did Sinclair have? If not a friend, not family, then who? Who helped hold her together when she was on the verge of shattering? Her sister was the only one of them to show a sliver of kindness to her, but from what she's told me, she only patched her up after taking a beating. She didn't protect her from it. No one did.

She's sleeping on her stomach with her head turned my way and her arms tucked under the pillow. The blanket dips low on her back, baring the graceful line of her spine. Slowly, without thinking, I drag the blanket lower, exposing the curve of her entire backside.

The jagged scar on her hipbone catches a sliver of light. I yearn to trace it with my fingers. To memorize every inch of her pain. But I restrain myself.

Instead, I pull the covers back up, shielding her again. I study her face as she slightly stirs, and a tiny sigh leaves her lips. She doesn't wake. She remains relaxed and unguarded.

No hint of a smirk. No mask concealing her pretty features. She's never looked more human. Just as she was meant to be.

My phone vibrates on the side table, and I snatch it up before it wakes her. She only stirs a little, but her breathing remains even. I pull myself out of bed and head into the bathroom to get washed up.

My father will send someone for me soon if I'm not quick. I take a short shower and throw on some joggers and a thermal shirt before leaving my room.

When I reach my father's office, he's already there. He's sitting behind his desk, still in his robe and a coffee mug in one hand. His hair is mussed, but his eyes are sharp on me.

"What the hell happened last night?" he demands without preamble.

Sighing, I flump into a chair across from him. "I don't know exactly. An argument between Beck and some other men." I rub the back of my neck sheepishly. I should know more by now. "Before I could intervene, it all went to hell." I shake my head. "I'm not sure," I mutter.

My father studies me, disappointment plain on his face. And it isn't unwarranted. What I should have done was stayed and locked down the scene. But instead, I left Scout to deal with it while I fled all for Sinclair's protection. I haven't spoken to Scout yet about the aftermath, and it's been hours.

This woman has my mind fucked.

"I'm sorry, *Baba*. Sinclair was there, and—"

"And she got involved," he finishes for me.

"Yes, and I felt it was imperative to remove her from the situation entirely."

"And why was one of Beck's guys brought back here?"

This is going to be fun to try and explain. "I'm not sure yet," I admit shamefully.

"Scout and Dane both said it was a request that came from Sinclair." He lets the words hang. "And that *you* approved it."

I scrub my palm down my face with a heavy hand, reminded of last night's panic. It still claws at my ribs as a reminder. How the thought of any harm coming to Sinclair had me coming apart. I finally nod in response.

His chuckle is low and knowing. I gawk at him as it grates on my every nerve. "Boy, that girl has you by the balls already."

I shake my head sharply. "No, it isn't like that."

He leans forward with his elbows on his desk and eyebrows lowered. "Growing feelings for your fiancée is not the issue, Blackwell. It's letting it cloud your judgement, especially in a situation like last night. It will only get you and possibly *her* killed." His words slam into me like a physical blow. "I understand you wanted to protect her. But don't you ever forget your role in this family. Where your duties lie."

A surge of resentment pulses through me. I feel offended he would imply my duties are above Sinclair. But he's fucking right. The family is first. Always.

"I understand, *Baba*." I bite down the urge to argue or explain. But I know he doesn't want excuses.

I can't let Sinclair be the reason I fail him or our family. Even if there's a part of me that knows it's already too late.

After clearing things up with my father, I leave his office in silence. I head next to the kitchen to have some breakfast made, balancing it on a serving tray myself to deliver.

Despite every warning ringing in my head and every vow I made to my father, I need to see her. To remember she's still breathing. That she made it out alive and she's still here.

I arrive back to my bedroom and close the door behind me still balancing the tray of food. The unmade bed is empty, but the sound of running water coming from the bathroom pulls my attention.

Placing the food down on a table, I follow the trail of steam inside the bathroom. The air is thick and warm, fogged up from the hot water in the shower. Through the misted glass, Sinclair's figure moves. So graceful and devastating. I lean back against the counter and cross my arms to refrain from going to her.

"Sorry, but I couldn't do the walk of shame without washing off all the makeup and dried-up sex on me," she says, her voice lazily amused.

I snort, biting back a grin. "No worries."

A glass sitting on the sink's vanity catches my eye. I pick it up to inspect the soapy and bloodied water. Inside, her rings sit at the bottom, glinting ominously through the suds. I fish one out and rest it on an open palm to study closely. What looked like a simple gold band last night is anything but. A tiny dagger folds neatly down, retractable like a switchblade.

A slow grin curves my lips as I drop it back into the glass. Sinclair Ortiz, always armed. I finger the other ring out and it too looks like a completely different one as well. Last night it was a gold band with a golden rosebud. But the flower is gone, revealing a small, needle-like spike.

Shaking my head with a chuckle low under my breath, I drop the second ring back into the sudsy water and turn my attention back to her in the present. "I have breakfast for when you're done."

"Oh, good. I'm starving."

I'm about to exit the bathroom when the water cuts off. She opens the glass door to stick her head out, her face bare and flushed from the heat. "Can I have a couple towels?"

I'm momentarily struck. It's a rare thing to see her without her armor of dark lipstick, winged eyeliner, and the scathing edge she hides behind. Just bare skin, damp hair, and a raw kind of beauty that hits like a physical punch. She's somehow even more lethal like this.

I have to wrench myself back to the present and grab two towels. When I hand them over, I'm careful not to brush her skin. One touch and I know I'll stop pretending I can resist her. Then I flee, escaping the bathroom before I do something reckless. Just imagining her body bare, wet, it has my fists flexing with a want I can't bury.

Adjusting my stiffening cock through my pants, I take a seat and wait for her to join me. Moments later, she comes sauntering out wrapped in a towel and using another to dry her hair.

I don't comment when she drops the wet towel on the ground, leaving it there, before taking a seat across from me with her legs tucked under her. She takes a napkin to lay over her lap like a fucking princess before snagging a piece of bacon for herself.

She is a walking contradiction, and it truly vexes me. Her good manners and bad habits so tangled together, I never know which to expect. Her unpredictability is frustrating yet alluring.

"Not hungry?" Her arrogant tone snaps me out of it. The smug smirk and knowing spark in her eyes have me slightly shifting and clearing my throat to buy a second of composure.

I don't answer her and begin digging in. I cut my eggs with too much force, causing the knife and fork to scrape against the plate. The high shriek is somehow less suffering than the silence stretching between us. How she can sit there without a goddamn care in the world when all I can do is bottle it all up and keep it together. It has my teeth aching.

"You can't ever do that again," I say, forcing my voice to stay level.

"Do what?" She's so calm as she stares back at me, all wide-eyed innocence, sipping her coffee as if we're discussing the weather.

I set my fork down and flex my hands on my thighs, so they won't shake. "Sinclair." She doesn't even blink. "You are not invincible."

"Neither are you," she bounces back.

I ignore her comeback. "You could have gotten seriously hurt—"

"I'm still standing," she cuts me off.

Her nonchalance has me counting to three before opening my mouth again. I may not have a total grasp of understanding her, but I do know that if I demand anything from her, she will only dig her heels in deeper. She's a creature who bends for no one, but if I change tactics, she might tilt for me.

"Sinclair. I'm asking you." I pause, my eye contact with her firm and unflinching. "Please, do not put yourself in immediate danger like that ever again. I do not want to see you hurt."

Something in my voice must reach her. She breaks character for a fleeting moment. Something flickers across her face before she can smother it.

"I can try, but I can't promise you anything." She tries for steeliness, but she's so transparent right now.

Knowing when to quit while I'm ahead when it comes to her, I move on. "So, is our guest a souvenir, or is there a purpose to detaining him?"

She looks at me as if startled by my question. "Haven't you questioned him yet?"

"Question him? For what exactly?" I counter, frowning.

Her expression runs the gamut—shock, suspicion, accusation, disappointment. Then she gets serious before speaking again. "This was planned, Blackwell. Any idea who?" I don't answer. "Alright." She wipes her hands on the towel as she stands up and stretches with effortless grace, showing off the tops of her tight thighs. "I'm going to get dressed, then we're going to go and question him." She even adds a little nod at the end and walks off as if she's calling the shots.

Normally, no one outside my bloodline dictates my next move, but Sinclair may be the exception I'm willing to entertain.

I wait at the bottom of the stairs after changing into a suit, glancing at my watch with impatience. Sinclair appears only minutes later, dressed in black head-to-toe. Her pants like second skin, hugging the trim curve of her waist, a sheer long-sleeved top with thumb holes, another pair of thick-soled boots, and a leather jacket dangling from one hand.

Her makeup is a toned-down version of her usual dark look, and her platinum hair is pulled back into a low, slick ponytail. If looks could kill, we'd all be on our knees.

Something reckless stirs in me. A compulsion to tell her how fucking good she looks. How there's a fiery halo wrapped around her. But I choose to bite it back and turn for the back of the estate without a word.

She shrugs on her jacket as we enter the chill of the early afternoon. Scout is waiting on an ATV next to an unoccupied one sitting, idling. I hop onto the empty one and expect Sinclair to join me, but she goes right up to Scout and says, "Thanks for keeping it warm, but I got it from here, Scout."

Scout cuts his eyes to me waiting on permission, and for fuck's sake, I nod. His nostrils flare with agitation before he dismounts.

Sinclair flashes me a Cheshire grin, swings her leg over, and revs the engine. "Race you there," she tosses over her shoulder, then bolts off as if knowing where she's going. I swear under my breath before gunning it.

Minutes later, we come to a screeching halt near the containment building. Sinclair hops off her vehicle and runs her hands over her hair, smoothing down the flyaways.

"Holy fuck, my face is frozen," she huffs, breathlessly.

I catch Spade approaching us as if waiting, a large black bag slung over his shoulder. He looks as wary as I feel. "What's that?" I ask.

"My supplies," Sinclair answers with a toothy grin. "Thanks, Spades." She flashes him a wink before turning her attention to me. "Shall we?"

My instincts light up like a goddamn inferno. I stalk over to Spade, my voice low. "Open it," I demand.

Spade promptly unzips the bag and opens the top for me to get a good view of the contents inside. When I recognize what they are, I level a grim look at Sinclair.

"What?" she says innocently, shrugging her shoulders.

"What are these for?"

"For interrogation, obviously," she sasses.

Considering they aren't ticking time bombs, I stifle a growl in my throat and lead us all inside. It's a one-story brick building built like a bunker, windowless with only one way in and one way out.

Inside, her prize sits slumped in a chair, bound wrist-to-ankle, his head hanging low. From the looks of it and the dried blood covering his face and chest, it seems as if Sinclair beat most of the fight out of him already.

And judging by the way Sinclair is chomping at the bit and strolling forward, last night was only a warm-up.

"Would it be possible to get him up?" she asks sweetly, peeling her jacket off and tossing it on the metal table full of tools.

She draws me in with her effortless authority that I decide to let her take point. So, I turn to Scout and mutter, "Just do as she says," while I settle in to watch the circus unfold.

"Spade?" she calls out, crooking a finger, and he approaches with the large bag. "Right there is fine." My eyes narrow as he sets the bag down obediently, as if he is entirely under her command. I'll have to arrange a new guy for her. I don't need anyone *too* loyal to her. After my father, everyone answers to me.

Scout and Spade drag the prisoner upright, binding his arms out and slightly above him with thick chains. His body hangs like dead weight, barely conscious, knees buckling beneath him. Blood has crusted over his face, painting him in dried violence, but every twitch, every shallow breath, opens his wounds anew. Fresh crimson seeping through cracked flesh.

His swollen eyes squint against the low light as he struggles to look around the room, disoriented and dangling like a carcass awaiting judgment.

I watch as Sinclair crouches beside the bag and picks up a softball, tossing it between her hands. "Thanks, boys," she says easily as they step back to stand behind me with anticipation buzzing in the air.

She prowls forward like a lioness sizing up an injured gazelle. "Hello," her voice rings out like a bird's song. The bloodied man squints at her through hooded eyes as he tries to focus. Recognition flashes across his ruined face as he stares back at her angelic yet twisted one. His face quickly blooms with hatred. "I'm only going to ask you once. Obviously, your boss was in on this failed attempt at Blackwell's life, but who else was in on it?"

He mumbles something unintelligible.

Sinclair responds with a step back. "Alright, then. Let's do this." She turns with a simple smile, walking back several paces like she's on a runway. Shoulders back, spine steeled. Her confidence is the most alluring aspect of her thus far.

Facing her victim again, she brings both hands up to clasp the softball at her chest. Placing her right foot forward, she swings the ball back with her right arm, then swings it forward and rotates it in a full windmill motion, stepping forward with her opposite foot, releasing it, throwing her weight into that leg.

The ball whizzes by him, cracking against the wall with a violent thud, missing him by a hair. "Well, that's embarrassing," she mutters with a hint of playfulness in her tone. "Just warming up, boys!" she announces.

Picking up another ball, I sit on the edge of my seat and watch her take another crack at it. Everyone hisses and groans behind me when it makes contact with his right shoulder. He howls, sagging further against the chains. Fuck, that had to have shattered it.

"Who else was behind the attack?" she asks with a sugary sweet tone, picking up another ball.

When he answers with a pained groan, she lines herself up with another shot, and this time, as the ball cuts through the air with even more speed than the last, it connects with his face with a sickening crack. It had to have been going at least sixty miles per hour.

I know it's lights out when blood sprays from the split flesh. She jumps forward with a gasp. "Oh, shit," she says, inspecting her work like a bored surgeon. "Oh, good. I didn't get your nose. You can still talk, right?"

"You fucking bitch!" he spits through the blood.

"Good. You can." She looks over her shoulder, smiling and shaking her head. "It's been a while, so my aim is a little off."

I sit back and rest one ankle over a knee. "As entertaining as this is, is any of this even necessary?"

Raising an eyebrow, she picks up another ball, twirling it inside her hand, both of us tuning out the withering man behind her. "You still don't think it was planned?" She looks behind me. "What about you, Scout? Some preening meatheads, or something more? Something calculated."

I twist my upper body and look at Scout. "Well?" I prod.

He bounces back and forth between Sinclair and me. Wanting to be anywhere else but this room. "Something wasn't right last night." He's right. I felt it, too. "It could have been random, or it could have been coordinated."

My stare remains fixed on his for another moment before swaying back to Sinclair. "Alright, darling. See if you can make him talk."

Predictably, the humor in her face morphs into gravity, taking my words as a challenge. Her eyes narrow as she rolls the next ball between her hands. Planting her feet, she pitches another one, crushing his ribs. He lets out a strained grunt, chains clinking above him.

"Ready to talk?" she asks coolly, the next ball ready to launch.

He spits a wad of blood out, and Sinclair's lips thin, lining up another pitch. Her shoulders square, and she launches it. This time, landing right in the center of his chest.

She is fucking radiant when the power is hers. When she owns absolute control. God, I want her. But wanting her is wanting her fire, and I'm not sure how long I can stand in it.

"Alright, alright," he gasps, wheezing for air and gurgling on blood.

Sinclair drops the next ball to the floor, taking deliberate steps forward. "Good boy," she coos.

"Beck," he pushes through heavy breaths.

"Beck, what?' she asks so softly, like hushing a crying baby as she encroaches his space.

"Beck—he set it up." The room falls into heavy, charged silence.

Behind me, I can physically feel Scout and the others stiffen. I sit forward, elbows resting on my knees, staring at the man hanging from chains like he's already a corpse.

"Yeah, no shit. But who else?" There's no humor or warmth left to Sinclair's voice.

"I don't know," he sputters. "Only know that Beck instructed us to..." he trails off.

"To what?" she snaps, bucking at him.

He flinches and *fuck*, I want her so badly.

"I don't know! Start shit!"

"You're going to have to do better than that," she sneers, and I rise to my feet.

"I don't know," he cries out. "We just do what we're told."

Her arm jerks, and he's throwing his head back, jaw dropping with a pained howl as she has a crushing grip on his shattered shoulder. "Better."

"Okay, okay! Beck was working with the Mendozas. They planned a brawl as a distraction to get to Blackwell," he spills in one breath.

The room is now deathly silent, and I can physically feel the way Scout and Spade go still.

She was right. This was a fucking assassination attempt.

Well, fuck. Me.

CHAPTER FIFTEEN

I did it. I actually did it.

My fingertips tingle with power as the thought ricochets in my skull. I feel high. Like in this moment, I can do anything. I can walk on the fucking moon or climb the tallest mountain.

I turn around with an uncontrollable grin on my face, struggling to play it cool. Adrenaline ripples through me like a second bloodstream as my chest heaves with sharp breaths.

When I lock eyes with Blackwell, triumph freezes in my throat. There's a fervid look on his face, making him look delirious and ravenous. He's motionless aside from his chest rising and falling heavily like mine. The heat smacks into me, punching the air out of my lungs and causing all the blood to rush to my core so violently I almost stumble. My cheeks relax when the smile drops from my face, and I find myself paralyzed.

"Everyone out!" he shouts with this guttural edge, never taking his eyes off me.

A fire stokes deep in my belly, so fierce that I have no recollection of who took the first step, but our bodies collide in only seconds.

We attack each other with zealous desire and animalistic urges. My body is hot all over, and I have never needed someone like this before in my life. Every time we collide, it's fucking fire. And every time, that fire burns hotter than before.

Metal clanks when he hoists me up onto the table of tools as some of them clatter to the ground. I roll my hips to find contact with him, and I even let a whimper out when he parts from me. He grabs at one boot, then starts yanking at my waistband. Once he has one leg out, he adheres his body and mouth to mine again.

There's no need for foreplay. We already had ours. Something about the violence has us both spiraling.

He pushes his way inside of me and fucks me savagely without delay. He dives in so deeply, as deep as he can go, but I somehow want more. I want my pussy to throb in both pain and desire.

Throwing my head back in ecstasy, I squeeze my eyes shut while I hit the peak of my orgasm so quickly, riding it out as he continues to slam into me over and over. As soon as I come down, I look at him through tiny slits and grab his tie to pull myself up to kiss him recklessly.

I moan as my tongue wrestles with his and I rock my hips to fuck him back. He senses my urgency for more and lifts me to carry me, and I'm sitting on his cock when he takes a seat in the chair.

He tears off my other pant leg and boot as I sit up and down on him, fucking him. Switching the angle of my hips and the pace. His shoulders tense up, and I know he's getting close, and all I can think about is seeing him detonate.

"I want to see you come," I rasp when I pull my tender lips from his. He gazes back at me with hooded eyes, and I could come from the sight of him.

Lifting my hips, I release his cock and hold it firmly in one hand. I stare down at the bulging head of his cock in fascination as I stroke the soft skin, causing a lewd sound of wetness that we both created.

I rock in his lap, letting my pussy rub against the base of his length and butting against my hand while I pull him to that salacious paradise. A growl erupts from his throat when he begins to come, and my body responds.

But I'm still not entirely sated. I have to have more. Smearing his milky cum over my sensitive pussy, I moan and mewl. Brushing his ear with my lips, I whisper, "I want more."

He has his cock inside me in the next instant, but my muscles are failing me.

Hooking his arms under my knees, he curls his biceps to slap me up and down at a lazy pace while he sucks all over my face, neck, and chest. Then he pushes me to my feet so abruptly that I wobble and catch myself on the back of the chair. It's precisely where he wants me to be.

Bent over, he grips my cheeks and thrusts his way back inside me. He hooks one of my thighs to crank up, and I plant my foot on the seat.

He eases his cock out of me and quickly replaces it with his fingers. Shoving them in harshly.

My head snaps back with my mouth wide open, and his fingers begin to work some ethereal witchcraft. Plunging deeply and hitting that spot that has my supporting leg shaking. I fuck his fingers back with uncouth movements, and suddenly, I'm paralyzed. My entire body locks up, and my eyes roll back as my pussy spasms, and I spew out an ample amount of liquid, splashing against his palm and running down my thighs. I whimper and whine as he drains the fuck out of me.

I'm still quivering from the quake when he replaces his fingers with his fat cock in one brutal, seamless motion. His hand glides up, his fingers slick with me, painting my bottom lip before dragging down to smear a glistening trail to my chin.

He turns my head, and before devouring my mouth with his, he stares at me for one agonizing moment. Time fractures, and I can't move.

I can hardly breathe.

His eyes have me completely under his control.

Burning me alive beneath the weight of his gaze.

I don't blink.

I just wait.

Wait for him to either save me or destroy me.

He finally puts me out of my misery and kisses me hard and unrelentingly. When he groans into my mouth, I want to cry. It's the sexiest sound. The vibration from it draws something raw and desperate from somewhere deep inside me.

I can't take it anymore. I squeeze my eyes shut, and he grips my chin with more strength and turns the kiss into an obliteration. His hips pick up pace, slamming into me until my leg is ready to give up. But I find just enough energy to lock it and ride another tidal wave of devastating pleasure.

He twitches inside of me as my muscles pulsate, sapping him. The vulgar sound of him withdrawing from me is the first sound I can register. Then all I hear is panting and hearts pounding. His body is coated in sweat as it still sticks to my backside, and I can feel his heart thundering in his chest. My mouth lazily hangs open just a breath away from his.

As feeling comes back to my limbs, I'm terrified to open my eyes. Terrified I will find that same look in his eyes that had me undone.

He's starting to scare me.

And like I had feared, when I peel my eyelids back, his gaze is no less heated. The embers in my belly engulf in flames. How can I crave more?

We're silent as we right our clothing, and I grow timid in my movements. Bashful to make eye contact. But he isn't at all abashed when he takes me by the hand and hauls me out of the building and to one of the ATVs.

I've lost the will to speak, let alone argue, when he easily lifts me and places me on the vehicle, climbing on behind me. I'm stiff and rigid as he revs the engine and slides an arm around my waist, and we're jolted forward.

The nerves are knotted in my gut, and I stare blankly ahead as the world whizzes by. I feel like I can't think, and at the same time, I feel like I'm overthinking everything. So lost inside my brain.

What the fuck is he doing to me? This needs to stop. How do I make it stop?

I remain amenable as we arrive back at the estate, and he cuts the engine. He's courteous with his touch, pulling me off our ride and steadying me on my feet. But when he clutches my hand, his hands are hot and randomly flex, as if he's trying to restrain himself.

I've never been so docile in my whole life. Never been so hesitant to regain some control. Never felt so...helpless.

It's a whirlwind flying up the stairs and into his bedroom. Not a single syllable is whispered the entire way. Not even when he pulls me into the bathroom and starts the shower.

Reality finally sets in when he releases my hand, and all senses return to full function. He turns to me, and I make the first move, toeing off my boots. His eyes remain glued to mine as he begins to peel his clothing off.

His skin is so rich in color and pulled taut over bulging muscles. He's so fucking sexy. I have the urge to lick him all over, tasting every inch of him.

His eyes grow heavy when he gives my naked body a perusal. The corners of his mouth twitch, and he takes in deep breaths.

I feel so desired by him. Not in such a crude way or an anticipated way, spurred on by my purposeful seduction. I'm not doing anything right now, but he's looking at me as if tormented by the very sight.

Wrapping his arms around my waist, my hands flatten against his chest. We both give a subtle smile as he takes a few backsteps until we're in the thick, warm fog. My hair is still damp from showering not long ago, but I don't say anything when he gently tugs on the hair tie and frees it.

It cascades around my upper back and shoulders. His fingers run through my hair to cradle my head, and I hold my breath.

"So, how did you know?" he asks, breaking the silence that was beginning to suffocate me.

I arch an eyebrow. "How did I know?" He gives a curt nod. "Question is, how did you not?"

"Humor me," he says with a controlled level. I hit a nerve.

I grin up at him smugly and slide my hands to meet around his neck, my body arching into his. "It was easy to read the room." I shrug casually. Truth is, I happened to see the men arguing first thing when I walked into the room. And not too far from the trouble brewing, there was a guy laser-focused on Blackwell. As if waiting for a signal to go for him.

"The tension is always high when we're all forced to share the same space." He narrows his eyes as if trying to read me. "What was it exactly? What tipped you off?"

I'm almost flattered he's looking at me with accusation. As if I'm someone important enough to be in on a scheme to take him down. I could take the opportunity to string him along. To fuck with him and have him questioning everything about me. But the rebellious spark in me isn't lighting up like it typically does. I blame the draining sex we just had.

"The dude was too obvious." I sigh and occupy my wandering hand by petting a scar on the front of his shoulder. "He stood there, all wide-eyed and mute. Eyes solely on you. He was waiting for his cue. The heated argument between Beck and whoever was meant to be a distraction."

He doesn't speak, and I'm afraid to look up. But that trepidation turns into curiosity. My eyes slowly roll up to his. He holds my stare, and I don't dare flinch.

A humorous grunt jolts his body, and his lips slowly curve into a sly grin. Then there isn't much more talking left.

After he eats my pussy like he's angry at it, we finally wash up and get out of the shower. "I want to show you something." His hesitation behind his tone has me looking at him. The towel hangs low on his hips, displaying that fucking 'v' us women tend to wet our panties for.

I groan and use a towel to start drying my hair. "I'm tired," I whine. Truthfully, I am. He has exhausted me with too many orgasms.

The corner of his mouth ticks. "Be ready in thirty."

CHAPTER SIXTEEN

He has the decency to warn me that we're going back outside again and on the ATVs.

So, I wrap my damp hair into a bun at the nape of my neck and tuck my head under a black beanie. My jacket zips all the way up over my chin, so I don't have to battle the freezing air against my face.

We walk side by side to exit out the back again, and when I realize there's only one vehicle there, I don't miss the little smirk on his face when he mounts it. Rolling my eyes, I climb on behind him and slip my arms around his waist.

The innocent gesture has those crescive feelings in the pit of my stomach festering. The sharp, unwelcoming knot twists with something I've tried to ignore since the moment I stepped foot on the estate. A pestering ache, heavier now, and impossible to ignore.

His scent envelops me, intoxicating and smothering. I made a vow to myself to never let anyone hold that kind of power that could crush me. But that control is unraveling thread by thread. And I fucking despise it.

Yet here I am, pressed against him, soaking in his warmth like it's salvation. Letting him thread himself deeper into my bones. And the worst part is, I'm not even trying to stop it.

I pay close attention to where we're going and realize we aren't heading in the direction of their little torture bunker. We're headed in a different direction. We reach one part of the iron gates, and he stops to hop off and enter a code into a keypad I almost didn't notice.

The gate opens and he climbs back on to drive us through, exiting the estate and entering into the thick tree line. A path is already stamped through the forest as if used frequently, and I sit quietly behind him until something materializes in the distance. A shadowy figure grows with each beat of the engine.

The figure rapidly takes shape. A house. Black, striking, and entirely unexpected. It's not massive, at least not in comparison to the estate we both grew up in, but it carries a grandeur that leaves me breathless.

The forest gives way to manicured landscaping, and the closer we get, the wider my eyes become. It's something straight out of my dreams. Gothic bones dressed in regal detail, with hints of mid-century lines and Victorian drama. A deliberate chaos of styles that somehow feels like dark poetry. A driveway curves around a freshly carved crater in the earth, suggesting something still being built or unearthed.

I'm in total and complete awe as the vehicle falls silent and I robotically dismount it. My eyes are unable to tear from the sight before me. The stunning architecture.

Movement dances in my periphery, snapping me back to reality. I blink the daze from my eyes and catch myself in time. I settle my cheeky mask into place and look to Blackwell, finding him already studying me coolly, and impossible to read.

"I don't care whose house this is," I murmur, eyebrow arched with mocked defiance, "but I will take it from them."

His smile spreads slowly, like he was anticipating this kind of reaction from me. Something about it is infuriatingly endearing. "Well, sorry to break it to you, but there's no need for bloodshed." He leaves a heavy pause. "This is our home."

I swallow hard, unsure if I heard him correctly. "Ours?" I parrot back, the word unfamiliar on my tongue.

His smile turns into a rare toothy grin. "Yes, *ours*." He chuckles, shaking his head when I narrow my eyes at him. "This isn't a trick, Sinclair. Come."

Still stunned, skeptical, and slightly uncomfortable, I follow him up the steps toward the front doors. Tall, maroon, and crowned with gilded hardware like something out of a forgotten cathedral.

We step into the barren space, yet the emptiness carries a strange, unexpected warmth. Something intangible that clings to the air and reverberates off the bleakness. A serenity settles over me like a blanket, unwelcome in its comfort. I don't know if it's the way he said *ours*, as in *his* and *mine*, or if it's the sheer absence of blood, betrayal, and memory. But something about this place feels sacred. Unspoiled. *Safe*. And that's what disturbs me the most.

"I wanted to leave it up to you to finish it out. Floors, kitchen—all the final touches." His voice seems far off as I cautiously explore, moving on autopilot.

The place is skeletal. Raw even. The floors are unfinished, the walls are stark, and what appears to be the kitchen lacks cabinets or appliances. Even the bathrooms are empty. Void of even a toilet. Yet, none of it feels hollow.

I decide to work from top to bottom. The stairs are grand, but not gaudy. It curves with elegance, understated and commanding. The only thing, other than the exterior, that's been completed. A blank canvas stretched in every direction.

Blackwell follows, but says nothing. His presence is quiet yet distant, granting me space as I meander from room to room, my eyes absorbing every detail while my mind overflows with ideas. Colors, textures, textiles, furnishings. I can see it all so vividly because this house *is* me. Not the curated persona I parade for survival. The *real* me. The one I bury under armor and performance. The truest version. Unguarded and aching to breathe.

We reach another stairwell, tight and tucked away. A contrast to the sweeping stairs that brought us here. "What's this?" I ask, my voice guarded.

He dips his chin, silently telling me to look for myself. Mixed emotions swarm inside me, and my heart plummets with elegiac memories. It was my choice to move my bedroom up to the attic back home. For seclusion, isolation, and security. My sanctuary as well as my cage. I chose to live above everyone. Not to feel safe, but because it gave the illusion of control. Up there, I could see the threat coming. I could pretend I had autonomy. It was the only space I ever felt belonged to me.

At the top, the room opens wide, swallowing me in quiet awe. The ceiling is steep, its angles dramatic, painted black and broken by heavy mahogany beams that stretch into the two-story space above. Below, black-stained floorboards, aged with time, creaks softly beneath my steps.

Everything soon fades into the background, rendered meaningless by the one thing that now holds my attention. My piano.

Swallowing the rock lodged in my throat, I amble with careful steps as if it may be a mirage. Like if I move too quickly, it might vanish.

But it isn't a figment of my imagination. It's real. It's really here. My pristine, sleek, stark white grand piano, I've had since before I was ten years old. It was my true sanctuary.

My fingers glide along the smooth keys, barely grazing the ivory surface, and I exhale shakily. Untouched by time. Not a scratch. Not a crack. Not even a speck of dust.

It's strategically placed near the double glass doors that lead into a glass and steel grid half-dome. The structure alone makes my breath hitch and draws me in. I catch the cold of the handles in my palms and swing them open. I step out into the cool air, and a smile breaks across my face before I can help it.

A widow's walk.

Iron railings curve around the edge of the platform, aged black and ornate, looking down on the yard and endless forest beyond. It feels like I've wandered into my own dream.

My back is to Blackwell when his voice splits through the fog my head is stuck in. "The house was built in the 1880s," he says, voice low and steady. "I tried to preserve some of the soul of the house, but I could only salvage the bones. Floors, foundation."

He sidles up next to me at the edge, and I turn my head slightly. He gives me this slow, annoyingly charming smile, and his annoyingly handsome face goes out of focus as the world tilts. I feel like I might faint. Or puke. Or just fucking drop dead.

How can he know me like this? *I* don't even know myself.

"Sinclair, are you alright?" His voice is muffled, like it's traveling through water. But when he touches my arm, I'm jerked out of whatever the fuck that was.

My stomach twists, and my head pounds. Everything is scrambled, but I manage to pull myself together and clear my throat. "I'm fine," I say with boredom, arching an eyebrow.

Okay, Sinclair. Get your shit together. It's a fucking house. A house. *Material.*

"Do you actually play, or is this another way to fuck with people?" His cheeky tone has my face heating.

I turn to give him a sardonic grin. "Now, why would I tell you outright?"

He chuckles and goddamn, I *swear* he's blushing. That's it. My knees betray me and wobble, and I struggle not to choke on my tongue. A chunk of dark hair falls over his forehead, and my fingers itch to touch it. He looks so unfairly good like this. Relaxed, thawed, and unarmed.

"Of course, not." He leans his forearms on the railing to take in the view.

We stand shoulder to shoulder, soaking in the silence, the trees, the distance between who we are and who we pretend to be.

A few minutes, maybe more, pass until he finally murmurs, "There's still more to see. We should move. Light's fading."

Walking at a leisurely pace, we make our way back down to the main floor. "Do we have a basement?" I ask with lucid enthusiasm.

He gives me a knowing smirk. "Sorry, but it's more like a crawl space. Should be enough room to drag your victims down into, though."

"Fair enough."

We float room to room until we get to the back of the house, where nearly the entire wall is glass, opening up to yet another gorgeous view of the forest. Sunlight spills across a cluster of moving boxes off to one side. My gaze snags on one in particular, my name scrawled across the top.

"It's ready for the final touches," he says from somewhere behind me. "I'll set up a meeting with an interior designer."

I run my fingers along the seam of one of the boxes taped shut. "What are these?"

There's a pause, then a barely restrained chuckle. I whip my head around in time to catch him rubbing his jaw to hide it. "The rest of your belongings from your bedroom." He moves his hand to the back of his neck to squeeze it. "And your *other* room."

My cheeks ache from trying to hide my grin. My *other room*. I laugh internally. "Is that what they called it?" I ask as I circle the box to another one.

"If you mean your family, yes. That's what they said."

"And if I didn't mean them?"

He's standing there all handsome and so assured, watching me. "Then I'd guess dungeon, lair, cave..." A corner of his mouth hitches upward.

I flash a toothy grin, then pretend to be more interested in the boxes. His attention is too intense for me right now. I've never been shy about my appetite or kinks, but there's something about his gaze that strips me bare.

Unclasping the golden chain around my neck, I remove the bottom half of the crucifix dangling from it to reveal the needle-like dagger. I stab the seam and slide it through, cutting it clean, the box giving way with a satisfying split.

Everything inside is individually bubble-wrapped. I pull out the first thing that catches my eye and unwrap it to find a pair of gold handcuffs. "Might as well get rid of most of this stuff." I dangle the cuffs from a finger and raise an eyebrow at him. "I'm sure you're too *macho* for any of it." Rolling my eyes, I toss them back in.

"Have *you* tried it?" he asks.

I turn and cross my arms with a hip popped. "They're mine, aren't they?"

He puts one foot in front of the other, daring to stalk me like prey. "I meant...on yourself." I don't answer because I don't need to. We both know the answer. "Have you ever given up complete control?"

His voice drops, and that vortex begins spinning in my gut. "To let yourself be vulnerable…"

"I'm not a stranger to helplessness," I snap, breaking character. But my stature remains fortified.

His eyes ignite, sharp and knowing, aware he struck a nerve. But he doesn't gloat. Just watches me closely, standing close enough to cage me in with his presence alone. He towers over me with unintentional intimidation.

Men no longer scare me. Insentient machines in human skin. I've known too many of them. Greedy in their violence and vacant in their cruelty. You learn quickly that there's no use fearing them because fear doesn't save you. And there is no saving you.

Only survival.

But with Blackwell, he's different.

He doesn't want to break me.

He means to unravel me.

He doesn't need to touch me to dominate me. Doesn't need to raise his voice or lift a hand. He saturates the room by simply standing in it. His dominance isn't rooted in brutality or degradation. It's quieter. Coiled. More insidious.

And that's the true danger of it. Because I have spent my whole life learning how to survive cruelty. But I have no idea what to do with kindness wrapped in control. With someone who sees me and chooses not to destroy me, but to dismantle me.

It's a total mindfuck.

"I'm not talking about control being taken from you, *joon-kharâsh*." He tugs at a piece of hair sticking out from underneath my hat. "I'm talking about surrender. On your terms. Voluntary."

I want to laugh in his face. Free will? That's a luxury I've rarely wasted. So, when the chance comes to take control of anything or anyone, I don't hesitate. I seize it. Always. And he knows that, because he's the same. Men in his position never loosen the reins of control. Not even in sleep.

One side of my mouth shifts. "Let's make a deal." He looks mused as he waits. "I'll give you one night," I say, plucking the gold cuffs from the box and dangling them between us. "Total control. But you give me one in return, where I'm in charge, and you're mine to do with as I please." His eyes hold mine like a challenge, and I could do this all day. I won't bend or break.

"Any rules to this?" he finally asks.

"Nope. Just one night each. Full control. No safeties. No safe words. No outs."

His eyes glint. "We're still talking sexually, right?"

"Yes." I hold my empty hand out. "Deal?"

He looks down, considering. Then he bites back a smile as he takes my hand and shakes it.

CHAPTER SEVENTEEN

Blackwell

I use the grip I have on her hand to yank her into me, the force just enough to hear the sharp catch of her breath as her body collides with mine.

I hardly took my eyes off her as I let her quietly explore our home. How her eyes swept over every corner like she was trying to memorize it. The near imperceptible softening around her eyes, the pause she took at the top of the stairs, and the way her fingers lingered on the edge of the banister.

It was subtle, something anyone else would miss, but I could see it. The tiniest hint of a reaction from her. Especially when we first arrived. It had my chest expanding with pride.

Everything about this place was designed with her in mind. Chosen with obsessive precision. Not to impress her, but for comfort. Entirely unlike the prison she was raised in. The opposite of what she's been living in for the last several months. A place meant to feel untouched by blood.

Nothing gaudy or garish. No flash, but still fit for a fucking goddess.

She's still a complete puzzle to me, but I am starting to find some of the pieces. Her ring, for example. I'm almost certain she has no idea what it is. Or how many hours I spent tracking it down. The negotiations with the previous owner. The favors I had to cash in. She's still wearing it, and Sinclair would not wear anything she didn't want to.

This will be her safe place. A home where she will feel unchained. Somewhere that makes it feel separate from our lives. Here, we aren't heirs or criminals.

I am content with the life I am destined for, but Sinclair deserves so much more. And I will spend my life giving that to her.

Because she will never be someone's pawn again.

Going into this, I had planned to respect her and maybe even enjoy her, but the need to protect her was unexpected. Her safety is my number one priority.

And I never thought I would want her as badly as I do. The fire she ignites with a single glance. The way she lives in my mind. The thoughts she consumes.

Everything is *her*.

Slanting my mouth over hers, she slightly tenses. I've learned to look past it. The day she no longer braces for pain will be the day that I know that I've won. Not control, but trust.

The kiss turns savage in seconds, and we're pulling at each other with the need for dominance. The end of our last conversation doesn't help any.

She climbs up my body to wrap her limbs around me, and I carry her to the windows, pressing her back against the cold glass. I break the kiss, and her feet touch the floor to start toeing off her boots, the same time my fingers slip beneath the waistband of her pants, tugging them low.

I pull one foot at a time out of her pants, her panties coming with it, and her jacket hits the floor. I stand up and wrap my fingers around her jaw, and we lock eyes. Breathing heavily and anticipating the burn that comes next.

I kiss her hard and deep, then I spin her around, her facing the windows now. Her back naturally arches, taunting me with her perfect ass. I have my cock out, hard and heavy in one hand, while I reach out with my other to rub the silky-smooth globes. Admiring my darker color against her flawless pale tone.

She rocks back and her head falls back. I press my body into hers, my hand sliding around her hip, slowly making its way between her thighs. My fingers glide right through her wetness and I fucking love the way her breath hitches like she's stopped breathing all together.

My teeth sink into her neck as I shove three fingers inside her, my palm slamming against her pussy. I nip and lick her and start thrusting my fingers in and out with brutality. My cock throbs against her ass and she rubs her perky ass into me.

"Fuck," she whispers with a gravelly voice, then starts riding my fingers. Chasing her high. I fuck her harder until her mouth falls open on a silent scream, her inner muscles contracting, and a torrent of her arousal spills free.

I allow her to come down slowly, prolonging her pleasure. As soon as her muscles stop twitching, I remove my fingers, slipping against her pussy the entire way. I lean back and use my hands to spread her cheeks, her dark pink hole between them has me salivating.

She tilts her ass up and I drag my wet fingers between her cheeks while using my other hand to guide my cock between her legs. Gripping her hips, I slam into her in one sharp motion. She moans, and her back bows more.

My hands move to her ass again and I can't stop gawking at her tight ring of muscles. I ram into her with swift efficiency. My groin meeting her ass over and over. Using my thumb, I rub that tight hole of hers, and she almost wilts under me. She wants it just as badly.

I press my thumb deep inside, and my hips speed up. I stab my thumb in and out, and I can't take it anymore.

My cock slips out of her and I have her on her hands in knees in the next moment. Gripping either side of her ass, I spread her and tongue the fuck out of her. Every inch of her most delicate areas. I dart my tongue in and out of her tight rim, then up and down the seams of her cunt.

I sit back, and she drops down to her elbows so she is open nicely for me. Pulling her ass cheeks apart, I spit on her asshole before using my thumb again to spread it and dip it inside.

She moans and rocks her body and curls her fists in sexual frustration. Not wanting to torture either us any further, I push the head of my cock in her ass at a leisurely pace until I bottom out.

Fuck. Fuck, it feels good.

I curl my body around her and begin moving. One hand fists her ass while my other snakes back between her thighs to bury inside her cunt. She cries out and tries to fuck me back. And it turns barbaric.

I rut her, her body jolting, my fingers anchored inside her, my cock ready to combust. She cries out and convulses, but I don't stop. I don't relent. I fuck both her holes harder. She tries to squirm away on instinct, her body overstimulated, but I own her.

I put more of my weight on her and piston my hips until I'm gritting my teeth with a groan caught in my throat. The base of my cock is sticky and her cum has my hand dripping.

I drop to my side, pulling her with me as we both try to clear the stars from our vision. I nuzzle my face into her hair and use her soothing scent to steady my breathing.

I'm more than content right now. I'm home. With Sinclair.

This was just a taste of what our life together will be like.

CHAPTER EIGHTEEN

I 'm just coming out of the hedge maze after hanging out with Blender when I see Blackwell.

He's standing at the top of the steps, hovering over like a Persian god, all regal and handsome as fuck. His hands are casually shoved into his pockets, and there's a black silk scarf around his neck, owning the fuck out of it.

It should be a sin to look that good while doing absolutely nothing.

It's infuriating how he can get my blood pumping without saying a word or moving an inch. He lets the silence speak for itself. It makes me want to choke him with his own scarf and demand he release me. To free me of whatever spell he's cast or whatever chemical imbalance he triggers in my system.

Because whatever this is, it's an illness I'm starting to like.

"You seem to like the garden," he states as I join him at the top of the steps.

"Just the maze."

He glances over at it and smirks. "It took Harlan till he was a teenager to find his way out of it."

"What about Dane?"

"He still can't find his way out."

I grin. "And you?"

"Took me a couple of days."

My grin turns smug, and I move past him, heading towards the back doors. I'm unsure of how to act around him. We're engaged to be married, but not in the traditional sense. We're certainly sexually compatible. There's no denying the chemistry there, but we're not lovers. And we're certainly not friends. If anything, we teeter on that line between love and hate.

"Aren't you going to tell me how long it took you?" he calls out after me.

I stop and face him. "Like you don't know?"

"How could I? You ditched my guys every time you went in." He walks to me, and my heart rate picks up. It's unnerving how tranquil he is when I'm one touch away from combusting.

I shrug nonchalantly as I resist the craving for some kind of physical touch from him. "I prefer exploring on my own."

"Well, considering we never had to send in a search party, you figured your way out fairly quickly."

I lift one shoulder with a smirk. "It was challenging enough. At least to keep me entertained for a day."

He's quiet for a moment while he stares at me. "We're invited to dinner tonight at your family's estate."

Right away, the mood shifts, and any pleasure I've had from this conversation quickly evaporates. "And it's necessary for me to attend?" He doesn't answer as he blankly stares back at me, and I huff in annoyance. "What time do I need to be ready?"

He glances down at his watch. "You have two hours to get yourself ready."

"Alright. I'll see you then."

It's just past six o'clock as I stare at my reflection in the mirror. My makeup is dark, my lips painted a bloodied maroon. My hair is wild with a crimped style, and I wish I had more warning so I could have dumped some color on it. Purple or anything loud enough to make my father sneer with disdain. He's always loathed whatever shade of rebellion I picked that month.

But it was better than the way he began looking at me once I had tits. That slow, slithering look that no father should give his daughter.

There's no one pounding on my door, no mother waiting to lecture me about appearances, propriety, and the endless shame I've supposedly brought to the family name. She hated my so-called 'gothic phase', but all her nagging did was make me double down. So, I wore more makeup, more leather and fishnets, and made my hair brighter, wilder.

What started as a petty "fuck you" turned into armor. Then into comfort. A phase that is no longer a phase, and now a part of me.

Picking out my outfit for tonight, I felt torn for the first time. Part of me wanted to put on something that would have my family steaming in embarrassment and clenching in resentment. But then the other part of me, the part that I hate, wanted to wear something with Blackwell in mind.

Something that would have his hands itching at his sides. Something that would have that muscle in his jaw twitch. Something that would drag those dark, dangerous looks from him that tell me we're about to combust together.

And I absolutely abhor it. I don't do anything for anyone but myself. People are selfish and greedy by nature, primarily driven by self-interest. A harsh lesson I had to learn the even harder way.

So, I ended up compromising. Only because I wanted to, not having any outside influence.

A black, form-fitting leather skirt, high-waisted, ending at my calves, and a slit up to my thigh to give a tease, as well as showing off an inch of midriff. Pointed black stiletto boots come up to my knees, and a sheer high-necked top that covers my arms and shoulders, but shows off the black lacy bra underneath. Neither wholesome nor obscene.

Giving my wild hair one more fluff, I grab my black trench coat and head downstairs, making sure to be a couple minutes late just to get under my fiancé's skin.

Though he seems to tolerate me more lately. Must have pulled that stick out of his ass.

As prophesied, Blackwell paces at the bottom of the stairs, looking at his watch and counting every second I make him wait. When he catches sight of me, he stops and freezes. Eyes raking over me with a heat that has my skin burning and my nipples hard against the fabric. I confidently hold his gaze and take the stairs as if I own the fucking world.

"Do you purposely arrive belatedly," he drawls, voice low and threaded with irritation, "or are you really that careless?"

I give him a cloying smile. "Now, why would I purposely arrive *belatedly*?" I respond cheekily and breeze past him to head out.

"To push my patience," he mutters, appearing at my side.

I give him a shocked look in mock offense. "Me? Oh, come now, Blacky. You wound me."

He beats me to the car door to open it for me like the gentleman he is not, all the while cursing under his breath. Guess he isn't so tolerant of me yet.

I slide in, and he gives me a dry, unimpressed look before shutting me inside and circling the vehicle before joining me from the other side. His moves are smooth as he settles in, unbuttoning his jacket with a practiced flick of his fingers and then giving a sharp tug on the lapels. All the while, I can't keep my eyes off his every move. How can I not? He's so annoyingly secure and alluring. From the way the veins pop out on the back of his hands as the muscles constrict, reminding me of how strong they are and how rough the pads of his fingers are against my skin.

Sometimes I'm not sure if I want him, or if I want to *be* him.

I tear my eyes from him to stare out the window as the car pulls into motion with a vehicle in front of us and another behind us. "Where's your father this time?" I ask, assuming he isn't joining us again because I haven't seen him. I wonder if it has anything to do with his heart condition I'm not supposed to know about.

"He's in the vehicle in front of us, and my brothers are behind us," he says with disinterest.

I snort. How pompous. The vehicles are lined in order of power and succession. "And your mother?"

"She won't be coming."

I look at his prominent profile. "Why does she get to skip this?" He refuses to answer me or even look my way. "So, is there a special reason we're all being summoned for *dinner* tonight?" I turn my head again.

"Do you need a special reason to join your family for dinner?" His voice dips in that maddening neutrality.

I snarl at my reflection in the tinted window. "There needed to be a special reason to even talk to me while living under the same roof," I mutter, immediately regretting commenting at all. I can feel his eyes on me, heavy and simmering in the quietness of the vehicle. I'm sure with pity.

"No," he finally says, releasing his hold on me. "No special occasion."

Liar.

The Ortiz family has never been the type to regale or break bread together, especially for the sake of it. There's always some ulterior motive.

It isn't a long ride to their private airstrip where there's a jet waiting for us. It's not very spacious, unlike the one I was forced to take when I came here. Not a lot of headspace and no private bedroom in the back. But it's luxurious, nonetheless.

I give his father and Dane amicable smiles and say hello, then Harlan a more genuine one as I take it upon myself to sit as far back as I can on one of the plush leather seats.

Blackwell stops near his family and looks torn, looking to me, then to his brothers. I school my features and pull out my phone to open a game of solitaire, then cross my legs, completely ignoring him.

He makes the wise decision and stays at the front to sit. We take off shortly, and as soon as a stewardess comes to see if I need anything, I order a bottle of wine without thinking. When she comes back with the bottle and a stemless glass for me, I request a side of bourbon to add.

Probably a horrible idea since I haven't eaten much today, but aw well. It'll make tonight slightly more tolerable.

I shoot the bourbon back and keep my face passive, even as it burns all the way down and fizzles like acid in my stomach. Then the real drinking begins.

The more my face heats from the alcohol consumption, the less tension I carry, and the more bored I get. Damnit, why didn't Harlan sit back here with me? At least he would've been a good distraction.

I reach for the wine, filling another glass with a shaky grace. Just as I bring it to my lips, I catch Blackwell closing in like a storm cloud. I lean back and smile up at him, casual and unbothered, drink in hand.

He takes the seat next to me, his face grim. "I think you should slow down," he says firmly, as if he's speaking some wise words.

Right away, I'm triggered.

Does he have any idea how difficult it is to even breathe the same air as them? How badly I wish never to see that scum called family ever again? That this isn't just discomfort. It's a punishment. And being expected to act civil? That's straight-up torture.

Out of defiance, I bring the rim of my glass to my lips and chug the whole thing. Then I snatch up the bottle to pour myself another, doing so with a very heavy hand. So heavy that I manage to fit what's left of the bottle, filling it to the rim.

My nostrils flare as he gets up without saying anything, and before I can feel the gratification of being victorious, he draws the curtains shut, secluding us. When he turns around, I swallow around the wine like it's a fucking rock.

Oh, shit. He's pissed. Like *really* pissed. But I relish it. He's so fucking adorable when he's mad. How does his calm demeanor scare me so much, but his rageful one turns me the fuck on?

Oh, right. Because I'm totally and completely fucked up in the head. I couldn't ever do anything right in my family's eyes, so I did everything in my power to defy them and do the total opposite. Now, it's just how my brain works. What normal people do and think, I typically go against.

His head is tilted to one side because he's too tall, but he looks no less daunting as he comes back for me. I lift the glass to my lips to drink, and the wine splashes over when he snatches it from my hand, spilling on me.

"What the fuck, Blackwell?" I shout as I look down at my lap, thanking God I wore all black. It sloshes over as he angrily takes it to the back, away from me.

This motherfucker.

I get up and practically crash into him as he's coming back out empty-handed. *Did he pour out my wine?!*

"What is your problem?" I sneer.

He grasps my jaw with a strong hand, and I am not having it right now. I'm furious. Furious, I have to see my family. Furious, he doesn't understand how it affects me. Furious, he dumped my goddamn wine!

I start yanking at his arm and swinging at him until I'm shoved back into my seat. I only falter a little, but then I add my legs into the fight. I'm trained, but right now I'm half drunk, and now, emotional. All I can do is flail my limbs, hoping I hurt him in some way.

"Clair," he seethes in a gravelly tone. "If you do not stop, I swear I will put your ass over my knee."

I stop. But my mind goes haywire. The *fucking audacity*.

"You do that, and I swear to God, you will regret it. You think I've been wreaking havoc before? I can be a shitstorm of a nightmare for you."

Through all the fury on his face, his mouth cracks, twitching at the corner as if he finds my threat cute. Growling, I start swinging again, and I don't know how, and I don't even know when, but my wrists are bound behind my back, and I'm forced against the back of the seat face first.

There's heavy breathing in my ear as his weight pins me there. "You just can't help yourself, can you?" His voice is so fucking dangerous, my pussy hurts.

"Fuck you, Blackwell," I spit through my clenched teeth.

He gives a dark chuckle and my back arches in response, bumping the bulge of his pants against my ass. His hand around my wrists constricts to a painful grip, and his other hand goes to my hip to hold me against his groin. My core is on fire with salacious need.

His nose touches the rim of my ear, and he exhales heavily out of it as if releasing all the air in his lungs. God, I want him so bad.

This time it's intentional when I tilt my hips to rub my ass against him, and that's all it takes. He keeps me contained and uses his other hand to search for the zipper on my skirt. I'm already panting like a bitch in heat, screaming inside for him to find it.

His fingers fumble with the obscured zipper at my side, but once he pulls it down, he yanks my skirt down.

"You are maddening, *joon-kharâsh*. Fucking maddening," he murmurs against my ear and shoves two fingers inside me from behind.

My upper body is relieved of his weight so I can push my ass out in offering. Silently begging him to keep doing exactly what he's doing. I moan and he grunts, fucking me hard with his skilled fingers. The hum of the engine drowns out the indecent noises coming from both my throat and the wetness increasing between my thighs.

My molars crunch together, and I come all over his hand, rocking my hips on instinct. He wastes no time at all. Lining his cock up, he pillages his way in. No time to let my muscles relax and welcome him. Stretching me, giving me that sliver of pain I crave.

His pelvis slaps against my ass over and over. His hand crushing my wrists, and his fingers digging into my hipbone with a bruising grip. It's the most I've allowed him to manhandle me, and I hate myself for it, but I don't hate it. Words I would never say out loud.

He fucks another orgasm out of me and before I can even think straight, he has me spun around and pushed down to my knees into front of him. It was so sudden that I had to brace myself against his strong thighs.

My eyes flick up to him, and he threads a hand through the back of my hair to fist it, yanking my head back. He's stroking himself in my face, and I know what he plans to do with what comes out of it.

I clamp my mouth shut in defiance and stare daggers up at him. "Open," he snaps.

My nostrils flare, and my eyes narrow. Fuck him. I know what kind of point he's trying to make here, and I will not go along with it. The head of his cock is wet with me when he bumps against the seam of my mouth. I thin my lips and clench my teeth harder.

"Very well, *zan-e sheytâne eslâh-nâpazir,*" *incorrigible she-devil,* he rasps, and my eyes widen in fear.

Ropes of cum shoot out of his cock and I struggle against his hold on me. My scalp burns and stings as he fists it harder and continues to stroke himself, coming all over my fucking face. He's going to fucking die. I will fucking kill him for this.

Despite my furor, my core sparks to life again, wishing for one more orgasm. I move without thinking, rubbing my sticky thighs together, chasing friction. But I lock it down and stave off my arousal by shoving it beneath the weight of my fury.

His hand comes to a still as he stands over me, eyes dark with violence and sex-crazed desire. His hair is out of place, locks hanging over his forehead to his cheekbones. Those lips of his are slightly parted as he pants, and I almost forget myself. Almost.

"I should've bit your dick off," I seethe.

His response is to break a smile and slowly unfurl his hand from my hair. I'm up on my feet before he has his cock put away. I lock horns with him as I force my skirt back into place, thinking of all the ways I could fucking annihilate him.

I return his smile, and he falters. I'm sure he's now worrying about my retaliation, as he should be.

Spinning, I stomp back to the bathroom, slamming the door shut, locking it with a satisfying click. I brace myself on the counter, sucking in a deep, ragged breath before looking in the mirror.

Luckily, his aim was off, and he only got my chin and a little on my neck, so it doesn't ruin my makeup. I go to grab some tissues to clean it off, but pause. Dragging my finger through the slick mess, I bring it to my mouth and create a suction with my lips around it. Goddamn, even his cum tastes divine.

Snap the fuck out of it!

I use the tissues to wipe at it angrily, but careful enough not to fuck up my face. After using the toilet and ensuring my clothing is right and my hair looks good, I exit the bathroom, dangerously calm.

I spot a bottle of red wine in the little kitchenette, and I uncork it like a professional. Then I march back into the cabin with a smile on my face.

Blackwell was prudent enough not to trust me alone again and now occupies the seat next to mine. I plop down and take a swig straight from the bottle like a classy bitch. The aggravation from him feels like a static charge between us.

I can't wipe the grin off my face. Proud as fuck of myself. I'm going to make tonight a night from hell he won't soon forget.

I've put a good dent in the bottle by the time we land. I get up before him, and before I can take two steps, he rips the bottle out of my hand and shoves me forward. Hard. I stumble out of the curtains, cheeks blazing.

Slowly, I turn my head back to him, and he's just as red with anger in his face. Flushed and tense. And for some reason, I retreat.

Not in surrender. It's not like there won't be plenty of alcohol and sharp objects where we're going.

Let him think he won.

Or let him think I'm silently plotting.

CHAPTER NINETEEN

Running off alcohol and violence, we pull up to the hellhole I was forced to call home.

I'm not consumed with feelings of nostalgia. No cleaving to any memories. Nothing to even reminisce on. Only malice and contempt fuel me. The thought of setting the estate ablaze and watching them burn alive, screaming for help, begging for mercy, stirs up something dark and almost euphoric inside me.

Blackwell keeps me close, but not for safety or affection. It feels heavy like a chain, not warm like a comfort. As if he's here to parade his trophy for winning a hunt for exotic creatures, and he plans to hand me over as a tribute.

He's not gentle when he pulls me out of the vehicle with him, and I glance up at the height of the estate. At the attic.

They thought that by banishing me up there, I would alleviate them of grief. In a way, it did. I kept myself hidden up there more often, lurking in my little tomb, rather than hunting down my next victim to drag their sorry ass through their polished halls. But every time I did emerge, it was open season.

A shudder trickles down my spine, imperceptible through my coat, when Blackwell drops his hand lower on my back. His touch still causes me stress, but for this moment, it steadies me, whether he knows it or not. I find some peace in it, like an anchor on my sanity and tranquility.

My mind drifts into a fog the second we walk through the doors. It smells the same as I remember. Cold. Lifeless. Embers and soot. The painful past tries to choke me, but I'm too checked out. So far detached, I feel nothing at all.

I have no idea who takes my coat, but my father materializes like the devil, that repulsive, poisonous smirk twisting his face, my brothers trailing behind him like pathetic pets. Thank God my mother isn't here. I somehow hate her most of all.

I plaster on a confident smile, ready to propel forward when Blackwell's fingers catch my hip in a subtle gesture, yet a warning undertone. "Let them come to you," Blackwell's voice pierces through the fog, rapping into my ear.

To anyone watching, it may look like a tender whisper, sweet nothings spilled against my ear. But to them, all they see is control and correction. A man reminding his woman of her tight leash.

His breath ghosts across my skin, chilling my spine. The torrid heat of his proximity almost has me wavering. But I've trained for this. To remain idle against dominance and tyranny.

Stillness is safe.
Stillness is survival.
Stillness is safe.
Stillness is survival.

I've worn a mask, impenetrable and bulletproof, for so long, I'm not even sure what's underneath it, if there's anything left at all.

Let them come to me.

When my father realizes we aren't advancing, he strolls forward to close the distance. He shakes Dario's hand first, then to Blackwell, and down the line. Everyone smiling like snakes.

"Sinclair," my father says in a dead, monotone. His chin only dipped slightly. His soulless eyes lingering on me for too long. A toned-down version of his beady stare when he had too much to drink, but I can see the fire and filthy thoughts swirling behind them.

When Royce's obsession with me came to light, he beat him to a pulp. But it was in no way a paternal reaction. It was jealousy. Because then he took it out on me, too.

"Hello, father," I reply, my posture unflappable.

Lincoln and Royce flank his sides to follow our father's lead with stiff handshakes and sneers posed as smiles. Lincoln gives me a cursory nod that I barely acknowledge, and I avoid looking in Royce's direction at all. I can physically feel him trying to suck me in with his eyes, or perhaps it could be Blackwell he's sizing up.

I'm suddenly regretting the outfit I chose for tonight. I resist the temptation of recoiling or bolting for the exit. I hate how easily they can still tear me down with one single look. I hate how they can make me *feel anything*. I hate *them*. And I hate being here. Why the fuck did I agree to this?

Because I refuse to cower, letting them win.

The only way to get through this evening is to imagine slicing them into pieces, basking in their anguished screams, and bathing in their blood. Picturing all the ways I would inflict pain and torture on them, murdering them in my head over and over again until I'm numb.

Well, *that*, and alcohol.

Blackwell's hand traces lazily up and down on my hip as he trades hollow words with the monsters of my past. Whether absentmindedly, like calming a wild animal, or consciously. Either way, I'm grateful for it, and so should everyone else be in this room. If he weren't touching me right now, I'd be ripping their throats out.

We're finally ushered to the cigar room, and I peel from his side without a glance back, heading straight for the minibar. I don't need his judgey looks right now. My buzz is waning, and I cannot stomach any of them sober.

Still maintaining the façade of enjoying dark liquor, I pour two glasses and carry them back to the loveseat where Blackwell is now sitting. I join him, careful to leave a few inches of space between us, and offer him his drink without a word.

I clam up internally, feeling his eyes hanging on my profile, maybe questioning me, maybe studying me. But I refuse to look at him.

I have no fucking idea why I did that?

I didn't even realize I did that.

Why in the fuck did I just serve him a drink?

Well, *fuck*. I'm fucking *fucked*.

I tip half the liquor back in one go and fight the bitter burn scraping down my throat. The men are already in whatever disingenuous conversation, talking around me, thinking I'm too vapid to hear.

But I'm here. Floating at the edges, detached and unnoticed, like a ghost through their words. Invisible but ever present, taking inventory, filing it all away to later sharpen as weapons.

It's when I become the center of attention that I can no longer play the fool. Like when my father asks Blackwell if I've been a problem for him, as if I'm not here. I allow my eyes to wander, letting their words wash over me. Playing the dazed idiot and disappointment, they've always seen me as.

But when my mother floats into the room, I can't ignore her. I feel the space getting smaller. The air is thicker and heavier like wet cement pouring into my lungs to be buried alive.

I can't breathe in here.

I can't fucking breathe.

I rise abruptly, saying I'll be back, and no one says a thing. No snide remark on how I no longer live here, or ask where I'm going, or tell me to wait for dismissal, or even a flat-out *no*. I throw a glance over my shoulder on my way out, and no one follows.

It's not because they trust me. It's because I'm in no way a threat to them.

Let them think that. That mistake will one day cost them everything.

I wander aimlessly, long enough to be sure that I'm really alone. Once I'm confident no one's shadowing me, I veer toward the back of the house. The soft clatter of dishes and muffled chatter leaks through the swinging door to the kitchen, and it gives me a light smile.

When I blow into the room, conversation instantly stalls. All heads turn, all eyes widen on me. It takes me less than two seconds to find the only pair that matters. Pale eyes framed by deepening lines that crease when he smiles at me.

"Miss Sinclair," Baxter says warmly, setting his knife down to wipe his hands before meeting me halfway.

We don't hug. Never have. But his smile is comforting enough because it's genuine.

"Hello, Baxter."

"Hello, little shadow," he says, smiling widely, and gives me a quick once-over. "It feels like it's been so long."

I smile. "It's only been a few months, hasn't it?"

"Several." His tone makes it feel like years.

"So, what is on the menu for tonight?"

The background hum of the kitchen chatter resumes, and I end up beside him, watching him move with adroit grace I've studied since I was a child. There's always been something about the noise here. The murmurs, the clanking of pots and pans, it's like white noise for me.

It was one of the few places untainted by my family's rot. It's too far beneath them. But it was my first sanctuary, before my attic.

Baxter launches into the night's dishes and low-stakes gossip. Mostly trivial drama between the staff. When you never get to leave the estate, spilled wine becomes scandal.

"How is your new life, girl?" he asks.

I study his profile and realize how much he's aged. I was so used to seeing him all the time, I hardly noticed as his hair turned gray and the crinkles turned to wrinkles.

"Just as subservient as it always has been," I say breezily, and pop a grape tomato in my mouth to avoid his look of pity for too long.

He sighs, eyes dropping back to the task at hand. "Could you say it is better than here?" he asks quietly.

"Depends on how you look at it," I rush out and pivot to a new subject before I speak too honestly. I shift the conversation to food, raving about how good the food is at the Golzar estate, but making sure he knows that none of it compares to his work.

I know the first course will be plated soon, and someone will come to hunt me down. "Well, it was nice catching up, Baxter." I give him a pat on the shoulder. He turns to give me his undivided attention, and I have to fight the ridiculous urge to wrap my arms around him and deeply inhale all the scents clinging to his jacket.

His looks soften, turning sentimental. "Take care of yourself, Miss Sinclair."

"Always have," I chirp and steal another grape tomato before spinning on my heels.

I leave the kitchen as swiftly as I entered, and can't help but think it could be the last time I see Baxter. He's getting older, slower. This house doesn't keep anything that can't serve. If he drops dead, they'll probably take him out with the trash. Or if he grows too weak, they'll probably take him out back and shoot him like an injured animal. Dig him a shallow grave to throw him in, next to all the rest of the nameless, loyal corpses buried around this place.

I round the corner and nearly slam into a broad, firm chest cloaked in expensive wool. My breath catches for a split second before registering it's Blackwell, not Royce. "You startled me," I say with a flippant chuckle, trying to pass it off even though my pulse thrums. He stands there silently, hands shoved in his pockets like he's posing for an oil painting of himself—brooding, rigid, and fucking handsome. "Dinner almost ready?"

"Not sure," he mutters grumpily, looking over my shoulder as if expecting someone to be with me. Then his hand finds my lower back to steer me back in the direction of the quaint dinner party from Hell.

"Came to make sure I was *behaving*?" The words are bitter on my tongue.

He doesn't answer as I stare at his profile, jaw tight, unreadable. He's more wound-up now than when we first arrived.

"Still mad at me?" I push. He still doesn't speak and it's grating on my last fucking nerve. I dig my heels in, refusing to take one step further.

Finally, he reacts. A faint growl rumbles in his chest, releasing from his nose, and he pins me with a dark stare. "Sinclair," he says my name so lowly, the timbre of it ripples down my spine.

"When will you and all those bombastic *fucks* get it through your thick skulls? I—"

The hallway spins, and I'm suddenly caged against the wall. His body covers mine, holding me with his weight, reminding me of the night of our engagement party. "And when will you stop giving them reason to look down on you?" he sneers.

I gawk at him in disbelief. "Excuse me?!" I shriek.

"Keep your voice down," he bites, and my blood boils. "You couldn't have just come here and—"

"And what? Keep my mouth shut? Sit there like your well-trained show dog? My *deepest* apologies for emasculating you by slipping my leash and forgetting to play the obedient bitch in front of your precious council. Didn't mean to break your fragile illusion of control, *darling*. Next time I'll crawl before I stand."

"This isn't about me," he snaps, his voice raw. His eyes bounce around my face. For a fleeting moment, there's softness flickering in his eyes. But it vanishes, and he's back to being surly and steeled. "Acting like a rebellious *drunk* only lets them win."

My eyes narrow on his. "I don't fucking care what they think," I hiss.

He keeps analyzing me, closer now. Scrutinizing every micro-expression, and I wish I had just kept my trap shut. "You're upset with me."

"I'd have to care to be upset." My response is instant.

His stare sharpens. "We all have a part to play, Sinclair. You know that." I turn my head, done with this conversation. But he's not.

His long fingers curl around my jaw, firm but maddeningly gentle when he turns my face. I don't want gentle. I don't need it. I'm not some fragile vase on the verge of tipping. I'm already chipped, and what's left doesn't break, it cuts.

"I have to be the man they expect me to be. But you know that's not me."

I blink. *What the fuck?* He's exactly who he portrays himself to be.

"I don't know you at all," I say, instantly wishing I could take it back. His face falters, almost crestfallen, and it stabs me somewhere I didn't even know could hurt. A lump rises in my throat, dragging my resolve down with it. And I *hate* him for it. "And you know nothing about *me*," I push, needing distance. "Don't act like this is anything other than an obligation for both of us." Nothing in his wrecking-ball eyes changes, and all I want to do is hurt him. "What? Because we've been fucking you think there's anything between us more than a fucking contract? I have *never* let you in, and I *never* will. And I don't even want to know you. You are no different than any of them!" I finish loud, coldly.

He slaps a hand over my mouth, and I burn, imagining how I'd like to kill him. I haven't forgotten about the little stunt he pulled on the jet.

The rage and rejection and humiliation all swirl into one violent storm. I start to shake as it all tears me to shreds. All I want to do is scream. Cry. Disappear.

He brings his head in, bypassing my face, and brushes his lips against my ear tenderly. I start thrashing in his hold, and he gives me more of his weight, taking the air out of me.

"I fucking love your lies," he whispers. The words crawl under my skin, digging up something buried too deep, too familiar. "It's so easy to see the truth beneath them."

A hairline fracture splinters through the barriers I've spent my life reinforcing.

No, no. Get the fuck out of my head!

That traitorous lump swells, and I can't swallow it down. My insides clench. I've felt pain. Real pain. My body's been scorched, twisted into something unrecognizable. But my mind—that was hallowed. Sacred. *Mine.* No one could ever touch it.

But now he's in. Infiltrating and prying it open, making me *feel*.

Stillness is safe.

Stillness is survival.

I chant the words in my head over and over like a mantra until I reel myself in and regain temperance. He feels it, I think. His hand falls from my mouth, and I turn my face enough to whisper back in his ear, "You're *really* killing my buzz."

And just like that, I see it. A crack in his armor. *Finally!* I knew he was part human. His body turns to stone, locking up like he forgot how to breathe. Fear tries to creep in, but I shut it down, putting myself back into that safe place. Cold, quiet, untouchable.

He leans away like he's been burned, finding it difficult to look at me. And when he releases me from his weight, I stumble, unsteady without the pressure of him holding me upright. I press a hand against the wall for support.

Without a sound, he places his hand at the small of my back like it never left and nudges me back in the direction of Hell. His silence is more domineering than any threat he's given me. Domineering and annoying as fuck.

We enter the room, and no one pays us any mind. I spot Harlan at the minibar, leaning an arm on it with one ankle crossed over the other. His face is the one everyone sees, but I see that twinkle in his eyes when they connect with mine.

Blackwell is prudent enough to withhold his tongue when I part ways with him again, heading straight for the dark liquor. "I was wondering where *this* Sinclair was hiding," Harlan murmurs for only me to hear.

I give him a smirk and turn to peruse the room with a new drink in hand. "Yeah?"

"I was beginning to think all the rumors about you were exaggerated."

"They were watered down." I sip my drink with a straight face. Anxious for the buzz to kick back in and send me into a state where I won't remember much of tonight.

He hides his low chuckle in his drink. "I don't know, *joon-kharâsh*. I was expecting the *Lady Lobotomy* everyone fears."

I abruptly spit out my liquor on an uncontrollable laugh. Heads turn and conversations halt as all the attention turns to me. But I ignore them and wipe my mouth with the back of my hand. Harlan is trying to hide his grin behind his glass, but I don't give two fucks.

After everyone is sure I'm not lighting a match, they go back to their conversations, and I'm back to being a nobody.

"Is that what they call me?" I ask Harlan.

He shrugs a shoulder, face back to neutrality. "Something like that."

"Did you just make that up?" The corner of his lips twitches, his eyes surveying the room like he's ignoring me, like everyone else. But I don't take offense, because unlike Blackwell, I do know Harlan. "Wow, that was pretty good. I like it. What else you got?"

"I'll tell you only if you promise not to spit your drink out again."

"I never make promises." He snorts. "Come on," I whine, feeling the effects of the liquor again. "Entertain me, Harlan." I go to drink, and only a drop comes out. *Damnit.* I pick up the crystal decanter to fill my glass, my pour sloppy.

"Fine." He pauses, and I watch him, zealous to hear what else he comes up with. "Batshit Barbie."

I snort. "That's alright, but you can do better."

"The Attic Witch."

I roll my eyes. "Heard that one already."

"Gotherella."

I look at him with confusion, creasing my brows. It takes me a moment, but then it finally hits me. I have to steady myself on the bar top when I giggle. "I like that one too. Almost as much as *Lady Lobotomy.*"

A dark cloud rolls in when Royce comes into the room. I only see him out of the corner of my eye, but I can feel his eyes on me. Another set of eyes burns into me, and I look up to clash with Blackwell's. Is that why he came looking for me? Because Royce left the room after I did?

Stop it, Sinclair. He doesn't care about you. If anything, he just wanted to make sure nobody was touching what he claims belongs to him. He wasn't concerned for your safety.

CHAPTER TWENTY

Blackwell

T he dining room is gleaming and gold.

Polished silver, expensive crystal, enough blood money in the tableware alone to fund a coup. And yet it feels oppressive.

Sinclair's too far gone now, loose but unfiltered and dangerous. She's drunk but not sloppy. She's too proud for that. Her face is flushed, and her eyes are glossed over. She's so obstinate in her opinion of me and convinced that my actions against her tonight are all out of my need to control her. That I demand to keep her on a taut leash.

My anger hasn't been towards her. It's been *for* her. Her entire demeanor changed since the moment we got onto the jet. She is constantly throwing me for a loop, but tonight it's different. She's using it to hide something deeper, more painful. Seeing her go through all the emotions in the last few hours has affected me in ways I never knew I was capable of.

She settles into her seat beside me, almost missing it entirely. But my hand is already there to steady her. She hardly notices as she starts drumming her fingers on the table, resting her chin in her propped hand like a bored heiress. Her mother clocks the movement, wrinkling her nose up in disdain.

"Still can't hold your liquor, I see," her father says, without looking at her. "Some things never change," he utters under his breath.

"Not for lack of trying," Sinclair chirps without slurring her words. She reaches for the wine as soon as it's poured, and I hold my tongue. I'll let her deal the way she wants to tonight.

Her brothers chuckle, low and cruel. Lincoln mutters some snide remark under his breath, and I fist the fabric on my leg.

"I see you've kept up with the theatrics. Always needing to be center of attention," her mother says, staring daggers at her like the sight of her daughter repulses her.

Sinclair grins after drinking some wine. "I like to give the people what they want."

My nostrils flare as I white-knuckle my fork. I glance at Dane and Harlan across from me and see them trying to hide their smirks. But I can't see the amusement here.

"And you still think leather and fishnets are formal wear," Royce jumps in. "What's next? Cosplay?"

"No, I save those for your dreams," she replies sweetly, ripping a large chunk of bread off to shove into her mouth.

She might as well have ripped a piece of my heart off. I don't know how much longer I can stomach this. I clench my teeth so hard I taste blood.

"Charming how you've never evolved past rebellion," her mother tries to say without retaliation.

"And it's charming how you've evolved into nothing more than skin, bones, bitterness, and Botox," Sinclair claps back so easily, it's impressive.

"I did warn you," her father says to me, trying to pass off passive aggression for fun banter with a chuckle. "You'd have your hands full."

"I'd rather have my hands full than empty," I say, stabbing at my food with enough force to crack the China.

"Those who crave silence seem to never shut up," Dane mutters, and the room falls dead silent. His words aren't directly pointed at the Ortizs, but we all know who they're for.

Dane hardly speaks up. It's typically Harlan tossing in comments, but they seem to have switched roles momentarily. Dane is past the point where he can no longer stay quiet, and Harlan is too, where he doesn't trust what will come out of his mouth if he opens it.

My father clears his throat. "Funny. Most families at least pretend to get along in public," he says in a way that is intended to lighten the mood, earning a chuckle from a few. But I know it isn't in humor.

"We've never been good at pretending," her father replies.

Sinclair falls back in her chair and laughs too loudly. But I don't watch her. I'm too preoccupied with keeping a vigilant eye on her father and brothers as their faces turn crimson. If they so much as flinch in her direction, so help me God, I won't be able to stop myself.

Her father, ever the coward, changes the subject. Veering towards safer terrain before Sinclair can recover and begin to spill, splaying all their dirty laundry.

I remain composed, putting on the façade of following along to the flow of conversation, but that's not where my attention lies. I'm fixated on the way Sinclair fists her hands in her lap under the table as she wears a careless, vacant smile. Putting on a flawless performance.

If I didn't witness her consuming all the alcohol myself, I'd swear she wasn't even drunk right now.

She's just that good at acting aloof to her family's cruelty, keeping hold of what little power she still possesses with them. She plays it so well. Detached. Dismissive. As if none of it gets to her. But I see right through the act. I see how deep it cuts.

And the worst part? She's used to it.

So, when the wine is again poured for her, I don't bat an eye.

If they make her out to be the villain, she might as well drink like one.

We're all silent on the flight home. No one questions my mood or dares to speak to me. No one rolls their eyes at my drunk fiancée. We were all witnesses to the same abominable treatment. How Sinclair was carved up by her family and then written off like a check. And how she took it. As if it were normal, expected.

Harlan takes it upon himself to sit next to Sinclair with an unspoken understanding. They all sense that I need time to myself. I need to keep my distance, stewing in my anger until it simmers before dealing with her.

After seeing her mistreatment for myself, I don't have the heart to take my anger out on her. It's not a question of whether she can take it or not, because it isn't a question. I know she can. But she deserves better.

I stare at her profile as she seems to be entertaining him right back, causing him to laugh a lot. But it isn't long before she passes out.

I don't know how she does it. Tonight was hardly a glimpse into her wretched life. She was treated like dirt and chewed on like a dog toy, yet never letting them rip her apart. The only purpose she served was to bleed for their entertainment.

If her sister hadn't swallowed death first, they'd have buried Sinclair long ago, simply for sport. And she would have let them do it if it meant not giving them the satisfaction of seeing her back down.

There's something holy in the way she endures.

She is no longer for their amusement. No longer their possession. She belongs to me, and she will have a life like no one has had before. Never again will she have to look over her shoulder, wondering if today is the day they finally break her for good.

By the time we land, the space given to me was not nearly enough to cool me down. And when Sinclair wakes up giggly and still intoxicated, it only rips control further out of my reach. I'd save the explosion for the morning, if only I could think straight, but I am only capable of so much.

As soon as we walk through the doors, I pull Sinclair by the hand and take her straight to my bedroom. She doesn't resist. Still giddy, still drunk on deflection.

I completely tune her out the entire way, and the moment I close the bedroom door behind us, I pin her against it. "What did Royce do to you?"

The smile dies. "Fuck off, Blackwell," she snarls, shoving hard at my chest.

I'm immovable. "Tell me what he did." My words are chopped up into tiny pieces.

"I said fuck off!" she shouts and pushes harder.

I'm tired of the secrets and mysteries and games. I want answers. Mostly where Royce is concerned.

I grip her jaw, squeezing and forcing her to remain focused on me. "What did he do?"

Her eyes glass over, and her mask reveals the pure rawness underneath. "I said," she growls through her teeth. "Fuck. Off!" she screams and starts flailing about, her fists slamming into me, wild and trembling. "Get off me! Get the fuck off me!"

My hand shakes on her face. "Tell me what he did!" I roar.

"Why do you care so much?!" She stops thrashing. "Huh?! Why? So, you can toss me on my ass when you realize how fucking ruined I am? How dirty I am?"

Ruined. The word hits like a brick to the sternum.

And the raw pain in her eyes is so tangible, I can feel it too. It has my knees buckling.

Her chin contorts as her glossy eyes bore into me. "I think you know what he did to me." Her voice cracks, ripping my heart out. "Just use your fucking imagination." She shoves at me with the last two words.

I swallow hard as my stomach churns. I need her to say it out loud, so that my imagination doesn't run wild like it has been. I know it's selfish of me, but the mystery of it all is gutting me from the inside out.

But then I remember the turmoil of her life. I don't wish to inflict more pain into it. I never want to cause her any real pain again. I wish I could build a protective cocoon around her.

I ease my grip and drop my forehead to her. She flinches, and it nearly sends me over the edge. But I stay there, breathing her in. Steadying us both.

Eventually, after several moments, our breath aligns.

Without withdrawing, I run my hands over her. Sliding up the back of her head, into her hair, then down to caress her neck and shoulders. Down her arms. Letting my touch say everything I can't right now. Everything I won't.

When I open my eyes, her eyes are open too, staring blankly. She's retreating behind the wall again, but tonight I'm going to tear a piece of that wall down. Permanently.

I don't say anything as I scoop her up, holding her protectively. She's never felt so tiny in my arms. I carry her to the bathroom, set her gently on her feet, and turn on the tub. She doesn't resist, and I don't dare disturb the silence.

I know her strength, but I undress her like she's breakable. Then I undress myself, my eyes never once straying from her beautifully broken features.

Once I'm satisfied with the water's temperature, I lift her again and lower her into the steaming water. Then I sink in, bringing her back to my chest.

Minutes creep by as her body remains stiff. So, I just hold her. No demands. No expectations. Only patience and warmth.

Just when I think it'll never happen, she melts back into me. Her body softens, and I keep my breath steady despite the victorious feeling bursting inside me.

When I begin running a soap bar over her silky skin, I do it slowly, reverently so. The scars on her back, ribs, and thighs...I study each one, touching them with care. No words.

Not tonight. I won't ruin this with questions, threats, or promises of revenge. Just solace as I hold her until the water turns to room temperature.

When we leave the bath, we don't speak. I wrap her in a towel and carry her to the bed. She doesn't ask for anything. Doesn't need to. Because I already know.

Every time we touch, we explode, coming together in a frenzy. Passion turns to hunger. Hunger turns to greed. Greed turns to dominance. Tonight, our gravitation is no less fervent. Our desire is no less parched. But I take my sweet time with her, and she lets me.

I sit on the edge of the bed with her still in my arms. Holding her for a few more moments, my nose pressed against her head, breathing her in. Her smell is so overpowering, I'm enslaved. She has no clue the possessive hold she has over me. I may be able to conquer her physically with pure brute and muscle. But she reaches places inside me that are unattainable. To everyone but *her*.

Dragging my lips across her forehead, I cup her delicate face, and she returns my gaze. Her eyes are pink with unshed tears and exhaustion. The pain is still evident, potent. I feel hopeless at this moment. I could give her anything in the world, but I can't wipe away her past.

Searing my lips to hers, they move together. Our tongues meet in the middle, and we remain unhurried. Her arms curl around my neck, clinging to me like it's the only thing that'll keep her from finally shattering.

She's pliant in my hands as I maneuver her to the bed, laying her down, covering her body with mine. All the while, she still holds onto me and kisses me so deeply, as if to make the rest of her world disappear.

The towels get tossed aside, and I rain down kisses on her face and neck. She has her eyes squeezed shut, but it's okay. If I am going to get anywhere with Sinclair, I need to take smaller steps with her. Learn more patience.

So tonight, when I settle my hips between her legs and I slide into her, there's no battle for dominance. No war between our bodies. We lay down our swords and surrender.

As I make languid, long thrusts, her nails dig into my back. But not in an animalistic way like she usually does. It's to anchor herself to me. To hold onto me for dear life.

When I feel her mouth in my hair, and a hand snakes up my back to thread her fingers through it, I feel it. That shift. It's faint, but it's there. Proof that she's still alive.

That no matter what they did to her, she survived.

And now, she's mine.

CHAPTER TWENTY-ONE

It's been days since the dinner from hell, followed by something more terrifying, but I still feel raw under my skin.

Like something foul I can't quite scrub out.

Outwardly, I'm the same. Wandering the vast estate, looking for something to get into. Touching things I'm not supposed to, peeking into rooms I'm not supposed to be in, all the while wearing an unbothered smirk, throwing a wink at every mob puppy I pass.

But inwardly, I'm frayed. I'm still stuck in that tub with Blackwell's arms around me, holding me like I'd fall apart if he didn't. It was something I didn't know I needed. It's why I can't let it ever happen again. I can't let him get that close again.

I'm afraid of what I might say if I do.

What I might *feel*.

So, I've been avoiding him as much as humanly possible. Going out on more shopping sprees, wandering the hedge maze with Blender, clinging to the shadows like a vengeful little plague.

But when we *do* cross paths, I do a great job at pretending like I'm as solid as ever. Neither of us brings it up, but he's different. In the way he touches me for the sake of touching me, so casually. A light caress down my cheek with the pad of his thumb. Brushing my fingers in passing. Kissing me without devouring me and tearing my clothes off.

And I let him. I don't pull away, but I don't lean into it either. And I never make the first move. Reciprocation is all I can offer. It's the only currency I trust.

We may come from the same world, but our lives were nothing alike. I've never had a relationship. Never even seen one up close. Not romantically, not platonically. Hell, I wasn't even friends with my siblings. Watching Dario and Jacqueline Golzar is the closest I've gotten, and it's fucking *weird*.

She was forced into her marriage like the rest of us ill-fated bitches, but she seems...*happy.*

It's so unnatural.

As if she had learned to love her captor. The whole Stockholm syndrome thing. Or maybe he somehow earned it.

I can't think too long about marrying Blackwell. Every time the thought tries to slither its way in, I shove it down with the rest of the bottom-feeders in my mental basement. Alongside shame, want, compassion, and trust.

I don't hate it here. Sure, I'm bored to death most days, but I don't always feel the need to keep my bedroom locked at all times, or sleep with one eye open. I don't trust any of them, or *anyone* in general, but I feel somewhat safe here.

Maybe *safe* isn't the right word.

I think it's content.

Yes, I feel content.

Turning a corner, half-expecting to be alone, there he is. Manifesting himself like he knew he was on my mind. All clean lines and subtle assuredness, standing there like he's been waiting for me.

I slow to a stop, letting him come to me. When he reaches, his arms automatically go around my waist, and his face softens. Without a word, he kisses me like he hasn't seen me in so long. Desperate but unhurried. With warmth that's reserved for something soft and real. Not for steeled mobsters like us.

I kiss him back with a smirk curving my lips. Cool and detached as always. "Stalking me, Blackwell?" I rest my arms on his shoulders.

"Always have," he rasps between kisses. "Losing your touch, *Sinister Sinclair?*"

I grin at the most common nickname people have for me. "I prefer *Lady Lobotomy.*"

He chuckles, pausing his lips for a moment. "I haven't heard that one yet."

"That's because your brother recently came up with that one."

He looks down at me, head tilted, half a smirk, eyes sparkling. I can't take it. "Fitting."

I need distance. Instead of running my fingers through his hair like I'm dying to, I drop my hands. He takes the hint and follows suit. His ease unwavering.

"So, where are you headed off to? Another meeting with plans of global domination? Or global annihilation?"

He sighs and runs a hand through his hair, averting his gaze. He's hiding something. "Just business as usual."

"So, murder then," I tease.

His half smirk stretches. "I'd like to have dinner tonight."

"Then have dinner. No one's stopping you." I breeze by him.

"Funny," he says dryly, matching my steps. "Six o'clock."

"Not going to tell me to wear something nice?" I sass.

"Would it matter if I did?"

I turn to grin at him, and he's already looking at me. "Never."

I start to veer off to disappear around the corner when I'm grabbed by the waist and spun into him like a move straight out of a fucking fairytale. My hands slap against his chest. Our bodies press flush.

He only tortures me with a heated stare for a moment before opening his mouth over mine for a kiss deeper than the one before. Leaving me breathless and my pussy wet with heat.

My mask slips when he pulls away. Not giving me any time to recover, he walks off wearing a cheeky grin like he didn't just set me on fire to leave me smoldering.

Asshole.

I head up to unwarp my mind and bleed out some tension. When I hit the top of the stairs, I hear some newcomers arriving. Quickening my steps, I duck around the corner to see who they are and what kind of evil they're adding to this place.

Curiosity is one hell of a drug.

I peek over the banister only enough to see but not be seen, and I spy the last people I'd expect to be visiting. What the fuck are the Bozzellis doing here?

Looks like my day just got a little more interesting.

I switch directions, walking away from my room and towards another. A little secret of mine. Making sure I'm not being watched, I close myself inside the empty bedroom that happens to be right above the office, where all their little secret meetings are held.

Same old trick I used back home. All the vents are connected in some way, acting like an intercom. And the closer you are, the louder they project.

Closing the door and flicking the lock, I kick my shoes off to get comfortable. Seeking the floor vent I've used for months now, I lay down on my belly and fold my arms to rest my head on them with my ear hovering over the vent.

I half-listen, half-doze. Nothing but egotistical babble. Men preening and comparing dick sizes.

I don't understand what kind of business they could have with the Bozzellis. They aren't well-connected. No solid ties to the inner circle. They have some bad blood with a few of the core families, mine being one of them. They're a total wild card. Unpredictable.

Which makes them dangerous.

Their loyalty to no one, and their allegiance for sale to everyone.

I'm about to check out with nothing holding my interest when I hear my name drop, and my ears perk up.

Is she as crazy as they say she is?

Do you keep her locked inside a cage?

Yawning through the usual, I turn my head to the other side to stretch my neck. Once they've exhausted all curiosity where I'm concerned—part freakshow, part cautionary tale—they move on to my family in general. They wear their disgust for them loud and proud. No pretense or diplomacy, even with Blackwell sitting right there, knowing he's about to marry an Ortiz.

But I can't blame them. I share their sentiments and revulsion. No offense taken here.

And like storm clouds rolling in, the conversation takes a dark turn. They want to take out the Ortizs. And not metaphorically. A sick thrill crackles through my chest like firecrackers. The thought of my family dead should be a joyous occasion, but there's no time to celebrate. Because technically, I'm an Ortiz, no matter how far I try to separate us and how much they like to disown me.

And without the family name, there's no leverage. No empire. No point or purpose.

If they kill my family, I'm *worthless*. Like I've always been.

I teeter on the edge of sanity, waiting, *begging* for Blackwell to speak up. To say something concerning me and our arrangement. To push back. To insist I'm off-limits. But why would he? Our marriage was transactional and strategic.

No family, no gain.

No gain, no value.

Worthless.

Just when I thought it couldn't get any worse, they drop the *real* bomb. They want into the circle. And to cement their seat, they want to take my family's place and offer their daughter to Blackwell. Replacing me.

Blood thunders in my ears. My throat throbs, and my chest caves. I feel it everywhere.

Betrayal. It ripples through me like fire in my veins.

Dario is the only one to speak. He doesn't object. He explains it will have to be further discussed.

Discussed.

Whether I live or die will be a simple matter of discussion.

But I know they won't refuse their offer. Why would they? If they don't take the deal, someone else will. And the outcome will remain the same.

I'll be left with no family, making me useless. Then I'll end up tossed onto the heap of corpses of my kin or cast aside like trash.

Either way?

Fuck. That.

It's finally time for me to take possession of my own life.

CHAPTER TWENTY-TWO

Blackwell

I 've been sitting here silently seething as every moment passes.

To walk in here and *demand* that I marry their daughter when I already have a fiancée. I agree that the Ortizs should be erased, their legacy burned to ash. They're weak. Corroded. Dangerous in the stupidest, sloppiest ways. But Sinclair is *not them*, only in name. And without the name, the marriage is no longer profitable.

But the idea of replacing her, discarding her like it means nothing, it's gut-punching, hitting somewhere deep. Somewhere I don't wish to acknowledge.

It makes it hard to breathe.

I haven't moved a muscle since the Bozzellis left. My body locked up so tight, I know my muscles will ache tomorrow. But when my father comes back into the room after escorting our guests out, I can't remain reticent anymore.

"I'm not doing it."

My father sighs as he lowers himself back down behind his desk. "I don't see any way around it, Blackwell. Refusing their offer, they would align themselves with someone else, making us their enemy."

"How so? We could still aid them and take out the Ortizs, but is it necessary to marry his daughter?"

"You know how this works," he says with a patronizing firmness that makes my fists twitch. "Your engagement to Sinclair was never out of affection. It was a power move."

"And now we're going to wipe them out. If they're so easy to uproot from the circle, why align ourselves to begin with?" I say more vehemently than intended. Trying to come up with every reason possible to refuse it.

His face hardens in disappointment. "She was not your only option. I gave you plenty to choose from, and after dragging your feet for years, you still chose the Ortizs."

Yes, I chose Sinclair.

Because the Ortizs were bottom of the barrel. Her father is aging out of relevance. Her brothers are arrogant, reckless, and vapid. Destined for an early grave. Their empire was a crumbling fortress I could walk into and claim without bloodshed. Little mess and no effort at all.

It was supposed to be the easiest choice.

But it's not so simple anymore.

I knew she would be a task, but I didn't realize she would be the entire complication. Until she became an addiction I refuse to quit.

Now, every time I earn one of those rare, genuine smiles, it feels like a prized victory. Knowing that I'm one of the very few to do so.

And when she truly laughs, the sound reverberates off the walls like a song no one dares to interrupt and miss a note. Out of admiration or fear. It's all the same to her.

And now, when I touch her, she doesn't flinch like she used to. That alone feels like something sacred. A privilege that *no one* else has.

He prattles on, but I'm not hearing anything he has to say. When he finally wraps up with, "I'll think it over," I nod once and leave.

Think it over my ass.

I go straight to the surveillance room. No searching her usual spots or asking around. I'm in no mood for a game of hide and seek. "Where is she?" I say as soon as my toes hit the threshold. The demanding desire to find her is torturous.

Whomever is manning the tech spins in surprise, not seeing me coming. "Last I saw, she was heading out to the hedge maze, sir."

There's no need to have him double-check or make sure she hasn't left that area, even though the sun is beginning to set. My girl thrives in the dark. She was born in it.

I move quickly and quietly through the hedge. Even after decades of exploring them, I still have to second-guess every turn I take. And Sinclair could walk it with her eyes closed only after months.

As I'm swiftly approaching the epicenter, I hear her voice. High-pitched and girlish. Not to give away my position, I stop to listen in.

"You're such a piggy," she coos. I blink, stunned. "After everything the world has done to you, you decide to trust *me*, of all people," she says, switching back to her caustic charm.

She has to be talking to some kind of animal. Most likely trying to coax it in, to slaughter and leave it for someone under their pillow like coins from the tooth fairy.

I strain my hearing in search of any distress I might find telling in her tone. I know she is always listening, and today couldn't have been a worse time to be eavesdropping on.

"Well," she sighs. "The sun is going down, meaning they'll send in a search party if I don't emerge from here soon." Her voice is just as dry-humored and impassive as always. "I'll come back to see you as soon as I can. *If* I can."

There's a cooling in my chest. She couldn't have heard anything. One thing Sinclair cannot act her way through is her nasty temper. If she thought for a second her life was on the line, that betrayal was afoot, she would be burning this place down in an instant.

I stand rooted with my hands shoved into my pockets, putting myself at enough distance to make it seem like I was just walking up. Her light footsteps over the gravel fall in a rhythm before she comes around some foliage and spots me immediately.

"Your stalking used to be impressively subtle." Her words are as smooth as honey. Her wit so effortless.

I pull her in around the waist. "I was just coming to find you." Her scent surrounds me—sharp like smoke, sweet like sugar. "Hungry?"

Her hands move up my chest with a casualness that can match mine. "Starved." She flashes me a toothy grin, the gold hoop under her top lip peeking out, and the diamonds ingrained in her teeth, blinding in the golden hour.

Nothing in her tone or demeanor resembles anger, putting my paranoia to rest.

CHAPTER TWENTY-THREE

Blackwell

Tension has been mounting at every turn.

Ever since the Bozzellis showed up with their proposition, everything has been unraveling. For two weeks, my father and I have been locked in a silent war over it. We've all gone round and round, trying to come up with a compatible deal. We offered them almost everything they wanted. We'd eliminate the Ortizs and give them a seat at the table. But they want insurance. And they want it in blood.

A marriage to tie our families is non-negotiable for them.

By refusing it, we'd be rejecting the entire offer and our alliance. Our first offense, and in our world, we never let anything go. We may have been their first choice, but we're not their only. They'll take their offer and bring it to another family. Cutting us out entirely, leaving me blind to their plans. And their plans include killing every single Ortiz. Including Sinclair.

I've been trying to stay levelheaded, especially with my father's health declining. His heart is failing and needs surgery soon. We've kept it quiet, but it weighs on every decision. I'm taking on more than my fair share to keep the pressure off him, but it's all too much. And time is working against us.

Through it all, Sinclair has been my quiet place, waiting for me in the eye of the storm where everything stands still. My only fucking peace. Her presence. Her oblivion. Knowing that she's safe and completely unaware of the danger lurking behind her. It's enough to keep me grounded.

The only thing that is for sure—Sinclair is mine.

If I have to agree to the marriage with the Bozzellis to buy us a window, then so be it. I'll tear that window into a door and walk Sinclair right through it. The ring is just a tool, but Sinclair is the only future for me.

She's had the green light to begin furnishing our estate, but she's been dragging her feet on it. Most likely, dreading the permanence of it. But I'm done waiting. It's time we finally have our space. No more his and hers when it comes to bedrooms and belongings.

It's late when I go to look for her. I haven't seen her since this morning. I left her in my bed, curled up in the sheets, naked and peaceful. Looking like she belonged there.

I haven't made it two steps up the stairs when my name is called out with urgency. Scout and Hawk come running up to me, faces flushed and out of breath. My mind instantly goes to Sinclair.

"What's wrong?" I rush out, bracing for the worst.

"We found two of our guys dead in the hedge maze," Scout says.

"How?"

"Stabbed to death. It looks like they were killed just outside of it and dragged in. I haven't made it to the control room yet," Scout explains.

Hawk nods. "I found them."

My blood chills, and I start beelining for the control room. "How did no one catch this?" I growl out.

There's no need for any of them to answer because I'm met with it as soon as we get there. Both men on duty are dead.

"Motherfucker," I say, seething. "Get everyone on this," I order without looking at them. "Now!"

I shove one of the bodies aside to start scrolling through footage for clues. My phone goes off and I answer it without seeing who it is. "Yeah," I clip.

"What the hell is going on?" My father demands on the other side of the call.

"Trying to figure that out right now."

He sighs. "Can you handle this?"

"Yes."

"Good. Call me when you do."

I hang up and focus on reviewing the footage. Starting with the one on the maze. Rolling it in reverse until something catches my eye. Feet first, a body being dragged. Then another figure steps into frame.

I freeze it there. "Start with this," I direct to Scout, then look to Hawk. "Where's Sinclair?" I ask even though I know the answer.

"I have everyone on it," he quickly replies.

I run out of the room and try calling her. I call over and over, all going unanswered. "Fuck!" I yell, taking the steps two at a time.

I try her room first. Barreling in, I already know she isn't here. I can feel it. Pivoting my head, I stomp over to the side table where my attention is being drawn.

Her phone.

Her ring.

And a note.

Left, but not gone.

Stepping into the dark to set the stage.

A kiss for the crowd, a dagger for the king.

The finale is mine.

I bare my teeth with an animalistic snarl, crushing the note in my hand. Jumping into action, I leave the room, knowing I'm not going to find anything helpful there.

I place my phone to my ear and my father picks up after the first ring. "Yeah."

"She knows," I say, running down the stairs.

"Where is she?"

"Haven't found her yet." And I don't think we will. At least not here.

He's silent for too long. "You should have told her."

Yeah, no shit.

"I have to ask you, Blackwell. Is it worth it?"

I halt in my steps. "Of course it's worth it. She's worth *everything*," I answer so hurriedly as if the words have been waiting on the tip of my tongue to spill out at the right moment.

"So, this is your decision."

"Yes." I start moving again.

"You understand the position this puts us in," he tries to remind me.

"I do."

He sighs before speaking again. "Well, she didn't have much of a head start," he points out. "We'll find her."

She wasn't supposed to find out this way. Not without hearing it from me. That I had no intention of going through with it. There could never be anyone else. Not for me. Not in this life or the next. It was always Sinclair.

But she knows, and now she's gone. Every minute she's out there, exposed and vulnerable, her life is on the line. The thought of someone getting their hands on her first punches a hole through my chest.

No matter how far she runs, how well she hides, I will find her.

And God help anyone who stands in my way.

CHAPTER TWENTY-FOUR

Blackwell

I t's been months without her.

No contact. No leads. No sightings. Just left reaching for her in the middle of the night, only to come up empty. Her side of the bed, cold to the touch. Left chasing shadows.

It isn't the fact that she left without a trace. Or that she ran from me. It's the fact that I still have no clue what goes on in that beautiful, twisted head of hers that is the most infuriating of all. That she can so easily play me.

She led me to believe she was oblivious. She gave absolutely nothing away. No cracks. Never wavered. She knew, and yet she withheld her reaction. Bottled up her vengeance. She kissed me back with every kiss. Shook with every orgasm. Curled into my side when she slept.

I've kept eyes on her family's estate around the clock, thinking that's where she may have run to take cover, but there hasn't been any detection of her. We haven't flat-out asked the Ortizs if she's there, in case she's not. They don't need to know that she's out there somewhere. No one does.

Once word gets out, there'll be a pretty price on her head from all their enemies.

As predicted, when we informed the Bozzellis that there would be no marriage arrangement between our families, the deal was taken off the table. There hasn't been anything brought forward about whether they went to another family or not. But it doesn't matter.

Deal or no deal, it's time to rid the world of the Ortizs. Sinclair excluded. Tonight is the night.

We come with no mercy. The Ortiz estate folds like paper. The gates are breached, the perimeter swallowed by our men like a tide rolling in to cleanse the land. Their men scatter like roaches when the floodlights slice through their manicured façade.

Screams echo, ripping through the dead of night. Gunfire cracks from all ends.

I stare up at the highest point of the house, half expecting to see Sinclair there, perched like a queen with a bag of popcorn, watching us dismantle her past with wicked delight. But only the ghost of her remains.

By the time I step foot in the foyer, the fight is already over.

Smoke still lingers from the flashbangs. Blood streaks with boot prints cover the marble floor. Windows are shattered, and doors hang from their hinges. Taking on the look of what this place has always been.

A well-decorated grave.

"Anything?" I ask over my earpiece.

"She's not here," Scout replies.

I already knew it. I knew she would rather burn than crawl back to the people who set her on fire. But their takedown was inevitable. And there might be some clue here to help me find her.

"Round up the staff!" I shout. "Anyone still breathing, bring them!"

Minutes later, the remaining help are lined up. Frightened, confused, barely clothed. I walk the line with slow, deliberate steps.

"Is there anyone Sinclair talked to on the staff?" I ask, studying everyone closely. Every twitch and tremble. "Anyone at all."

The more I pace, the more they tremor. The women are crying. A few whisper prayers under their breath. But no one speaks up.

I'm about to give them an incentive using someone's blood when an older man steps forward at the end of the line. I stand in front of him, and he bravely meets me in the eye. "I've known Miss Sinclair since she was a child. She would hide away in the kitchen a lot."

I watch him for another heavy moment before deciding he's telling the truth. I nod to Scout. "Take him. We'll question him later," I tell him.

The rest of the staff are free to go. We already have enough bodies to dispose of. And it's finally time to deal with the real infestation.

They kneel before me, stripped of dignity, fallen from grace. All of them, and I wish Sinclair were here to witness it herself. Lincoln is bleeding from his nose. Royce can hardly breathe through his fear.

Anthony has a few cuts and bruises of his own as he glares at me. And her mother reeks of piss and shame.

My blood boils hottest when I stand directly in front of her father. "If you're going to kill me, just get it over with," he sneers.

My grin is slow. "I'm not here to kill you." He frowns, obviously confused. "Not tonight, that is."

"Then what do you want?" he snaps.

I crouch down. Letting a moment of silence make him squirm. "What was it you hated so much about her?" Lincoln starts throwing curses at me, but I let them bounce off. Still, Scout clubs him on the head with the butt of a gun. "Was it because you envied her strength and tenaciousness, or because you wanted her so badly in such an unnatural way? That if she ever told you to kneel, you'd fall right then and there."

I struck a nerve. He's frothing at the mouth now. "If you don't kill me now, I will kill you later," he hisses.

I stand up smiling, then I look at her mother and see how she's shriveling up on herself. Pitiful. Then I look at Lincoln and he bares his teeth. And, when my eyes move to Royce, I laugh.

I side-step to stand in front of him. "I think she'll have the most fun with you, ripping you to shreds. Peeling your skin off one layer at a time." A tear escapes, trickling down his face. A puddle forms between his knees, and I scowl in disdain. "Not because she hates you the most, because she'd have to care to hate you, but because you'll probably scream the loudest."

I give Scout another nod, and he barks orders to take them all away. Lincoln and Anthony resist and curse at me, Royce and her mother start begging for mercy and sobbing, which falls on deaf ears.

They'll be tossed in cells to rot while they wait for Sinclair to bring justice down on them. A fitting wedding gift. Hers to unwrap and dissect at her leisure.

CHAPTER TWENTY-FIVE

Today will be a reckoning.

The last scene before the final act.

The stage is set. Now, all we need is our performers. Thanks to my old pal, Baxter, I know that Blackwell knows my location. He called me with the heads-up yesterday, right before he left town with the money gifted to him. If I know Blackwell at all, he's on his way right now, bringing the cavalry.

I finish the final touches to my makeup. "Well?" I glance over at Blender. "What do you think?" She flicks her tail once, unimpressed.

She looks like a totally different cat, now that her fur has filled out and she has some meat on her bones. Her black fur is long with a red tint in it under the sun. There's a patch of white on her chest, and the hair is thicker around her neck, giving her a lion's mane. Her eyes haven't changed, though. Still a yellow-green, piercing, and soulful. She's the definition of majestic.

I was apprehensive about bringing Blender on the road, but she's always been a contradiction. Untamed, yet tethered to me in her own quiet way. She roams freely, capable of surviving anywhere, but never strays far.

I stick my tongue out at her playfully, then turn back to the cracked mirror hanging crooked off the wall. I wanted to look extra special for my ex-lover for our brief reunion. Remind him of who he fucked with.

I wanted to create an image that'll haunt him for the rest of his life. Possibly the last image he'll ever see.

I grin at my reflection. "I'm really digging this look."

I was going for dramatic, but it morphed into a goth clown glam style. My skin is porcelain-pale, a contrast to the rest of the makeup. My eyes are framed by elongated, black lines drawn both above and below like wicked clown tears. The red, matte color on my lips is sharply defined at the corners of my mouth, giving me that sinister grin. And to top it all off, the classic red nose tip. Not humorous in appearance, but provocative and eerie.

I pull the black hood up over my head and blow a kiss at the mirror. "Alright, girlfriend. Time to finish setting the stage. Our leading man will be here soon."

Double- and triple-checking all my booby traps and trip wires, I make my way up to the top floor for the best seat in the house. Lighting up a cigarette to help calm the nerves, I wait.

The petite mansion is old and forgotten. Places like this always call to me. Abandoned. Ghostly. Full of stories and pain. It feels like home.

The loud chirping tells me that one of my perimeter sensors has been triggered. I spit out the wad of gum I've been chomping on for too long and stretch my body like a feline. "Alright, Blender." I turn and look at her with a grin. "You might want to make yourself scarce." Another chirping rings out, alerting that the sensors on the other side of the property have gone off, too. So far, everything is going as planned. "It's showtime."

They breach quietly and methodically, but not cautiously enough. One by one, my traps spring. Silent darts with paralyzing serum of my own little invention hit their marks. They go down like a sack of potatoes, one thud after another. I lurk in the shadows, picking off the stragglers with my dart gun. None of them see me coming.

Blackwell goes down very last. He's stronger, more stubborn. But eventually, he ends up sprawled out on the dusty floorboards. A couple more twitches as he tries to move his arms, then he's still. Only his chest heaves.

That's my cue.

I step out of the dark and into the warm light filtering as the sun is getting low. Hood up and knife in hand. I straddle him slowly, tilting my head. Our eyes lock, and it tries to move something inside of me. But I slam it shut and shut it down.

He tries to lift a hand to stop me or pull me closer. Either way, I don't care. "Hello, lover," I say, grinning, revealing the knife. "Miss me?"

I slice and chop at his Kevlar with careful precision. Then I rip his shirt open. I almost salivate when I see the brute muscles bulge under the rich skin. Glistening with a sheen of sweat, his chest heaving.

Okay, focus, you huzzy.

I tease him some, coming at him with the knife with slow movements. But it'd be too easy to kill him like this. Very anti-climactic. Instead, I delicately carve a heart into his chest. Not too deep, but deep enough to bleed and scar.

I drag the blade along my tongue and mewl. "Mmm." Then I flip the blade over to wipe the rest of the blood across my lips like lipstick.

Lowering my head, I kiss him. Sloppily and possessively. But I force myself to think I'm kissing someone else. Anyone else.

The illusion almost cracks when he kisses me back. It's sluggish, but his lips move with mine. And I hate myself for letting the kiss linger a second longer than intended.

I pull back and smile down at him, unfazed. "Don't blink, darling. The grand finale is closer than you think," I rasp.

At the front door, I sling my backpack over one shoulder, then pick up the red gas can. I whistle a happy tune as I make a trail of gasoline from the stoop and down the path. Blender is already waiting for me there. Twitching her tail and watching with disinterest.

I light up another cigarette and take a few puffs as I pause. What a shame to destroy something so beautifully broken.

I flick the cigarette, and seconds later, it catches flame. The fire races, slithering up the path like a serpent. It doesn't take long to grow, and it somehow adds more beauty to the withering estate.

"Beautiful," I whisper.

I hear male voices in the distance. The second team. And they're coming in hot. Probably because Blackwell isn't answering them. No one is.

"Time to go." I slip off the backpack and open it for Blender. She jumps right in, and I swing it across my back, snug to me, and take off into the woods.

Hopping on my bike, the engine roars to life, and I take off without a glance back.

CHAPTER TWENTY-SIX

Blackwell

I'm wrathful as we get back home, empty-handed.

"Goddamn—*kīram to khodam!*" *Fuck me*! I pick up a chair and arch it over my head and release it. I hardly register the crash. "That fucking—" I grab another piece of furniture and slam it on the ground over and over, growling through gnashing teeth. "*Kīram to mādar-e kasi ke... kīram to in zendegi,*" *Motherfucker...fuck everything*, I snarl as pieces of another chair go flying. But no amount of damage could relieve the ire scorching my insides.

She was right there. "*Goh khordam,*" *I fucked up*, I mutter and pace furiously. Literally right on top of me. But I was helpless. Paralyzed from whatever she shot us all with. I couldn't even speak. I couldn't tell her that she was never on my hit list. That she was under my protection. That she will always be under my protection. Tell her that I refuse to marry someone else for power. That she is empowering enough, no matter her surname.

That yes, I do miss her. My hand goes to my bloodied chest on instinct.

My lungs are burning, my muscles are all constricting, and my head pounds with rage. "*Dāram divoone misham...che ghalati kardam?*" *I'm fucking losing it...what the fuck did I do*, I mutter, the words muddled.

"Are you done?" Dane says dryly. My head snaps in his direction, glaring at him like I'm locked in on my prey as he sits casually on the windowsill.

"Easy, Blackwell," Harlan chimes in, going for a soothing voice.

"Don't," I snap between gnashing teeth.

He waits a long moment before speaking again. "We'll find her. We did once, and we'll do it again."

Now my eyes snap to lock on Harlan. "She tried to kill me!"

He chuckles and shakes his head. I'm seeing red, a hair from snapping. "She was fucking with you. If she wanted you dead, she would have done it."

"What the fuck do you mean?" I roar, advancing on him. "She tried to fucking burn me alive!"

"But she didn't," he argues. I walk away, shaking my head at his nonsense. "Sinclair is more cognizant of our world and how it works than you think. Than *any one* of us thinks. She knew that there was a second team and that they would come in just in time to get you out of there."

I'm staring at the ground, still panting with fury. I turn my head slightly to see him. "You don't know that."

He shoves his hands in his pockets. "I *do* know that. And you do too. You're just too wrapped up in your own emotional turmoil to think straight. You're upset you didn't get her, I get it. We were so close to bringing her home. She outsmarted us." I find it difficult to look at Harlan when he's wearing a smirk and trying to hide it.

"I don't see anything funny about this," I chop up each word, seething.

"I'm sorry," he says, his smirk growing and still trying to conceal it. "I know this isn't funny, but—" He shakes his head more.

"It was brilliant," Dane pipes in. He stands up, posture straight. "Harlan's right. If she wanted to kill you, she would have done it. Probably before she even left. But she didn't."

"She's fucking with you. You know how Sinclair loves games," Harlan says.

My mind begins going through everything I have catalogued about Sinclair and the way her mind works. Everything she does is unpredictable. Yet calculated.

Then it hits me. My head pops up. "The chef."

CHAPTER TWENTY-SEVEN

My head pounds and my ears ring as I try to regain consciousness.

The smell of blood and urine invades my senses, slapping me awake and burning my throat. Opening my eyes is like lifting concrete, but I somehow manage. Groaning, every muscle in my body screams in agony as I try to sit up. The hard ground is cool beneath my palms.

"Fuck," I hiss through a dry throat and wince, squeezing my eyes shut. My hands shoot up to cradle my skull and apply pressure. I rub at my temples to desperately try to allay the pain.

I force my eyes open again. I need to bear my surroundings as I focus on the blurry fragments. A single light bulb flickering sways above my head. Even though it's dull, it still hurts to look at.

Nausea washes over me, and I rest my eyes to breathe through it until it passes. The foul smells do not help any.

Okay, focus.

One more deep breath.

I slowly open my eyes for the final time and peruse the rest of the small room. Cement walls, a bucket, one door with no handle, and nothing else.

Oh, no. No, no, no, no, no.

How?

My memories are jumbled, and I cannot remember how I got here, but I know where *here* is.

Knowing there's no sense in trying, I have to anyway. Using the wall for support, I stand up and give myself a few moments to steady my legs and find my balance. I don't have time to waste.

Here goes nothing.

Gearing up my strength, I sprint forward, then angle my body to ram my shoulder into it. "Ohh," I groan in agony, holding my shoulder. That fucking hurt like a bitch.

I rotate my arm a few times to work out the kinks and shake off the pain. This is not the time to be a pussy. I've been through worse.

I give it two more goes before my body gives out and I slump to the floor. My energy is completely depleted. There's no use in crying out because anyone out there is the same people who put me in here.

The will to survive does not stem from the will to *live*. It's about pride. I will decide when, how, and where I will go out. Not any of them. Me. My choice.

The longer I sit here, the more my memories start to reveal themselves. It's all my fault. I let my guard down. I thought I was in the clear. I walked around in broad daylight thinking my newly darkened hair would be a disguise enough to remain unnoticed.

I barely saw it coming. I was caught and bagged.

And it wasn't by accident. They knew exactly who I was.

"The last of the Ortizs."

"Her head is worth millions."

"No. We were ordered not to kill her. She's going to the auction."

"Her bid will be worth more."

The underground auction where women are lined up and sold like cattle to the highest bidder. Paraded on a stage to be broken and humiliated in front of a crowd of men with deep pockets, and by invitation only. Politicians, old money, new money. Anyone with a sick fetish of an unwilling woman and the pocket to fit the bill.

An unexpected laugh escapes me just thinking about the sorry motherfucker who wins the bid on me. The prize will not be worth the price.

The door opens with a shrill, ear-piercing sound. Two men step inside. They're armed with brawn muscle, but they still have no clue they just stepped on a hornet's nest.

"You need to eat," one of them says robotically, tossing me a plastic-wrapped sandwich, as the other guy gives me a look that turns my stomach.

I curl into myself, trembling and wide-eyed. Like a frightened little bird with a broken wing. And it works like a charm.

As soon as they get close, I strike like a feral beast. Teeth gnashing and claws ripping at flesh in a frenzy. I sink my teeth into the neck of one as the other tries to pry me off him. Copper floods my tongue, and I spit out a chunk of flesh as I'm yanked away.

I don't hesitate as I turn on the next. My nails tearing his face apart, and I catch his eye. His hands slap over it on instinct. He stumbles back, and I throw my weight into him, knocking him down and straddling him.

Using my thumbs, I hook them into his eyes and push all my weight into them. Instead of trying to remove my body from his, he only scratches and claws at my hands. But they're anchored in by my nails. I'm shaking from using so much force, and I scream through my teeth. Blood curdles out of the sockets as they give way, and my thumbs sink into his skull.

I'm yanked off and tossed back, hitting the ground with a thud. But it does not stop me. I'm too high on adrenaline to feel anything. The first victim is mobile again, holding one hand to his neck as he bleeds. "I'm going to fucking kill you, bitch," he seethes through blood-stained teeth.

I give him a bloody smile right back and scream like a Banshee, flying through the air, talons extended. On instinct, he removes his hand to use both of his to try and fight me off. I use a finger and stab into the open wound close to his throat. He screams out, and the more he flails, striking me anywhere he can get to, the more my finger disappears into his neck. All the way to my knuckle.

The sickening sound of flesh and gurgling breath brings me joy, sparking the adrenaline coursing through my veins like a rush of heroin.

My body is lifted by my arms with harsh grips restraining me. I start cackling as I watch the gory picture I painted. Blood still running, still warm.

"Goddamnit! I told them to watch her carefully!" someone shouts. I keep laughing like a fucking lunatic. "Get them out of here."

I'm tossed into a corner and watch them with a splintering grin as they drag out the bodies, and guard the door to make sure I don't make a run for it. The one who was barking orders is the last one to leave. He sneers at me. "Crazy whore." He spits on the floor, then slams the door shut.

They return only minutes later, stronger in number. I'm crouching in the corner like a feral, covered from head to toe in blood. I'm no match for them, but that doesn't stop me. Nothing will stop me until they physically put me down.

My efforts are futile, and I'm easily overpowered. A pinch on my neck has me stilling. Cold trickles through my veins, burning them. I go limp, let my grin die. They drop me to my feet, and I stumble back and fall to the floor.

"Fucking cunt. She made me bleed," one of them says.

A few of them chuckle as I let them think I'm down. I'm weakened, but I am not done.

I tune out everything else they say, then when they haul me up, I keep the weak façade going. They drag me to a tiled room and strip me. The water is freezing as they blast me unmercifully. The daze I'm in isn't pretend as I watch the water disappearing into the drain go from red to a pale pink until it runs clear.

"Who's going to want her? She's all carved up already," someone says, talking about my scars.

"She's still an Ortiz," someone else says.

I want to laugh, but I won't. Not yet.

My wrists and ankles are shackled. I'm kept naked, display-ready. My head swims, but I'm not gone yet. I'm aware, caught between haze and fire. My steps are uncouth, trying to keep my feet under me as they pull me along. Down a hall—left, then right, turning another left, then I lose count.

I'm shoved into a glass box. "Behave or you will be put under," someone warns in my ear with hot, rancid breath. My mouth twitches, but I remain in a murk.

Lights blind me, shining bright on the display case. It's impossible to see anything past them, but I know they're there. Out there, licking their chops, readjusting their tiny dicks in their overly expensive slacks.

The sound of someone over an announcer saying a few things to rile up the crowd is just background noise. I don't even pay attention when the bidding begins, nor care about the price for me.

I shuffle my feet forward, the shackles clanking. I move until I can lean my forehead against the glass, staring out with broad focus, so that everyone thinks it's them I have my sights locked on.

I smile, a wolfish, toothy grin. All malice and no warmth. I roll my head back and forth listlessly. The background noise fades into nothing.

Good. I have your attention.

Standing up straight, I crane my neck back, then connect my head with blunt force against the glass. I don't feel a thing. Not when I do it again, and once again before I'm dragged away, roaring in laughter, leaving a streak of my blood left on display. Symbolic, really.

I'm handled with zero care, tossed around, and shoved down. But I go down with spirit. A sharp jab at my neck stands me to attention.

And the very last thing I remember is...*he didn't come.*

CHAPTER TWENTY-EIGHT

Blackwell

My knee bounces with fury and nerves as I sit crammed in the back of the surveillance van, watching her through someone else's eyes.

Sinclair. Shackled. Beaten. Vulnerable and exposed. Her knees are unscathed because she refuses to kneel. She's caged like a prized pig, yet still holding court like a goddamn queen.

The feed glitches from the covert cams our men on the inside wear as they move through the crowd. Our ties with the De Lucas paid off. In addition to their alliance with the Abramovs, who have ties to another Russian family. They gave us a rare in.

Russian alliances are hard-earned and even harder to maintain. But desperation makes excellent diplomats.

If the Bozzellis had never come to us with that deal or moved in on the Ortizs sooner, we would never have been put in this position. Sinclair would still be home, safe. Still mine. Wrapped in silk and sin, not displayed like motherfucking merchandise.

My molars grind. "Why are we waiting again?" I growl lowly.

"Patience, Blackwell," Harlan cautions, while Dane sits there unmoving since we got here. Rigid and hasn't spoken or unclenched his fists once.

Scout shifts beside me. "You know we can't move yet. Your father—"

I slice him a look. "Mention him again and I will put *you* on the auction floor."

The space quiets. All I hear is my heartbeat thrumming in my ears. But even that goes quiet when Sinclair moves.

Slowly. Her chin up, wearing that smirk that usually precedes carnage. "What are you about to do, *joon-kharâsh*?" I whisper.

We're on the edges of our seats, waiting for our *Sinister Sinclair* to make her presence known. She has her head resting on the glass ominously. I feel it in my blood, thick and hot when her eyes light up. Wild with sparks spraying.

Then she slams her head into the glass. I don't know how many times. Maybe twice, maybe ten times. It all happens so fast. The sound doesn't reach us, but I feel it vibrate every bone. She begins laughing, blood running down her face. Then she's grabbed up and hauled away like a slab of meat. Hands wrapped around her bare body, touching her. I explode. "We're going in. *Now.*" My voice is lethal.

"Blackwell—" Harlan tries to cut through the black haze with reason.

I'm in a blind heat when I jump up with an inhuman snarl. "I said now!"

She's no longer in our sights. Knowing I am helpless to see what they are doing to her, it amplifies my ire, turning it into molten carnage. I'm deranged and black out for the next few moments. My brothers are restraining me before I hulk out entirely in the small space.

I'm no help to her if I can't keep myself in check, so I inhale through my nose, slow and controlled, trying to wrestle back a sliver of composure.

"You good?" Dane murmurs, and I nod once.

"Gear up," I say evenly.

We hit the building hard. I don't hold back, waiting for the immediate danger to be dealt with first. I take the lead at the front of the line.

Gunfire goes off like a goddamn symphony of death. I move like a man possessed. Breaking bones with my hands, taking bullets. But I feel none of it. Nothing but the carnal need to reach her.

I burst through people like obstacles. "Where is she?" I roar at no one in particular. A man points, and I shoot him anyway before pressing on.

"In here, sir," someone shouts to me, standing at a closed door.

I barge in, and like that, I feel whole again.

The room reeks of chemicals and blood, but none of it registers. Only Sinclair. She's slumped over, barely holding onto consciousness. I rush to her and drop to my knees. Her head lifts, just barely, eyes glazed over, but she sees me. I cup her precious face and brush strands of her newly darkened hair away from her eyes, revealing the wreckage of the woman I would burn the world for.

"Get me something to cover her with," I snap loudly, rage coiling inside me. *Why the fuck hasn't someone already done that?* "Come here, *jâné del-am.*" *The life of my heart.* I gather her in my arms, and she's limp in my embrace. "Where the fuck is something to cover her?" I shout out. Louder and angrier.

"Here you go, sir," someone says in a winded voice, handing me a large jacket over my shoulder.

I snatch it without looking. "Get the fuck out," I growl, shielding her from every gaze with my body curled protectively around hers.

I wrap her in the jacket and hold her close. One arm under her knees, the other around her back, pressing her gently to my chest as I stand. Her body folds in with trust and surrender.

I turn with her and pause at the threshold.

"All clear. We can move out," Harlan says, his eyes drifting down to Sinclair repeatedly.

I follow behind him, flanked on all sides by our men while I carry Sinclair out of hell and into the only safety she has—me.

I look down at Sinclair, so small in my arms. She stirs, eyes fluttering open, unfocused but still defiant. She may be sedated, but Sinclair will always be Sinclair. Even half-gone, she stares up at me like she's weighing her options.

I lean down, voice low and razor-sharp, I warn, "You fight me, and it'll be the last thing you fucking do."

CHAPTER TWENTY-NINE

Waking up, I expect to be shackled in hell, not resting peacefully in paradise.

My head is pounding, but I can still feel the lushness of the pillow behind my head and the blankets surrounding me as plush as clouds. Everything doused in the emollient scent of the one who ruined me. The vengeful deity that tore through the place, bathed in blood, eyes like hellfire.

The memories of Blackwell coming to save me like he had any right to are fuzzy, and after that, I remember nothing. Between the heavier sedative they injected me with and the adrenal exhaustion, I was pulled under so deep there was nothing.

There's a pounding in my head like a war drum. Pain blooming behind my eyes as I try to sit up slowly. I feel it when I crinkle my forehead in pain, the stiff bandages. I reach up to tentatively run my fingertips over the coarse fabric covering my forehead.

Oh, right. From bashing my own head in. *Worth it.*

That's when everything became distorted. Only fragments of the events happening after that.

Panic sets in as my gaze sweeps the room, the only light coming through the curtains. Where the hell am I? The scent is familiar but alien in every other way.

Fuck.

Did I hallucinate Blackwell?

Fuck.

I was sold, wasn't I? His familiar scent is just my imagination fucking with me.

I throw off the covers and lurch to my feet. The hammering in my head screams, but I ignore it. My heart palpitates violently in my chest, and my stomach turns in terror.

My gut tells me to run, but my head tells me to fight. I rip open the bedside table's drawer. Empty. It's too dark in here. I walk to the curtains and shove them open to help illuminate the room more. Enough to make out some details.

The four-post bed is dark and ornate. A canopy tangled in vines hangs overhead, and the sheets are the color of fresh blood. A facelift to my old bedroom in the attic.

My eyes frantically dart to the door. Deep, masculine voices echo on the other side of it. My stomach knots violently. My eyes sweep wildly around the room, searching for something I can use as a weapon.

I have no recollection of what I grab. Only that it's blunt and heavy. My chest thumps from my pounding heart as I clutch the object and prepare myself for what's to come.

The door opens, and my lord steps through. Blackwell, calm and unhurried as he shuts the door behind him. Every emotion instantly bubbles to the surface, boiling. Smoldering from the inside out.

He walks further in the room, towards me, then stops several feet away. He stands there stoically and unbothered. The well-kept scruff on his face is scruffier than usual to match his unkempt hair. He's dressed down in dark joggers and a gray shirt with the sleeves pushed up to showcase his forearms with sculpted muscles.

He's so fucking handsome. I hate it. I hate him. How can I see him as anything other than evil?

He pins me with his stare and walks toward me with meticulous steps, and I feel like I can't breathe. Everything inside me contorts when he steps into the light. Every muscle of mine, powerless.

He's merciful, stopping, and leaving several feet between us. "How are you feeling?"

"What am I doing here?" My voice has more venom than I knew I had left. "Why did you—how—why—" I stutter and trip over my words. My thoughts scattered like broken glass. I give myself a few breaths before trying again. "Why am I here, Blackwell?"

"You mean, why are you still alive after trying to kill me?" He holds a hand out, silently demanding the makeshift weapon I'm white knuckling like I'm a child.

"If I wanted you dead, you would be dead," I snarl, slapping the object in his palm.

The corner of his dark lips tick. "Really? Then what was that, huh?"

"It was a message." I swallow around the nauseous lump in my throat as I sway on my feet, a wave of exhaustion washing over me. My vision tilts, and my knees wobble. He steps forward with a deep frown, and I throw a hand up. "Don't!"

He stops in his tracks, an alarmed look on his face that he recovers from in the next beat. "You should sit down, Sinclair. You need some food in your stomach and some more rest."

I chuckle bitterly. "Don't act like you fucking care." He doesn't even flinch, and it's infuriating. "Why didn't you just leave me to rot?"

His eyes take on a dangerous look, and he proceeds to close the distance between us. I'm afraid that if I try to shout again, I might puke. "Because you are *mine*."

"Yours?" I aim for venom but epically fail. I'm growing weaker by the second. "You were planning to switch me out for someone more worthy. To slaughter me for being cursed with my last name."

He's only a couple of feet in front of me now. His chin low as he studies me closely with the tiniest hint of warmth. "Slaughter *you*?"

"You and the Bozzellis," I pant and hold my stomach with my hand as if that'll help ease back the nausea. "You—I heard you meeting with them. They wanted you to help take out my family. And you agreed. You agreed to everything."

"I agreed to nothing. You need to sit, Clair."

He reaches for me and I recoil, screaming. A burst of energy surges through me. "No! You don't get to touch me!" My chin quivers as despair engulfs me. He gawks at me as if my outburst were unseemly.

He played me. Played me like a *fool*. He made me think he actually gave a damn. That I was more to him than some cursed bloodline, but all I've ever been to him was an asset. Just as disposable as the rest.

"Clair—"

"No!" I scream and shake my head as my eyes blur with fat tears. He jumps the gap and wraps his arms around me tightly, and the dam bursts. "No!" I try hitting him, slamming weak fists against his chest. "Get off me! Please." I try pushing at him, but he doesn't budge. I sob so hard I can't breathe. "Let me go," I say with a cracked voice through snot and tears.

He holds me through it all. All the years, maybe a lifetime, of anguished pain bleeds from me. The air rushes out of me as I wilt against him. Finally succumbing to the epic meltdown.

Resentment.

Hate.

Fury.

Heartbreak.

Betrayal.

Abandonment.

It storms through me, breaking me until nothing is left but the wreckage. And then the blackness takes back over.

"Clair." A deep voice stirs me from my torture-induced slumber.

The room is dim and quiet when I open my eyes. I'm back in bed with puffy eyes and a raw throat. I turn to meet Blackwell's bloodshot eyes. He's crouched beside me, looking more disheveled than before. The longer I stare at him, the more the embarrassment begins to creep in, and I can't look at him.

"You need to eat something," he insists quietly.

"I need water." I push myself upright.

I feel his eyes on me for another moment before he stands up and grabs something off the table. "Here." I glance at the glass of water and the tiny white pills offered on an open palm. My eyes roll up as if asking if he's serious. "They're for your pain."

Suddenly, everything hurts. My head, my throat, every muscle in my body. My instinct is to fight him on this and refuse the medicine. I've been through worse physical pain, I'll live. But at this very moment, I don't want to fight.

So, I take the pills and down all the water in one go. I put the cup on the nightstand myself, ignoring his hand, and I look around the room. "So, where are we?"

"Our estate." My eyes widen on him. "You were dragging your feet on furnishing it, so I had the designer start."

My nostrils flare with a violent breath as I tear my eyes away from him. *Our* estate? Is he fucking mental?

There's a polite knock on the door. Blackwell answers without a word. When he closes the door and returns, he's carrying a large tray piled high with steaming, hot food. My eyes lock on the delicious spread, and I swear I start drooling. It looks sinfully fulfilling. It takes everything in me not to dive in headfirst like a beast crazed with starvation.

"Eat," he orders, and I choose to ignore his curt tone. He can scream in my ear all he wants right now. All I can see is *food*. "Then, if you're up to it later, you can venture out for a look around. See what has been done so far."

I keep my eyes down on the food, pretending he doesn't exist. After he lets out a dramatic sigh, he heads for the door. "Oh, and Sinclair?" I still don't look at him. "There's no point in trying to run. Even if you were to escape, I will find you. And I will bring you right back here. And it'll be a long time before I ever let you out of my sight again."

I grind my molars until I hear him finally leave, the door clicking softly shut behind him. Then, I fucking dig it.

CHAPTER THIRTY

Blackwell

I haven't slept next to her since I brought her home.

Three nights. Three fucking, sleepless nights. I've been camped out in my office putting out fire after fire. Clean-up and damage control from the takedown. We've made ourselves countless enemies, but our allies are still more valuable to retaliate against.

My neck aches, and my back is bent, but I don't move from the chair. Because if I crawl into that bed with her and she turns her back on me, or recoils if I reach for her, or tells me to go to hell if I whisper her name, I don't know what I will do to her.

The thin line between restraint and desire.

Part of me wishes to hold her so tight she can't ever leave again. Tell her how I wish I had told her about what was going on behind closed doors. That I would never let her go, even if it costs me everything.

Then there's the other part of me that wants to fucking throttle her. For gutting me with that note. For having me chase her through blood and fire, only to look at me the way she does now. Like I am the center of all her scars, old and new. As if I made every one of them.

I either want to hold her or strangle her.

Sometimes both.

My hands fist on the arms of the chair, nails biting into leather. I need more time. We both do.

Still, I feel her like a phantom limb. Every breath she takes echoes in my spine. Every word she won't say to me cuts me to the bone. And

I can hear her laugh in my fucking skull. Especially when the house is dead silent.

If I go to her, I will cage her. And that's not what I want. I love the rebel in her, the side eyes, the dry tone, the defiance. I don't want to break her to reconstruct her. I want her as she is. I only want her to trust me enough to stay.

However, I need to step it up, just as my father trusts me to do. Sinclair is home and safe. The worst is over. I need to focus back on work. The time apart will only be good for us.

So, I stay where I am. Because if I break first, she could actually break me. And I won't survive.

And neither will she.

CHAPTER THIRTY-ONE

Sinclair

I've hardly left my room since I've been once again caged.

Only to scope out the place. Every door beeps when I open it, no doubt an alert going straight to Blackwell. And every window is the same. Mob pups are posted up at every exit possible, but he doesn't have me followed around by them. A slight improvement.

I'm not stupid, and I know that Blackwell isn't either. If he claims escape to be more difficult this time, I believe him. But it doesn't mean impossible. It just means it'll take more time to plan.

The room I'm sleeping in is gorgeous. Eerily similar to my bedroom back at my family's estate, only better somehow. Warmer and cozier. The sheets smell of something familiar that I can't put my finger on. It acts as a natural sedative, making sleepless nights bearable.

Blackwell's clothes are in the same closet as mine, but he doesn't sleep in here. Probably afraid I might slit his throat as soon as he falls asleep. And he isn't wrong.

There's a fresh-blood hatred brewing in me for him that's raw and pulsing. I can't explain it. How can you loathe someone so completely, yet still hand them the blade that cuts you? How do they manage to hurt you precisely the way you expected, and still make it feel like betrayal?

There's been this dark cloud hanging over me for days, and I think I've finally gotten the courage to swallow my pride and go to Blackwell for a favor.

It's still kind of early, and I'm not even sure if he's home, but I check his office first. The door is left ajar with one pup hanging around the outside. He steels when he sees me, as if I might bite unprovoked.

I walk in confidently, and he immediately stops what he's doing, fingers hovering above the keyboard, sitting behind his mahogany desk. Why do they all have a mahogany desk? My father, his father, and now he. Is it like a rite of passage or something?

He doesn't speak as I approach his desk. "I need a favor," I say boldly. Deciding to rip the bandage clean off.

A half smirk takes over his face as he leans back in his chair. *Pompous prick*. "A favor?"

"Yes," I say tightly, and he gestures with a hand to continue. "I need to go to Oglesby."

"Why?" he fires back.

"I left something there." I sigh, exacerbated when he looks confounded. "It's where I was." I look down and pick at my nails. "Before I got caught," I mutter.

"You were in Oglesby?" he asks in disbelief.

I take a peek at him before lifting my head again. "Yup."

He gawks at me for a long moment before shaking himself out of it. It makes me want to laugh. I was so close. Close enough to not look there. Anyone would assume I would try to put as much distance between the danger as possible. So, I kept close.

He relaxes. "And what is it you left behind?"

I huff and roll my eyes. "Does it matter? This isn't a ruse to try and run. It's just something that has become important to me that was left there that I would like back."

"Tell me what it is, and I'll have it retrieved for you."

My lips thin and I feel like stomping my foot. "Why can't you just take me there? Put a fucking chain on me if it'll make you feel better. I don't care."

He leans forward to place his forearms on top of the desk, eyes sharpening. "Why can't you tell me what it is?"

"Will you take me there, yes or no?" I snap.

"No." His answer is curt and final, and he goes back to his laptop.

Inhaling deeply, I wrestle my temper into submission and reach for a semblance of civility. "Blackwell," I say evenly, and he looks up. "It's...my cat."

This time, he's braced for the absurdity. "A cat," he echoes flatly. When I nod, he huffs a disbelieving laugh and shakes his head, retreating to his laptop as if the matter no longer warrants energy.

"I'm serious, Blackwell." He looks at me with dead eyes. "You don't believe me." He doesn't respond, and his face doesn't change. "What if I can prove it?"

"Prove that you have a cat."

"Yes. If I can prove to you that I have a cat, will you take me to go get her?"

He watches me for a solid moment, his face unreadable. He stands up and rounds the desk, and I try not to make direct eye contact with him as he nears me. "Show me."

Less than fifteen minutes later, we're arriving at the hedge maze on his parents' estate on an ATV. The ride was painful, being so close to him and not wanting to touch him, but being forced to unless I wanted to fall off.

We walk side by side, and I stuff my hands inside my pockets to hide the shaking. We're silent the entire time, until we finally come to the middle, where the bench is. I had this crazy feeling that she would find her way home and be there waiting for me. Or come jumping out of the bushes at any second, but she isn't there.

Kneeling, I start pulling out the cans of cat food and bottled water. Some full and some long emptied and forgotten. A lump forms in my throat, thinking I might never see her again.

"I started feeding this stray that would hide out around here and—" I shrug a shoulder. "Felt kinda bad for the thing. She was all matted and looked like she had been chewed up and spit out. When I left, I took her with me. Obviously, when I was taken from where I had been hiding, she was left behind. I don't even know if she'll still be there or not, but I'd like to see."

I'm already abashed when I look up at him. He's staring back at me as if I'm a puzzle he might never solve. Both a threat and a myth. Like I've just revealed a new piece of myself, and he has no clue where it fits.

"Never mind," I mutter and try to walk away.

Some attachments aren't meant to be retrieved. Some are left to be mourned. And some are better left in the wild.

When he jets an arm out to stop me, I freeze in fear that he might touch me. "Alright," he says, and I slowly turn to look at him. His brown eyes start to thaw. "I'll send some men out there to look. You're going to need to give me the exact location, though."

"I'll give you the coordinates."

He shakes his head again in disbelief. Then we make our way back to the house without talking.

CHAPTER THIRTY-TWO

Blackwell

I t began with two men and has since grown into a small team.

All of them dispatched for the singular task of tracking down Sinclair's unexpected companion. An elusive cat as wild and feral in spirit as her mistress.

I first sent out two men to scope out the perimeter, confirm her old hideout, and determine what kind of camp Sinclair had established for herself. I needed the full picture. The fact that she'd been just miles away from me for weeks, undetected, still claws at my sanity. I can't decide if I'm impressed or infuriated. Probably both. She's always been that paradox to me. My fascination and my torment.

It's what I love about her, and what drives me out of my goddamn mind.

Traps were set. Cameras were installed. The area was monitored around the clock, and nothing. When I broke the news to her, nearly two weeks into the search, she barely reacted. She accepted the report with a shrug, but I felt it. The subtle change in the air around her. Like my failure gutted her, and it doesn't sit well with me. It tears at me.

So, I continued with the search party. Expanding it and telling my men they will not come home until the job is done. They could build themselves a fucking cabin if they had to.

Finally, she was spotted. But as soon as she appeared, she would vanish like smoke, leaving only the echo of her defiance behind. She's Sinclair in feline form. Prickly, proud, and ferociously free. Slippery and too cunning for a cage. Catching her was like trying to snare a storm.

They're creatures not meant to be caught. You wait until they choose to be.

Yet she stuck close to the camp, as if waiting for her person to come back.

I couldn't take Sinclair up there, though. Not with the threat level of what occurred at the underground auction. Not after everything we've been through. She doesn't know it yet, but she will not be leaving the confines of the estate for quite some time.

But I had an idea.

Her scent. Comfort. Familiarity.

I sent over a box of her recently worn clothing and instructed the men to line the traps with it. Something to entice the small beast.

Turns out, that's all she needed the entire time. Reassurance of returning to the one soul she trusts.

With a carrier in hand, occupied by a peeved cat hissing and planning to kill me, I enter the house. As soon as I do, I halt.

Music.

Delicate notes curling through the air, ghosting down the staircase.

"I want everyone out," I say to Hawk, who has been promoted to being head of security at my estate, without looking at him.

No one else gets this moment. It's far too precious to be shared. Not the sound of her playing. Not the glimpse into something so raw and pure it makes my chest ache. I want to kill those who heard it before me.

Another piece of Sinclair, and I will not have it shared with anyone. I want it all for myself.

I take the stairs carefully. Not to be discreet, but not to taint the most ethereal sound with even a footstep.

My hand furls around the handle of the crate as I near the bottom of the attic stairs in a daze. I wasn't sure if she could even play the piano, or if it was just decoration in her old bedroom. But I should've known.

It suits her. The control in her fingers. The emotion laced in every chord. It's her voice, her escape, the only language I've yet to hear her speak without any walls.

I remain at the stairs landing, afraid to move. Scared she will stop as soon as she senses my presence.

"Shhh," I try hushing the cat when she starts meowing, but it only makes her meow louder. As if she knows exactly how to spoil this moment for me.

The music stops, and I want to strangle the being for ruining it. Instead, I drop to one knee and open the crate to release her. She doesn't hesitate. She bolts right up the stairs as if she already knows exactly where to go.

Sinclair's audible gasp echoes, and quick footsteps follow as the two reunite. I give them their moment. But when I hear her soft, warm, and impossibly sweet voice, I can't stay away.

I ascend quietly, as if it were sacrilege. Interrupting something sacred.

I'm not prepared for what I see. Sinclair on the floor, curled around the cat, her face nuzzled into thick fur, her expression radiant. Not smirking. Not smug.

Smiling.

I swear I can visibly see her now whole, and I envy the cat for being that missing piece of her.

She suddenly notices me, and just like a bucket of ice water, the walls are back up. The dry smirk tugs at her lips, and her voice morphs into that familiar flippancy.

"I hope it wasn't too much trouble," she mutters her version of gratitude.

I don't answer right away. I only stare. No matter how hard she tries to play it cool, I now know what lies behind the façade. I caught a glimpse, and I won't soon forget it.

"It was worth it," I say, and her eyes dart to mine. Surprised by the authentic softness of my tone. "So, you *do* play."

She shrugs, occupying herself with petting the cat. "A little."

I snort. I may not know much about music, but I do know that what I heard was extraordinary. "You're good."

Just when I think she won't comment, she says, "I taught myself, starting when I was like six. Something to help disappear without leaving the room."

An escape.

I nod slowly, understanding her more in these last few moments than I have over the last year she's been upheaving my life.

I want to tell her that she doesn't have to disappear anymore. That she's safe here. That she can now feel like she's home. But I don't.

I let the words hang in the attic, hoping she'll one day discover them for herself.

When she's ready.

CHAPTER THIRTY-THREE

I'm sprawled out on the velvety chaise in one of the sitting rooms of the obnoxiously perfect house.

From the colors to the textures, everything in this place is perfect. Whoever designed this place nailed it on the head. Dark, seducing, warm, intense. I love it all.

"So, how come I never see your wife or your kids?" I ask over my wine glass.

"You think I would let you anywhere near them?" Harlan responds with slight amusement.

I narrow my eyes at him. "I should've poisoned your drink."

He grins. "You'd miss me too much, *Lady Lobotomy*."

"I'd have to care for you to miss you."

"Lies. I'm the only one you don't want to kill."

I arch an eyebrow. "You sure about that?"

"Well, Blackwell and I."

I reach down and pet Blender, who's curled up against the nook of my bent legs. "That right is reserved only for Blender." She's never been so content since I've met her. When she sleeps, she doesn't leave one eye open and snap awake at every noise. Doesn't startle if I touch her.

"Bullshit," he teases.

"Don't say I didn't warn you."

He chuckles, causing me to grin. There's a sibling-like comfortability between the two of us. I wouldn't turn my back on him, though.

And I don't think he actually trusts me, but he would definitely have to provoke me to snap on him. Most people don't need much to get me to spill blood.

I gaze over at Blender again, letting her silky fur slide between my fingers. "He wouldn't stop looking, you know."

I blink, but I can't look at him. "What?"

"The cat," he says. "Blackwell wouldn't pull his men off the job until it was found."

"*She*," I correct him.

"Sure. *She*," he says dismissively. "He wouldn't let it go."

I scoff, pretending that doesn't strike somewhere raw. "He sent some of his disposable henchmen, it's not like he—"

"He did more than that," Harlan interrupts, tone suddenly serious. "He obsessed." I glance up. "Had surveillance around the clock and sent your fucking dirty clothes to put in all the traps. Dane and I thought he had just about lost his goddamn mind." I stiffen and have to look away. "When the wily beast was finally caught, he flew out there himself to retrieve her. Took her to a vet and had her flown here on a private jet like goddamn royalty."

"Harlan," I growl in warning. I can't hear any more of this. I won't let him get inside my head with these false hopes.

"Look around, Sinclair." He leans forward, elbows on knees, voice soft but sharp. "This entire estate? He built it all for you. Every inch. Every thread. Every detail screams *you*."

"An interior decorator did all this," I argue.

"And how the hell did the decorator know you this well? Huh?"

I scream inside my head, begging him to stop. I can't take it. I've been avoiding these intrusive thoughts for so long.

"He's trying," he says simply. "After your family fell, the alliance died with it." I know that. "Marrying you doesn't get him a goddamn thing. If anything, it weakens our standing. You're a pariah in our circle."

That stings, even though it's true.

"He doesn't need to win you over," he continues. "He wants to. It's no longer about power or politics, Sinclair. It's about you. The sucker fucking fell in love with you."

I swallow around the lump in my throat and grind my teeth. I want to stab him right now to shut him the fuck up.

"That, or he's clinically insane. Actually, both. Because he'd have to be crazy to be in love with you."

I give him a scowl, biting back a smirk.

"Look," his voice drops an octave. "You want to stab him? Go for it. God knows he deserves it. But don't ignore the fact that he's bleeding out trying to make you happy."

"He's holding me here prisoner."

"And yet you've remained content." I open my mouth, but he continues before I can make a sound. "Don't give me that bullshit there's no escape. That's never stopped you before." I refrain from arguing. What's the point? "He's never going to recite poetry or sprinkle rose petals on the bed. He's doing what he knows how to do. He's *trying*." He stands and stretches with a grunt. *Good, leave.* "Oh, and one more thing. Your ring."

I automatically glance down at the finger my engagement ring used to adorn. "What about it?"

"It's the Blue Moon." I frown at him, and he doesn't allow me to question it. "You aren't stupid, Sinclair. So, don't act like it."

My eyes snap up with anger, but I don't comment. I let him go without another word, then sit there still and silent, trying to make his words leave with him. But no such luck.

The glass of wine feels like dead weight in my hand. I stare at it blankly, then throw it. I watch the red liquid and glass scatter like something deeper broken.

He's wrong. He has to be. Because if he isn't, it means I've spent all this time hating a man who has been trying to cage me, not to control me, but to keep me. And I don't know which is worse.

The idea of Blackwell tailoring this place for me, knowing me so well, is ludicrous. Fucking unfathomable. No. I don't believe it. I *won't* believe it. Believing it would be letting him in. And no one gets in.

No. He hunted down the cat as a means to make me content, not happy.

No.

He's still the man who so readily agreed to slaughter my family. The one who schemed behind my back. The man who held me down and told me I was his, as if I were a possession to be possessed, like every man has seen me. He is no different from them.

And yet, he came for me. Even after I tried to kill him, he still came for me.

I deluded myself into thinking I spared him because death was too easy. That living in fear, always looking over his shoulder, wondering when I might pop up at any moment with a blade to his throat, was the sweeter revenge. But what if it's because I *couldn't* kill him? That I didn't want to?

Because he's still here.

And so am I.

I hate him.

I want to so badly.

I hate how disheveled he looked when I finally woke up. I hate how red his eyes were, how messy his hair was. How a mess *he* was. I hate that my stupid heart lodged in my throat when Blender barreled into the room and leapt into my arms, knowing he was the one to make it happen. I hated how, in that moment, I felt warm and safe and *whole* for the very first time in my life.

I hate him.

I hate him for making me feel everything I swore I wouldn't.

And the worst thing isn't that Blackwell might love me. If anything, it gives me more power over him.

The worst part is that I might be starting to love him back. Or something like it.

And I won't survive it.

Love is for fools, and I am no fool. So, what the fuck is happening? How is this happening to me? How can I make it stop? Can it be stopped?

My fingers curl into fists, knuckles bone-white.

What now?

Do I ignore it all and pretend this prison with soft pillows and velvet drapes isn't exactly where I want to be?

Or do I risk it all?

CHAPTER THIRTY-FOUR

Sinclair

I can't stop thinking about it.

The cat. The estate. The scent-worn clothing. The feelings.

The image of Blackwell, a man who commands death with the flick of his wrist, carrying the cat carrier off that plane like he was carrying valuable goods to be illegally sold...it haunts me.

No one has ever gone that far for me.

And on top of all that, I know how his father is in poor health these days, and I feel bad for him. Not for his father. No, no, no. His father is nothing to me. But he's someone to Blackwell, and the fact that it affects him, it affects me. I've never thought twice about anything that does not directly affect me. But I feel for Blackwell. The stress, the inevitable loss. Something inside me wishes that I could do something to make it better. Like how he did for me with Blender.

To find his 'cat' and deliver it to him.

He hasn't spoken to me since the day he brought home Blender. Not really, that is. He's here, physically close to me, yet he feels miles away.

He continues to fall asleep in his office. I've peeked in on him, finding him passed out, shoulders tense, and brows furrowed like he's bracing for an explosion. Scrunched up in a chair half his size.

It's obvious he's avoiding me, but why?

Is he pissed at me for trying to kill him?

Does he regret bringing me back?

Second-guessing it all? Me?

The questions echo louder the longer I go without answers, each one louder than the last, until it's a full-blown cacophony inside my skull.

Tonight, I give in to the chaos. To the curiosity. To the pull.

Draped in my black lace robe, I flit through the halls on silent feet. The place is dead-quiet this late in the night.

When I reach the office, the door is left cracked open. I nudge it and peek inside. There he is. Shoes off, dress shirt unbuttoned and spread open to display the heart-shaped scar, sleeves shoved halfway up his forearms. One arm draped over his eyes as if shielding himself from the world. From me. From whatever the hell he's battling behind those lashes.

Blender is curled up on the desk like she owns the place. Like she's claimed him in my absence.

Traitor.

I slip in and quietly shut the door behind me. I don't even bother with stealth. If he's going to wake up, he'll wake up. But I move slowly, more from reverence than fear. There's something sacred about this moment. About seeing him like this, unguarded and unaware.

He looks exhausted.

No. He looks wrecked.

I climb over him with calculated movements, straddling his hips with my knees tucked around his sides. His body stiffens instantly, and his hand shoots up like instinct, clamping around my throat. His eyes wild and vigilant.

I don't flinch.

We just stare at each other.

The room is bathed in low amber light, the soft glow catching on the sweat beading at his temples, the harsh cut of his jaw, the faint red rim of sleep-deprived eyes.

My heavy breathing picks up with his. His hand tightens, thumb pressed to my pulse. Like he's waiting for me to crack. To run. To prove I'm still the danger he thinks I am. But I don't.

Instead, I lean down slowly, letting my lips hover over his. Close enough to touch but not touching. Just enough space to feel the heat. Just enough to make his pupils deepen.

Then I kiss him. Slow. Sure. Seething with every unspoken word we've both been swallowing for so long.

He doesn't hesitate. He kisses me back with all the torment he's been bottling up, with all the questions neither of us knows how to ask, and all the answers we're too afraid to give.

This could be a mistake. But right now, it's the only thing making any sense. And neither of us is willing to stop. It's far too late for that.

My hips begin moving, grinding into him. His hands vanish into my hair while mine roam the hard lines of his chest and abs. Tracing the jagged edges of the heart I gave him.

Then I tear my lips from his, and we pause, breathing heavily, eyes dark and drowning. He's almost wrecked when I remove myself, but it's fleeting when I drop to my knees and go for the waist of his pants. The moment my fingers brush the silk of his length, his eyelids droop.

I've only done this a few times. I've always felt it degrading. On my knees, their cock shoved down my throat. As if they were in control. But the way Blackwell is quickly unraveling right before me, watching my hand as if it were hypnotizing, I see it everywhere in his face. In his mouth, by the way his bottom lip hangs slack, as shallow breaths come in short repetitions. In his cheeks as they flush. Even his body slumps like he's been darted by yours truly again.

I see that it's I who is in control.

Wrapping my fingers around his cock, I stroke the soft skin, paper-thin, stretched over the firmness. I gawk at it and pull up and down with a closed fist. His breath hitches, and my eyes snap up to his. He's now watching me with a daring look.

I focus on his cock again, my hand stroking it, and a bead of cum dribbles out of the top. It glistens like a beacon, causing me to lick my lips, suddenly famished.

When I close my lips around him, he hisses through his teeth, and his hands fly up to my hair. His fingers flex, but he doesn't fist it. He simply cradles my head as I begin to bob my head up and down. Taking him as far back as I can, then sliding it along by tongue back to the tip.

"Fuck," he whispers, followed by muttered words in Farsi. To hear him muttering words uncontrollably, it does something to me. Something I could never try to explain. But it has me working him harder. Desperate to bring him endless pleasure.

His fists curl, and my head is yanked back, his cock popping out of my mouth. He glowers down at me as he holds me there, still on my knees. It was so abrupt, I can only gawk up at him, silently questioning if I had done something wrong.

His grip on me softens the same time his face does. "Come here," he rasps, reaching for me.

I meet him halfway, standing to my feet, and he pulls me over his lap, my knees hugging his hips. His fingers disappear into my hair again, gentle yet with sexual intent. We're both transfixed, unable to look away. Then he breaks a smile and pulls me in for a searing kiss that has my toes curling and my hips rocking.

His tongue licks mine and he uses one hand to cup my ass, lifting me. I reach between us to angle his cock, and he fists my ass to slam me down on it.

The air catches in my lungs as my body takes over, doing whatever feels so natural. Bouncing up and down, my arms wrapped around his neck. Our kisses become sloppy and uncoordinated, and I have to break away to breathe.

My head falls back, and my mouth drops open as pleasure blooms in every inch of my body. It really is like a fucking high when he's inside me. As if I would do anything for this feeling. *Anything.*

He drags his lips and teeth and tongue along the column of my neck, and I feel myself creeping towards the edge. I crane my neck forward, and my forehead touches his. Our faces tilted slightly downward to watch, mesmerized by where our bodies come together. My pussy wrapped snuggly around his cock. The length of him sliding in and out. Shiny and wet.

We pant in tandem, and my muscles begin to coil as I teeter on that cliff, so close to the precipice. He takes over, fisting my ass, and thrusting his hips upwards when my body locks up, continuing to fuck me.

I moan and whimper through it, then find his mouth with mine to kiss him unhurriedly while I quiver over him. My body gives a couple more twitches, then my eyes pop open as I'm airborne.

He strategically places me up on my knees on the cushion of the loveseat, my back to him. My head falls back on instinct when he comes up behind me. His body connects with mine, and he kisses my shoulder where my robe has slid off. His arms wrap around me, and he fists one breast, and his other hand coasts down the center of my body where my robe splays open, and his fingers meet the apex of my thighs.

His lips trail lazily all over me as he starts playing me like a fucking fiddle with his skilled fingers. "Sinclair," he whispers in my ear, sending a physical chill over me and a wave of arousal.

With his fingers still moving, he slips his cock back inside of me and presses in until his hips meet my ass. Then his other hand clamps down on my hip, and he begins slamming into me. My ass slapping against him and my breasts bouncing heavily.

I moan when he removes his hand from between my thighs to hold my throat. His fingers wrapped around, giving it a firm grasp. It bleeds more lust from me than when his hand was on my pussy. The animality and carnality of it.

His breath is hot in my ear as he moves inside me. Then he groans in my ear, and it's the most beautiful sound. It has me seeing stars and gushing all over him. His hips move faster, his cock slamming into me harder, and the fleshly fulfillment again has me limp.

His fingers flex around my throat, and his nails dig into my hip. I bite through the pain, and it sends me an aftershock. It rocks me, and

I scream out and convulse. He groans more and then pistons his hips faster and harder until he exhales on a shaky breath, stilling behind me. He sucks in sharply when he pulls out, barely, then slides back in. Two more times, twitching here and there, then he finally stops.

We're both breathing hard, his chest bumping into the back of my shoulders. His hands are still holding my neck and hip, as if he's unable to let go. That we both might crumble if he does.

Then his lips find my shoulder, placing soft, sensual kisses along the ridge of it. When he pulls out, I feel wetness dripping down my inner thighs. His hands soften before both of them go to my hips to guide my feet to the floor, and I slowly turn around to face him.

His shoulders are still rising and falling with labored breath, and his body is slick with sweat. I cannot believe how fucking devastatingly handsome he is. How sexy he is. How evil he is not.

I can feel my head spinning, and I begin to spiral like I always do when things get too heavy between us. He must sense it because he takes me around the waist and lowers his head to hover his lips over mine. My eyes automatically close, and my breath stills, as does the world around us. Everything falls silent.

It feels like an eternity before he kisses me.

We don't speak, we don't leave the office. We end up curling up on the small loveseat, his fingers toying with my hair, my body draped over his, and I fall asleep to the sound of his beating heart with my head on his chest.

CHAPTER THIRTY-FIVE

The sun is just beginning to bleed in through the curtains when I wake.

The office is still dark, still quiet, save for the slow, even rhythm of her breathing, steady against my chest.

Sinclair's body molds to mine, fitting like she belongs there. Her bare leg hooked possessively around my waist, one hand splayed over the heart she carved out as if to anchor herself in place. Her skin is warm, flushed from sleep, and she hasn't stirred once. I wonder if sleep hasn't come easily these last several days, like it's been for me.

Last night's memories still burn beneath my skin. Her hands, her mouth, her softness, fury, and surrender. All tangled together, building up until we finally collapsed into sleep. The first time in so long, I felt at peace.

The thin lines of dried blood on her hip catches my eye. I drag my thumb over the four crescent-shaped reminders of where my nails dug in. They edged the old scar her brother left behind when he tried to brand her. She claimed it back, making it hers. My touch left its own markings behind, and I should feel guilt or shame. I shouldn't like it, but I do.

I brush a knuckle gently across her temple. "Sinclair," I murmur softly, then press a kiss to her head, taking in her scent. Her eyes flutter, lashes twitching before she peeks up at me with the haze of sleep still veiling her gaze. "We're going to bed," I tell her quietly.

She blinks a few times, slowly coming to. She doesn't speak. Her nod is barely a movement, but I feel it move against my chest.

I reach for the lace robe discarded on the floor and carefully drape it over her shoulders, slipping her arms through the sleeves like she's the most fragile thing. She doesn't protest, just watches me with a strange softness I've rarely ever witnessed.

After pulling on a pair of briefs, I turn back to her and offer her my hand. For a moment, she stares at it, brows faintly drawn together as if it's something she's unsure of how to accept. Or like it has teeth. Although hesitantly, she reaches for it.

Her fingers slide into mine, tentative but warm. Slightly stiff, but steady. Something feels different, as if we're finally unified. Like something has been repaired or at least patched enough to hold for now.

We pad through our estate, silent, and our hands still clasped like something sacred. When we reach the stairs, she starts to move ahead, but I stop her. Her eyes lift right before I scoop her up into my arms.

She lets out a squeal of surprise that turns into a giggle, girlish and unfiltered. It's so unlike her and so unguarded that I grin down at her like a fucking fool as I carry her.

Her arms loop around my neck, and she tries hiding her grin, but it's wide and uncontainable. So fucking beautiful.

"Brute," she mutters, her voice light and breathy.

"Never denied it," I murmur back.

By the time we reach our bed, the sun has continued to climb. I lower her onto the bed we should have been sharing all along. The one I've left her alone in. But never again.

I slide in beside her, where I belong.

As soon as my skin is flush with hers, her breathing begins to quicken and her skin heats. That fire only we can make starts. Soon it will engulf us both in the flames.

I can't keep my lips off her skin, my hands off her curves, my nose buried in her dark hair. God, I love her dark hair. It's as if she's shed a layer of her armor. Giving me more of her authentic self.

I turn her on her back, my body over hers, and I stare down at her. *"Lanati, to kheili zibāyi,"* *Fuck, you're so beautiful,* I whisper. Her hazel eyes have never looked so soft. They bounce around my face, and she remains docile.

My lips press to her neck, dragging down her body in a heated trail, my rough stubble reddening her skin. Her breath trembles, and her fingers twist in my hair.

I look up at her, my shoulders locking between her thighs. She stares down at me, breath caught in anticipation. Then one side of her mouth quirks in a familiar, wicked smile. That flash of the Sinclair I know strips me of every other thought.

I open my mouth and eat her pussy. My tongue flattens, then flutters. My lips close around her, sucking and pulling. I stab at her core and slurp up her sinful nectar. Her knees hike up, and she moans, her hips rolling. I selfishly drink from her, pulling some of her pleasure for myself.

I could live with my face in her cunt.

"Fuck," she whines, her back arching off the bed.

I push her legs back, folding her, and crush my face against her. Her body quakes, and her legs fight me, but I continue to feed. Feed until she's convulsing again.

"Damnit, Blackwell," she rasps, still trying to squirm from me.

Easing up, I crawl up beside her. Keeping her on her back, I lie on my side, hooking an arm under her knee. Then I slide my cock inside of her, stealing her breath and mine.

Her chin tilts towards the ceiling on a gasp, then she snaps her head down and slaps a hand on the back of my neck to yank me in for a deep kiss. It's messy and raunchy as we both try to get as many kisses in as possible, like we're running out of time.

Our arms become tangled, and her other leg joins the one I still have hiked up. She's folded in half as I pound into her. She mewls in my mouth, and I bite her bottom lip. She whines and crushes her face against mine. Diving her tongue into my mouth.

Using my bicep to clamp her legs down, I slide my fingers against the tautness of her pussy. Flicking the sensitive bundle of nerves in rhythm with my thrusts. As soon as she cries out with yet another orgasm, I wrap my fingers around her jaw to hold her close. Our foreheads pressed together, we share the same breath.

Just as that tingle at the base of my spine spikes and makes its way to my balls, I pull out and explode all over her cunt. Exhaling with every spurt. My hips are still moving. My lungs are still struggling.

Once my body allows me to function, I press my lips to her forehead, eyes closed, breathing her in. I let the kiss linger before parting from her. Only to grab something to clean her off. Then I slink back into bed.

She's pliant in my arms, her breath ghosting over my chest in soft, slow intervals. The sun is now high in the sky, casting a golden streak across her skin, turning her into something unreal.

Her eyes are closed, her lashes resting against her rosy cheeks, her lips swollen from the way I kissed her. But I know she isn't asleep.

We're lying on our sides, our ankles entwined, and her hair tangled. My fingers twist around the strands, over and over, slow and reverent. I could stare at her for hours.

"Why did you come to me last night?" I ask quietly, brushing a lock of hair away from her face.

She hesitates, then opens her eyes and stares back at me for a long moment. "I wanted to thank you. For finding Blender." She doesn't need to say it, but what she meant was she didn't know how else to thank me. I won't call her on it, though. "Harlan said you were pretty determined," she says, softer this time.

"It was important to you," I say simply, like it should be reason enough.

She tries to shrink away, like she always does when I get too close. When the truth creeps up, and she doesn't know what to do with it.

"Sinclair." Her name slips from me like a promise.

She looks at me, those eyes holding a vulnerability that cuts through me. She's already retreating in her mind, searching for her next exit. But not this time.

I curl an arm around her waist, pulling her in so she has no choice but to stay. No choice but to hear me.

"There will always be games to be played. But *this*. *This* is not a game. You and I are *not* a game." I see it then. The panic flaring in her eyes. The instinct to run. I hold onto her even more tightly. "You ask anything of me, and you have it," I say, each word deliberate. "Every want, every need, it's yours. Everything I have, every fucking inch of me, is yours."

Her eyes glass over with something I can't name, but I recognize it. She doesn't know how to receive love, let alone see it when it's laid bare in front of her.

She shakes her head like she's trying to physically cast the words off her. "Please, stop," she whispers.

"No," I say too harshly. "Not until I'm finished."

"You said anything I ask of you. Is mine. So, please. Stop saying these things."

"Once I'm finished." I tilt her chin up with a curled finger until her shining and wounded eyes meet mine. "Clair." Her name is a breath of air on my lips. Reverent like a prayer. "I love you."

It hangs there for a beat. Then another. A breathless silence stretched between two people unraveling in real time.

She blinks slowly. Twice. Then a single tear breaks free, and she swallows it down like poison. But I can see the way her mind is splintering, the way her body trembles like it wants to believe me but doesn't know how.

Because Sinclair isn't built for love. She's fire and smoke. A creature of chaos and independence. She's unpredictable. Fearsome. Brilliant.

She's also strong and brazen.

Resilient to a fault.

Loud without making a sound.

Possesses just enough compassion to prove she has a beating heart beneath the armor she forged from pain.

She's everything I never thought to want. Everything I never dared to believe could exist. Everything I can't live without.

And somehow, she's planted something inside of me, and it's growing into a man born only for her.

She doesn't try pushing me away.

She doesn't say something vile to tarnish the moment.

She lets the words continue to hang there between us.

CHAPTER THIRTY-SIX

Blackwell

The sun casts a golden hue over the outdoor venue.

The string quartet, lush gardens, and lights strung up over our heads set a romantic ambiance. My cousin Kamea is celebrating her one-year wedding anniversary with a large party. They're calling it their wedding ceremony do-over, since an unexpected visit ruined theirs.

After the champagne toasts and the formalities, I find myself sitting next to an attractive woman, politely humoring a conversation with her. Her name already forgotten.

I feel the shift in the air and look right at the storm in heels approaching with bad intentions. Strutting, hips hypnotic, over the pavement, eyes locked onto me and ablaze.

She says nothing when she reaches me, then slides right onto my lap, an arm looped around my shoulders, perching herself there like a throne that she owns. Her back pointedly turned towards the woman in the middle of a sentence. Deliberately ignoring her and effectively dismissing her.

My arm instinctively goes around her waist, anchoring her against me, while I don't even attempt to hide my grin. "Jealous, sweetheart?"

She gives a subtle roll of her eyes, avoiding eye contact. "No." She finally gives in and meets my eye. "Fine. Possessive maybe. Who knew?" She sips her wine casually.

"You're even more intimidating like this," I rasp, my lips brushing against her temple. "Like you're one mood swing away from chopping a man's balls clean off."

"I'm pretty sure that's Alexia Bonnetti's signature strike."

"You mean Alexia De Luca, and you're right. Your style is more like a widow spider. Ripping a man's head off after fucking him."

She turns to me with a smirk. "You're thinking praying mantis. Widow spiders simply kill their lover after sex. No theatrics. Just lethal efficiency."

"I stand corrected." I slide my hand up and down her bare back, voice dropping. "Point is, you were jealous."

She scoffs. "I am not the jealous one in this relationship. That title belongs to you."

I don't need to argue. My silence is its own quiet denial.

She leans in. "So, if I were to walk up to an attractive man right now, and flirt, you wouldn't react?" I don't reply. "Care to wager on it?"

I raise an eyebrow. "As in a bet?"

"Yup." She drains the rest of her wine. "If I go and flirt with a random stranger, you'll blow your lid." I don't bite. "If I get him to walk away with me, you'll be murderous," she says with a sultry voice.

"Pass," I murmur and drag a finger down the length of her arm.

"Why, because you know you'll lose?"

"You are overly confident in your seduction skills," I murmur, tugging her close.

"Are you saying I don't have any game?"

I smile. "I'm saying you scare men off too easily."

Her gasp is affronted, but before she can sass me, I trail kisses down her neck, and she leans into it. My fingers brush along the swell of her breasts.

"You better quit it," she breathes. "You can see everything through silk. Including a wet spot if you don't cool it."

I chuckle. "Is that why you're wearing panties tonight?" My thumb rubs over her hardened nipple.

"Yes," she says through a small giggle. "Now, stop trying to change the subject. The bet."

"What bet?" I feign ignorance only to mess with her.

She clucks her tongue. "Blackwell," she warns, only half serious.

I sigh, conceding like I often do with her. "Fine. If I win, you dance with me."

She looks at me like I'm delusional. "Seriously? That's your big prize? A dance?"

"Not everything has to end with blood or orgasms, Sinclair." I sip my drink, eyes watching hers amorously. "And you?"

Those enchanting eyes of hers roll once again. "If I win, it's a surprise." She grins proudly.

"Alright, *joon-kharâsh*. Do your worst."

She leans all the way in and then uses her tongue to give me a good, wet swipe up the middle of my face. I chuckle, but the moment she struts away, hips swaying, locking eyes with a tall, unsuspecting man near the bar, I know I'm fucked.

The man who looks like he should be guarding the door, not sipping champagne, looks unsure. I watch, bemused, confident in her reputation's ability to deter any advances. She's notorious. No man in their right mind would entertain the idea of Sinclair. No matter how gorgeous and sexy she is.

But then the man relaxes and smiles at her. He leans in closer, and she touches his arm. I sit up straighter and finish my drink. The amusement in all this disintegrates.

When he offers her his arm and she takes it, the air around me drops ten degrees. I'm on my feet as they walk off together.

With the world narrowed to a singular focus, I follow them inside, my steps purposeful as my blood pulses with a surge of rage.

I find them in the hallway, and I don't wait. Spinning him by the shoulder, I slam him against the wall. He recognizes me instantly and is wise enough not to fight me.

"I'm so sorry, sir. She said that you wanted me to escort her to the ladies' room," he stammers.

"And snitches get stitches," Sinclair mutters from behind me.

"Fuck off," I seethe, shoving the guy away.

He runs like the devil is on his heels, but my focus is back on the she-devil. I pull her by the hips and cage her against the wall as my temper begins to simmer. "You cheated."

Her eyes widen. "How did I cheat?"

My eyes narrow. "You know how."

"The bet was that I could get a man to flirt with me, even leave with me, and you would lose it. And you did. So, I win." She grins, her eyes gleaming.

"He thought he was escorting you to the restroom."

"And yet you still freaked the fuck out," she teases. "How about this?" She hangs her arms over my shoulders casually. "We both win."

I break my resolve and let my lips curl slightly at the corners, showing my surrender. Her flippancy is sometimes contagious. "My reward first."

She sighs dramatically. "Let's get this over with," she utters under her breath.

I take her by the hand and lead her back out to the dance floor just as the next slow song begins. I pick a spot with a good enough clearing and pull her in close. My hand pressing into the curve of her back, and keeping her hand in mine.

"So," she says, her eyes glancing around. "Why this?"

I take my time answering her. "Think of it as exposure therapy."

She looks up at me, eyebrows lowered. "Exposure therapy?"

My arm snakes around her waist to bring her in closer. I brush my lips along the shell of her ear and whisper, "One day, things like this won't make you uncomfortable. You'll realize this is real."

I feel her breath slightly hitch. Her body freezes for a moment before she tucks her head and hides her face into my shoulder. And I let her.

As the song ends, she looks up at me, eyes wide and searching. My lips find purchase with her ear again. "I love you," I murmur against it. It's something I've said only a handful of times to her. Each time, I mean every word of it.

I lean away to watch her reaction. She blinks, then she masks it with her usual smirk. But I caught it. "Kay, my turn."

This time, she takes my hand and leads the way. Bringing us around the venue's building to a darkened pool. The only lights are those in the distance and the moon.

She drops my hand and kicks her shoes off. "What are you doing?" She gives me that hellish grin of hers right before she slips her dress off, leaving her stark naked. "Clair," I warn.

"Blackwell," she says in a mocking tone.

"Clair," I say her name sharply when she leaps into the air and makes a splash in the water.

Her head surfaces. "Get in here."

"Pass." I shove my hands in my pockets.

"Um, excuse me. We had a deal." She lowers her head into the water up to her nose, then pops up again to try and spit water at me and fails. "Chicken shit."

Because I'm not one to break a vow, I begin to strip. I neatly lay out my clothes and pick up her crumpled, silk gown off the ground to do the same with hers.

Then, I do something wholly uncharacteristic. Two long strides, one reckless leap, and I'm crashing into the water, sending a wave over her head. I pop up to the surface grinning, sending her into a boisterous laugh. Loud and true.

We tread water, drawing ourselves in closer. Then her face turns serious. Almost, fear-struck. "I won't ever be what you want me to be," she blurts out.

I frown. "And what is it you think I want you to be?"

"Normal."

I snort. "What the fuck makes you think I want normal?"

What the fuck is normal anyways?

She sighs, getting frustrated with me already. "Maybe not normal, but...I'm fucked in the head, Blackwell. All kinds of fucked up." My lips thin, and I don't know whether to laugh or fucking shake her. "I'm never going to let my guard down because it's not even about being guarded at this point. It's just me! Guarded. Jaded. Chip on my shoulder. Pessimist. Cynical—"

"Defiant. Stubborn. Rebellious. Devious. Batshit fucking crazy," I add, partly to lighten the mood.

She gives me that dry look that means she's about to reach for her knife. "I'm serious." She pauses, digging for the strength to continue. "For a moment, I thought maybe, just *maybe*, I could give you a sliver of my trust. But you killed it. It's gone, and it's never coming back." Her chin is trembling by the time she's finished.

I diminish the gap between us, sneaking my arms around her waist to adhere her body to mine. "I'm sorry, Sinclair." She bites down on her bottom lip. Knowing that if she dares to speak, she might fall apart. "I'm sorry for not telling you about what was going on. For not telling you right away that it was never a question." I admitted to her that I was in the wrong, but I had never said the words, 'I'm sorry'. "There was never a chance in fucking hell I would ever let *anyone* touch one hair on your beautiful head. And that you are the one I am going to marry, no matter what I lose or gain from it. I'm so fucking sorry, *jāné del-am.*" *The life of my heart.*

Her glistening eyes come to a boiling point. A tear falls. Then another and another. Spilling over silently.

"I fucked up, yes. I'll fuck up again. And so will you. You'll continue to be irascible and difficult. Because I'm not asking you to be someone else. But I in no way lied to you. I did not betray you. I kept it from you because it was not an option. And I didn't want it to hurt you." Her nostrils flare. "Clair." I drop my forehead to hers, and she closes her eyes. "Your family treated you less than dirt. Made you feel worthless and disposable. I didn't—" My words are deep, and my voice is raw. She slowly opens her eyes. "I fucking hated that for you. I couldn't allow you ever to feel that way again. No one gets to make you feel that way ever fucking again." My teeth clench with rising anger.

"Do you understand me?" I grip her jaw. "No one gets to treat you like anything less than royalty. Than sacred. Than untouchable." My grip tightens. "Anyone who dares to will be dead on sight. Do you understand?"

She blinks, not to bury the tears, but to break through them. Not to avoid the ache, but to walk straight into it. For once, she lets herself feel the sting. Lets the tears rise, hover, then pass. Not denied. Not hidden. Just released.

Then she nods. Slow, steady, fierce. Like she's choosing herself for the first time. She blinks away the last of her tears. Not in retreat. But in resurrection.

Our lips collide. If I could kiss away all her scarring memories and take them as my own, I would. Kiss away every scar, from the inside out, I would. But I can't change the past. All I can do is give her a better future. One that can help her move on from the darkness that was once her life.

Her legs circle my waist on reflex, and I spin us to pin her against the side of the pool. She begins grinding, her pussy warm against my torso. My cock is aching for her, but right now, this is all about her. I would deny myself anything to put her first.

Always.

I break the kiss to lift her out of the water, propping her on the concrete edge. She stares down at me with desire weighing her eyelids down. She curls her nails into my shoulders before releasing them.

Keeping our eyes locked, I part her knees and drape her legs over my shoulders. I watch her eyes spark, brimming with hunger, as I brush my lips over the silkiest part of her body.

Dropping my jaw, I flatten my tongue and swipe upwards, savoring her. "The tastiest fucking cunt, *joon-kharâsh*."

Her breath hitches, and the fire in her eyes burns. I know if I don't put her out of her misery, and soon, she'll snap. Part of me would love to push her to unleash the beast in her, but again, this isn't for me and my desires.

Inhaling her pussy into my mouth, her hand dives into my hair, her nails scraping my scalp. She snaps her head back and moans without shame into the darkened sky as I eat her pussy until she's quivering.

CHAPTER THIRTY-SEVEN

T onight is mine.

One night. No limits. No rules. That was the deal. And Blackwell, so far, has not broken a deal.

The room smells like candlewax and sandalwood, soft lighting flickering around, casting shadows along the walls like smoke. Our bed is neatly made with the black silk sheets, but I removed the comforter for this special occasion. Everything feels better on silk.

I timed it just right, knowing Blackwell will be calling it quits about now, and coming to find me for dinner. So, I sit on the edge of the bed, legs crossed, in a simple black silk teddy, swinging a pair of gold cuffs lazily around one finger.

The deal started as a question of power and surrender through the art of sex. But tonight, it's more than that. It's about trust. I want to see how far he'll let me go. How much he'll give me without question. Trusting me.

The door opens, and he steps inside the room, already peeling his jacket off. He notices me right away and falters. A smirk twitches on my lips. I always love seeing him visibly affected by just the sight of me.

The door clicks shut behind him, and I stand up to meet him halfway. His hands immediately slide around my waist, and his crooked smile is fucking adorable.

"I hope you're not too hungry," I say.

"Oh, I'm starved," he murmurs, making me grin.

"Well, we have some unfinished business, you and I." He arches a brow, his expression still amused and his eyes heated. "The deal. For one night, I have total control."

His lips twitch as he swivels his gaze all over me. "And tonight is the night," he mutters.

"Nervous?" I tease.

His arms tighten around me, leaving no space between us. His only response is a dry look.

"Because Blackwell," I whisper, brushing a finger along his jaw, "if I'm going to be yours. Then you sure as hell better learn how to be mine."

His look turns dangerous, and his head slowly lowers, his lips almost touching mine. "Do your worst, darling," he whispers back, then kisses me.

His body is spread out like an 'x' in the center of the bed. His wrists are cuffed to the bed frame under the headboard, and his ankles are bound by ropes tied to the frame at the foot of the bed.

Deliciously bare and exposed.

I stand there to admire my work and his mouth-watering naked body for a few moments. He readjusts a wrist, pulling me out of the daze.

I head over to one of the side tables and pull the drawer all the way out, dumping the contents on the bed. He cranks his neck to try and get a good look at what toys I brought to the party.

I cluck my tongue. "Uh-uh," I chastise, and he looks at me. "No peeking, my love."

He smirks, then narrows his eyes. "You're beginning to make me nervous," he says lowly.

I give him a grin, diamonds sparkling in the dark. "You should always be nervous around me, Blacky."

I reveal a red silk scarf, and he eyes it with more caution. Slipping the thin straps off my shoulders, his nostrils flare when the soft fabric hits the floor. I crawl on my hands and knees over the bed and climb over to straddle him. I can't wipe the giddy grin off my face. Seeing him tied up, vulnerable, and helpless. It's picturesque. A vision that'll stick out in my memories for eternity.

He already expects it, so he doesn't protest when I wrap the scarf around his head to cover his eyes. I take another beat to admire him again, then I lean down and kiss him. Deepening it just enough to leave him panting when I tear my lips away.

I scoot down his body and start kissing him everywhere. Licking him from his neck to his chest. Landing soft kisses over his pecs and the rough lines of my marking. Then I look up at him as I use my teeth to pinch a nipple. His body tenses up and he bares his teeth, but he doesn't say anything.

I lick it, then move to the next one to do the same thing. This time, I give it a little more bite. He goes rigid and growls. A deep, animalistic sound in the base of his throat. "Sinclair," he warns.

A giggle threatens to spoil this moment, so I distract myself by using my tongue to soothe his reddened little bud. His cock is like steel under me, pressing into my pelvic area. I undulate my body to grind against him and continue a wet trail of kisses and tongue lashing down his torso.

My chin brushes through the well-groomed hair and up the length of his hardened cock. I wrap my fingers around it, the girth almost too much for them. I rub the smooth head over my chin, lips, and cheeks. Teasing him, but also basking in the silkiness.

I stare down at the opening, stroking him lazily, eager to see that tiny bit of pre-cum appear like a pearl. My chin drops on a wanton gasp when it does. I dart my tongue out and I lick it up. His body slightly jumps, and the cuffs groan under pressure.

I use only my tongue to cover every inch of his cock. Licking him like a fucking lollipop. There's a hiss here and there from him, but I want to make him groan. Make him moan. Make him beg for release.

I scoot down further, my body balled up between his legs. I stroke his cock more, keeping the slow pace, and I work his balls with my tongue. Curling it around one at a time. Inching my way further south.

When the tip of my tongue makes contact with his tight little hole behind his balls, he instantly clenches up. His whole body goes rigid, the muscles in his arms bulging.

He's not ready for that. And even though this is supposed to be my night, I still want it to be equally pleasurable for both of us.

Another time then.

I open my mouth, taking his balls inside, and sucking on them. He tries to stifle his body's resistance. Trying to restrain himself for me. It makes me smile.

Humming, I slide my tongue up his cock again and then close my mouth around the crown of it. I tease it some. Swirling my tongue under the ridge then along the tiny slit at the top. More little tasty pearls leak out and die on my tongue.

Since this is supposed to be about pleasure and not punishment, I take his entire cock in my mouth, letting it butt against the back of my throat. I have zero gag reflex, so I easily breathe through it.

He sharply inhales through his clenched teeth, and it gets me going. I suck his fat cock with zeal. Like it's the most delicious thing known to mankind.

But it's much too early for him to finish.

I gasp for air when his cock pops out of my mouth. A sheen of sweat glistens off his body solely from desire.

Giving his length one last swipe with the flat of my tongue and two languid strokes of my hand, I begin to ascend his body. Teasing him all the way.

My bare pussy sticks to his abdomen as I sit. He's clenching his teeth behind tight lips, breathing smoke out of his nose. God, he's so fucking devastating. I just can't with him.

I'm becoming obsessed.

And I'm not instinctively fighting it. I'm craving it.

I grind myself on him thinking about how much I fucking enjoy this. *Fucking hell.*

He growls through his nose and tries bucking his hips.

Grinning, I run my hands up his chest and lean down to kiss him. He's eager as fuck when he kisses me back. Getting frustrated and coiled tightly. Especially when I pull away.

I chuckle, and it has his nostrils flaring with every sharp inhale. I admire him more. The defined features of his face. While he's unable to see the way I'm looking at him, I take advantage of it for a little longer.

I reach behind me to grab his cock, then I sit back on it. He jerks at the cuffs and restraints on his ankles in reaction. I lift my hips up and down, watching every single twitch on his face. His mouth bobs open and shut. His head rolls. His breath shallows. More sweat leaks from his pores.

My hands flatten on his hard chest, bracing myself as a wave of desire is about to wash over me. My eyelashes flutter, and I pant, chasing it quickly, but careful not to get him off. I chomp down on my bottom lip and let the wave finally crash, taking me under.

When I come up for air, I open my eyes and still. He's shaking under me. The veins in his muscles are now popping out as he strains. Not in anger, but in refusal to snap.

"You've been a good boy," I purr. It's time for him to see everything. I ease my fingers under the blindfold and remove it. When I do, I freeze.

He looks wild. Fucking crazed. I'm almost afraid to uncuff him. My pussy flutters thinking about how savage he'll go on me.

With a smirk, I pivot my body around, sitting on his chest with my back to him. Bending over, I thrust my ass in his face and he goes completely still. "Bite it," I command.

He isn't hesitant to pick his head up to bury his face in it. His chin brushes the raw flesh on my pussy. I spread my cheeks with my hands to assist him, granting him better access.

I gasp and hollow my body when I feel his teeth clamp down on the plug. My eyes practically roll to the back of my head. I hiss and moan, rocking only slightly. Enjoying the push and pull of the toy and the way it throbs and burns.

Slowly, I ease forward, all the way until it pops out, and my breath stills. I sit up and look at him over my shoulder. He dropped the plug, and he looks furious now. God, he's so fucking hot. My hips rock just looking at him with his hair all a mess and his lustful eyes.

"You better sit on my fucking face," he growls. The animalistic undertone has my pussy clenching and my eyelids sagging.

This is my gig, but I'm too far gone in a desirous haze. My body obeys.

I spin around again because I need to see him. Watch him as I fuck his face until he chokes on my cum.

My thighs hug his head, and I brace myself on the headboard. He tries diving in, but I lift my hips with a smirk. His eyes snap up with a dark look of warning. Biting my lip, I sit.

I cry out instantly, unable to hold anything back. I grind myself on him as his mouth works its ethereal magic. My lower back bends, and my hand dives in his hair to clutch onto a chunk of it. I don't fucking care if he can breathe or not. I fuck his face until I scream.

He doesn't let up, and I can't take it anymore. I sit back on his chest, fighting for air. His full lips are puffy and bright in color as they glisten with the hair around his mouth. He looks good with me on him.

His eyes are endlessly black as he glowers at me, disheveled looking and seconds away from hulking out. The threatening charge sizzles from him, and I tentatively climb off him to grab the key.

I go to his ankles first. My hands are shaking as I release the tethers. When I make my way to the head of the bed, I hesitate. He's watching me. Daring me to fuck with him right now. But letting him go is like unleashing a starved tiger.

You know you're the first thing it'll sink its teeth into.

I unlock one cuff, and he drops his arm, his fist red and angry. I kneel on the bed and lean across him to do the other. As soon as it clicks, he's on me.

CHAPTER THIRTY-EIGHT

He's fucking insane.

Sex between us is already intense. Cringe-worthy even. Too much for most people to ever bear witness to. But right now, it's me who's afraid.

I'm slammed to the mattress by my hips with a grunt and a growl. My eyes go wide, and I can smell myself on him when he covers me with his sweaty body. Then I taste it when he kisses me. Or what is supposed to be a kiss. It's punishing and bruising. But it doesn't stop me from kissing him back.

I wrap my arms around him and fist his hair. His massive hands grip my ass and spreads me wide for him. He's so fucking hard he needs no assistance in finding his way inside of me. He spears into me with a violent thrust. Giving me no time at all to accommodate him, he fucks me with brutality and animosity. As if he fucking hates me.

Yes, fuck me like you hate me, baby.

He props himself up with his arms locked and slams into me with a vicious sneer on his face. Lip curled up and nostrils flaring. My body jolts, and my breath stutters with every penetration. There's hardly a rhythm to his madness. Just lost to his own craze.

One of my legs is hoisted up over his shoulder. It hits at a new angle, and I cry in raw pleasure. He has me coming so fucking fast, I hardly get to enjoy it. But it leaves a lingering sensation on me and he's already pushing me up that fucking mountain again.

He pulls out, and I try to focus on his face. He's still unhinged. Hair falling over his face, and sweat now dripping from him. He spits in his hand and I suck in sharply, knowing exactly what comes next.

Of course it is. I teased him with it. But I didn't anticipate the lust-laced frenzy he'd be in when he fucked me in my ass.

He pushes my legs together, twisting my lower half to the side, my upper body still flat on the bed. Then he smears his spit up and down my cracks and creases. Mixing it with my natural wetness. I clench on instinct when he shoves two fingers in my ass and I can barely keep my vision straight.

There's no pause for me to adjust. No patience. He thrusts his fingers in and out, and I soon feel my muscles loosen. His face mimics mine as I feel the pleasure in every single inch of my body and soul. Lips slack, eyes sleepy, face flushed.

Fucking hell.

His eyes dart up like something caught them. Then he reaches above my head, grabbing something. I don't see what it is, I'm too fucking far gone to even care.

He almost scrambles off the bed and swiftly yanks me to the edge of it, forcing me on my hands and knees. I rock back, opening myself like a fucking flower.

The object that was in my ass only minutes ago it felt like, is shoved in my face. "Fuck yourself with this," he rasps, voice rough and breathy.

My eyes light up, and I glance at him before accepting it. I hear him spit a split second before feeling it land in my crack and drip down. I reach between my legs and gently slide the plug in my raw-fucked pussy. It burns from his barbarity. He's the only one who has ever fucked me so thoroughly my pussy swells up and it hurts to sit for days.

I hear him spitting again before pressing his cock against me. He keeps the momentum going, his head dipping into my ass an inch at a time. Until the very last inch, he slams in. My body lurches forward from the impact, causing me to fall to my elbows, giving him a better position.

My breath catches when he lands a good smack to my ass. His hips already in motion. "I said fuck yourself," he says with a whipping tone.

I had completely forgotten about the toy just chilling in my pussy. I begin doing as he says, but it's hard to concentrate when all I can feel is his cock stretching me so painfully good.

My eyes pop open wide when he lands another hard slap to the same area, making it sting more. I have never been spanked during sex before. I assume it's because men were much too afraid to strike me.

Or maybe it was because I usually had them bound and entirely under my control, it was impossible for them to do so.

But *fuck*, I love it when he adds the perfect touch of pain to pleasure.

"Start moving or I will find something bigger than my cock to fuck you with while I tear this ass up," he rushes out, his words jumbled and tight.

Gulping, I begin flicking my wrist faster. Faster until it makes a lewd slapping sound. I can't take it. Fuck, I can't take it. It's too much. Too. Fucking. Much.

I bury my face into the mattress and scream. And despite his threat, I can't fucking move anymore. I twitch and convulse as liquid shoots out of my pussy.

"Tell me where you want it." His voice hardly reaches me. I'm still reeling from the explosion. *Smack!* Like when someone is losing consciousness and you smack them hard across their face, enough to come back. That's what it's like when he gives me a smack on my ass that'll leave his handprint for days. I'm suddenly alert. His pelvis slows, and he curls his body over me. His hot breath hits my ear with short breaks. "Where do you want it, baby?" he whispers, then nibbles on my earlobe. "Hm?"

"Inside me," I whisper back, my voice hoarse and my throat raw.

I'm left confused when he pulls out, then I'm flying through the air for only a second when he tosses my body like it's nothing. My head landing up near the pillows.

I automatically roll to my back with my knees up. He has this devilish yet boyish smirk when he sits back on his haunches between my legs. His muscles are more defined from exertion, and his face no longer holds that daunting anger, but the threat still lingers.

"One more," he says, then tugs on the plug I had abandoned in my pussy.

I hiss and try to scramble back, but he clamps a hand down on my thigh, his face stone again. I don't think I can take any more. "No," I let the word tumble weakly out of my lips by accident.

He ignores my concerns and gently removes the toy, only to rub my pussy with his fingers. I'm so fucking sensitive, I can't tell if it feels good or bad. My heels dig into the mattress, my back comes up, my head rolls back, my eyes squeeze shut, my fists furl around the sheets.

Then he stops, and I think he's finally done. I crack an open only to see him spitting in his hand to rub over the head of his cock. His eyes fall to mine, refusing to let me go. Gripping my thighs, he spreads them and nudges at my asshole.

I start panting, and I shake my head even though I begged my body not to. He pushes his way in, and I try to refuse him. Locking my muscles up and trying to scoot away.

"Shh—shh—shh," he hushes and lies on top of me. He moves slowly while trying to console me. His lips find mine, and I can't reject him when he kisses me.

My body is still tense, and I'm still trying to rebuff, but he won't let me. Yet he does show mercy. Going slowly until I finally relax under him. The more I do, the faster he goes, and the more I want it again.

His hand wraps around the back of my neck, cradling my head as he kisses me, pouring so much passion into it. His other hand fists my one tender ass cheek, pulling it apart. I gasp and whimper into his mouth, kissing him more aggressively. Desperately.

I cling to him with my arms around him, my nails digging into his back. Warning him that if he tries to leave, I will rip him in half.

He switches the position of his hips so that his body rubs against my pussy. This time, I welcome the friction. The burn only makes it that much better. I'm shaking, and small noises keep spilling from me.

"Blackwell," I cry his name into a kiss and begin to convulse. He groans in response, jerking inside of me without warning. Like he could have gone longer if it weren't for me crying out his name mid-orgasm. Like that's what lit the fuse.

His breath shutters and his thrusts turn to small jerks, and when he groans again, my pussy gushes.

This man has fucked me up forever.

And you know what?

Fuck it. Take me.

Our hearts finally come down from dangerous heights, still thunderous but steadying.

Our limbs remain tangled in the afterglow, warm and worn. The room is heavy with sex and smoke, but it's him I breathe. Salt and cedar. His scent is now a part of mine.

He's becoming the center of everything.

I know it will all eventually end in more pain. Everything does. Not just for me, but for everyone. That's the nature of wanting something too much.

But I'm in too deep to care anymore. I will be the one who decides my fate, and I choose him. If he kills me, then so be it. It was my final act of defiance disguised as devotion.

Tonight, he gave me a piece of his trust. It's only fair he gets a tiny piece of me. He's earned it. I'll never let my guard down, but I'll give him something he's been trying to reach all along.

"I was nine when it started happening," I say quietly, and he almost stops breathing. In fear or fury, I'm not sure. But I do know that he wants to hear this. "Royce—" I swallow his name like poison. The embarrassment and shame have been plaguing me lately. Not for what happened, but what it might do to *him*. "He's always been...off. Like seriously sick. The kind of wrong that doesn't need a reason. Just born rotten." I pause, and he controls his breathing. Each inhale measured.

"Tortured animals and all that serial killer shit. You know, how they all start." I breathe, my breath ghosting across his broad chest. "We were close, once upon a time. Born only three years apart... He was never kind to me or anything, but we got along as kids. Always finding trouble."

"Then he started looking at me differently. The kind that made me uncomfortable. Even at nine, I could feel it." The bile rises, but I push through it. "So, I began distancing myself, but that only made it worse. For months, he stalked me. He would appear out of nowhere. Straight from the shadows, waiting to strike."

I close my eyes, and my breath shudders. Blackwell doesn't say anything, but his hand moves, slightly tightening around me. "One night, I woke up, and he was just standing there. Watching me sleep." I swallow. "Then he crawled under the covers and...held me." My throat tightens. "That's how it started."

"It only escalated from there. Not only behind closed doors, but publicly. He was possessive, yet still merciless when we'd train. Probably battling with the fact that he was obsessed with his own sister. Why wouldn't he take it out on me?" I snort. "The scar on my hip," I start. "He carved his initials in it. Branding me like fucking livestock. That did something to me. Maybe it was the final straw, but it's what made me finally snap. I wasn't rolling over anymore. I mean, I used to fight back when things were getting worse, but I gave up easily. Because what was the point? I never stood a chance. But then I stopped caring what happened to me if I tried. So, I did. That's when my father found out about it. We were beating each other to a pulp one night and woke everyone up. And I told my father everything."

I'll never forget the way he looked at me.

Not Royce.

Me.

Like I was the sickness.

"Anyways. We were both punished." He goes rigid under me. "It didn't stop him, though. He was just more careful. He'd try to catch me alone anywhere in the house. But I wasn't playing his games anymore. And he knew better than to get caught again, so as long as I fought back hard enough, he'd eventually back off."

I take another breath. "Then it stopped. No more ambushes. No shadow games. But I knew better than to believe he was done. That he gave up. It had me even more paranoid, a whole new fucked up game.

So, I began stalking him. That's how I found out he was sneaking into Gwen's room." My voice cracks on her name. I haven't said it out loud since she died. "I didn't even think about it. I acted. I thought I had to save her. Turns out, she didn't need saving. She didn't *want* it."

I thought she didn't, but knowing everything I know now, she was doing it for me. Her only way of protecting me. She took the damage so I wouldn't.

I clear my throat, choking down the wretched memories like bile. "I cut his initials out. Obviously."

I stop talking. I'm done. Mentally drained. The vulnerability has me sick to my stomach. My head pounds with an overwhelming rush. But I don't regret it.

Blackwell gently pushes me to my back, his handsome face unreadable as he hovers over me. There's no pity, no disgust, nothing but calm.

Without a word, he comes down to kiss me. There's nothing different about it, at least not in the alarming sense. When he pulls away, my hand reaches up to brush a dark lock of his hair out of his face. The moment feels surreal.

"I know the deal was sexually based, but..." he trails off.

"But what?"

"My night won't be."

I squint at him. "Meaning?"

He takes a moment to answer. "For my one night, I want to see you play."

I blink. "Play...the piano?" He nods, and I stare at him for a moment before breaking into laughter. "Really? First the dance, now seeing me play the piano?" His expression is unwavering.

It has me sobering, my laughter dying. He's serious. He's actually fucking serious. Instead of staking his claim and trying to push me further, he wants *this*.

I roll out from underneath him, and he lets me. Slipping my silk teddy back on, I get to my feet and glance at him over my shoulder. He's lying on his side, displayed in all his naked glory, only wearing a smirk. "Well, come on."

"Now?"

I shrug. "Why not? Or are you too tired, grandpa?" I grin, and he gives me a scowl. "I get it. You're what, forty-nine, fifty?"

He grunts and slides off the bed to stand in front of me. "Forty," he mutters dryly. "And no, I'm not too tired."

CHAPTER THIRTY-NINE

Blackwell

S he walks ahead of me, barefoot, barely covered in silk.

The hall is dim. The moonlight coming in from the high window at the end of the hallway.

She doesn't look back to check if I'm following her. She knows I am. Knows I will follow her anywhere.

We reach the stairs and she begins to ascend. No snark. No smirk. Just an eerie stillness she wears when she feels the need to protect herself.

It grows darker until we reach the landing at the top. Then moonlight floods in through the glass dome that leads out to her widow's walk. Illuminating the room and reflecting off the alabaster surface of her piano.

White.

She lives in black. Surrounds herself in it. Weaponizes it. It was intentional, separating it from the dark. A deliberate choice to keep it untouched by the poison.

The piano has been her true sanctuary. Music is her clean place.

Her proof that, despite everything, she still yearned for some light in her life.

Her exterior remains calm, but I know there's a storm of emotion going on inside her. In the way her jaw is too tight, looking like she's bracing for something. Her music is sacramental and private. Quite possibly the most personal piece of her that she holds closest.

In the short time she's been back, she's added to the space. Velvet furniture in deep jewel tones. Floor-to-ceiling bookshelves lined with worn spines. Several thriving plants scattered about. I haven't made the connection between her and the plants, but they're alive and well-tended.

She sits down on the piano bench, and I hover several feet back, unsure of what to do. Sit or stand. I'm sure she wishes for me to vanish altogether, so I take a seat to fade into the background as if I'm not even here.

She hasn't looked at me once since we left the bedroom.

Silence stretches, but I can be patient. For her. For this.

Finally, she lifts her hands. And plays.

No music sheet, no familiar tune, no effort. I could be wrong, but it feels like improvising. Raw and cracked open. Her fingers glide and strike, notes swelling and retreating. She bleeds into every key she hits.

This doesn't feel like a performance. It feels like a confession.

I've seen so many dark shades of Sinclair. Wild. Violent. Seductive. Manic and heartbroken. And right now, I can see her soul.

She's sorrow incarnate. A phoenix not just rising from the ashes, but she stayed in it, lived in it, and made it her kingdom. Built a throne on top of her own ruin, reigning where others would perish.

Every note she plays is a truth she would never dare to speak. And I understand it. God help me, I do.

It's mourning and rage. It's the sound of a girl who never got to be soft, still trying to remember what softness feels like.

The crescendo builds louder, more violent. Her hands slamming the keys, notes shattering like glass. I feel it in my chest. Like she's trying to cut the music out of herself with each stroke.

Then—silence.

She freezes, hands still hovering over the keys. She's breathing heavily, but her lips are sealed tight. Slowly, she lowers her hands into her lap.

I stay silent and still. Knowing she needs some time to process and avoid the retreat into herself. Her head finally turns to me. Her face impassive, as if she didn't just splay her soul for me.

I know she's going to act as if this meant nothing. But I know what I saw. She let me see the part of her no one touches.

Her lips curl. "So, was it worth it? Giving up your one night for this?"

I crack a smile and shake my head, feeling heat rush to my face. "It was," I say lowly, chin dipped.

EPILOGUE

Blackwell

I carry the papers as if they're made of stone.

Every step toward Sinclair feels heavier, as if she can already sense what's coming. She's lounging in the shade by the pool with the ocean in the background, toned legs stretched out, sunglasses on, and giving the illusion of not a care in the world.

Her black bikini is simple. Minimal. But she makes it look like sin in the flesh. And her hair is almost as dark, back to its natural shade.

She doesn't glance up when I come up on her. She's focused on her phone screen, playing solitaire. She's addicted to the damn game. Another quirk that doesn't fit but somehow belongs.

I take the lounge chair beside her, and she ignores me. So, I slap the papers down next to her. She eyes them with uninterest, one eyebrow raised, then takes a short glance up at me before going back to her game.

"What are those?" she asks.

I calmly take her phone away, and she scowls at me. "I need you to sign these," I say evenly. She stares at me, then I tilt my head towards them in a gesture.

Giving a dramatic sigh and eye roll when she removes her sunglasses, she picks them up, and something in me tightens. The longer her eyes read each line, flicking back and forth like a machine built to detect bullshit, the more anxious I get. It isn't nerves. It's readiness.

After skimming through the second paper, her expression hasn't changed. But I can see it behind her eyes when she looks at me. She's affected by this.

"A marriage license," she says flatly. My eyes flick to her engagement ring back on her finger, and I nod once. She squints her eyes in suspicion. "And...you want me to sign it."

"I'm asking you to."

Her eyebrows practically hit her hairline. "Asking?" she echoes, like it's a foreign word in her mouth.

"Yes." My voice stays steady. I'm giving her a choice. Her first life-altering choice. Though if she refuses, I'll sign it for her anyway. She'll eventually get over it. But I want her to make this choice. To choose me. To choose this life.

She holds my gaze, quiet but calculating. Always reading between the lines. Always deciding who she needs to be in any given moment. The rebel. The threat. The untouchable. Her reactions are never careless. They're crafted for impact. To protect. To provoke. To keep control.

The recklessness of hers still lives strong, itching to rear its head. But beneath it, something else is stirring. Sinclair is still learning who she is without the venom. She's so used to keeping the world at arm's length.

Her face drops a little, and I almost hold my breath. "Are you going to give me a pen?" The levity of her tone is armor and somewhat aggravating. But I hand a pen over casually.

I watch, feeling every second tick by. She pauses, the pen hovering over the paper. Then, without any more hesitation, she signs. No flourish. Just that elegant, sharp signature of hers. A slash of ink that feels like a vow.

She hands the papers back to me and reclines like nothing happened. Eyes closed, chin tilted up.

Joon-kharâsh.

My soul-scraper. The one who grinds me down to my rawest form and makes me grateful for the pain.

Sinclair never wanted a wedding. She may tear through the room like a tornado, wreaking havoc, but she doesn't enjoy the spotlight. She would never stand up in front of a crowd, big or intimate, and promise anything. Not to me. Not to anyone. Hell, even in private, she hardly expresses her feelings for me. Not in words, anyway.

She's afraid of both permanence and abandonment. Terrified of feeling like she belongs to anything that could break her. Even more terrified of being discarded. Of being told she's not enough. Not wanted. Not valuable in a world that deals in blood, currency, and leverage.

The doubts always lingering in her mind.

So, I gave her something that doesn't ask her to perform. Just choose.

And she did.

Setting the papers aside, I join her on her lounger. She looks at me, one eyebrow raised. I manage to contain my elation and push her knees apart.

She's fighting back a smile. The little she-devil is almost as debauched as I. The number of nights she has woken me up with her hand or mouth on my cock as if we didn't just have sex a couple hours ago. Or like we won't fuck again in the morning before I get up for work. Plus, however many times in between.

Tugging at the strings tied into bows high up on her hips, they unravel, and the fabric covering her hidden slice of paradise falls slack. My eyes on hers, I peel her bottoms off and lower my head.

I give her sex a sensual kiss and enjoy watching her react instantly. Her head relaxing against the chair, eyes wilting, and lips parting. She reaches down to run her fingers through my hair with one hand and pulls her top to the side to grope her supple breast with the other.

Haroomzāde-ye vasvasashi. Fucking seductress.

I sink two fingers inside of her and eat her fucking pussy. *Goddamn, I love this fucking cunt.* I tongue her little bud and fuck her with my fingers and her hand pulls at my hair, forcing me closer.

I know what you want, baby. My fucking nasty girl.

Curling my middle and ring finger, creating a hook, I remove my mouth and fuck her harder. Slapping my palm against her, and the more her body reacts, the harder and faster I work.

I sit up and watch her face as it contorts uncontrollably, lost in ecstasy. Fighting it, begging for it, wanting to savor it. I see it all. Painted like a fucking masterpiece.

My lips thin, and my nostrils flare as I put more into it. Her jaw goes unhinged on a raspy cry, her back bowing, head back, and cunt gripping my fingers.

Her back slams down and hollows, and her head snaps up. Her eyes watching my hand through heavy lids. She takes in sharp breaths, higher and higher. Then she fucking snaps. Her entire body steeling, and I pull my fingers out to rub her pussy vigorously as she squirts everywhere. Her hips rise and fall as she rides it out.

Before I can pull my cock out, she's already fully recovered and pushing me to lie back. Her diamond-studded teeth and golden hoop peeking from under her upper lip flash with her grin when she mounts me and sinks down. Taking the breath straight from my lungs.

I grab her shapely hips as she undulates on top of me. With a single tug behind her neck, her top falls effortlessly. I sit up and attack her breasts with my mouth.

This is my fucking life now.

There's another weight hanging in the air. One I've been carrying for several months. And it's time she knew.

Sinclair settles into the window seat of the jet, toned legs crossed, sun-kissed skin from ten days of temporary peace. A soft glow clings to her, a looseness in her that didn't exist before. And it fills a piece of me that I was unaware of.

Wine in hand, she flashes me a lazy smirk before turning to watch the sky swallow us on takeoff. She's beautiful in a way that doesn't try to be.

I take the seat across rather than beside her. I want to study her every tick, every twitch. She's impossible to read unless you know where to look. And I do. I can read her face, but I still can't predict her. With Sinclair, knowing the feeling never guarantees the outcome.

I wait until she's on her second glass of wine to begin. "I have something I want to show you."

She turns to me, innocently blinking. "A wedding gift?" she teases.

I crack a smile. "Sort of." Only because I'm still unsure of it.

"Well? Are you going to tell me, or are you just teasing me?"

I let silence wash over us. This will go one of two ways. She could hate me for this, shoving me ten steps back.

Or she'll think it's the most romantic gesture, because that's Sinclair.

"When the Ortiz estate was—"

"Razed?" she says, sharp but playful.

"Yes." I pause.

She's never asked what happened. To her family, her home, or her family's legacy and enterprise. So, I've never brought it up. Until now.

"Territories were redistributed, and businesses were liquidated." I stop again and decide my next words carefully. "But I thought it was only fair you had a say in some of it."

She snorts bitterly. "You just said they were all handed out." She looks away, jaw set tight. She's retreating into herself, walls standing firm.

I need to press on before I lose her completely. "The house is yours."

She looks up at me, frown lines creasing between her eyebrows. "What the fuck would I want that for?"

Fair question.

I sigh. Now second-guessing the second half of this. Perhaps it would be best to let her see for herself. "It should be you to decide what to do with it."

EPILOGUE TWO

The silence on the ride from the air strip to the ruins of my childhood is haunting.

Blackwell doesn't speak, and I don't ask questions. That's our language when something is too raw. Say nothing, breathe through it, and pretend it doesn't feel like being skinned alive.

The further we drive, the more familiar the land becomes, and the more chilling it is. I feel it in my bones. Like a map burned into me of a past I can never seem to outrun.

Then it appears. The Ortiz estate. Home. Hell. Both.

I stare out the window. Still and silent. He said it was mine now. To do whatever I want with it. Those words weigh more than the marriage contract itself. A wedding gift, supposedly. Or maybe just another strategic move in a long-running game.

Because I still have no trust in men. Especially not the powerful ones who say the right things and hand over power like charity. So, is this a boon? Or a burden?

A way to give me closure, out of love?

Or is this him dangling my past in front of me like a leash I can never cut? Just because he can.

That's the way my mind works. Fucked up, defensive, and programmed for betrayal like it's religion. I've never had anyone give me anything other than another scar. But I would be a fucking fool to be led by blind faith.

As the car creeps up the drive and the devastation comes into full view, I realize something. I'm not triggered. Not really.

I expected the walls to close in, the nausea, and the bile to rise. The weight of everything I lost here. But instead, I feel...lighter.

The closer we get, the easier it is to see the damage that had been done the night of their final demise. Like a mirror reflecting my version of a dream come true.

My wildest dreams never looked like weddings or fairy tales. They looked like this. Ashes. Destruction. My family getting exactly what they deserve.

The night's darkness is perfect. There's no light to soften the edges. No birds chirping. No blue skies and sunshine. No disguise to make it feel like anything that it's not.

It looks like a fucking warzone. The garish doors I've always despised blown apart. Windows all shattered. Parts of the iron gate twisted and flattened, like the perimeter lost its will to protect the vile scum inside.

There's no sign of life. No soul. Just ruins.

Imagining my family being slaughtered like pigs, whether Blackwell's intentions, I see the appeal to this.

I open the door before the engine is shut off. The gravel crunches beneath my boots, sharp and satisfying, like tiny fragments of bones snapping.

The front steps are cracked and uneven. I take my time climbing them, lost inside my memories. Memories I wished to rewrite.

Stepping over splintered wood and bullet casings, I step inside and I'm instantly hit with the smell of blood and death. It's baked into the floors, the walls, the very bones of this place. I inhale deeply, letting it fill my lungs, and I grin. It doesn't choke me. It feeds me.

Blackwell is silent, following several paces behind me. He knows better than to get too close when I'm like this. On edge and half feral.

The grand staircase is covered in more blood and debris. The chandelier my mother obsessed over hangs low, one side blown out, crystals scattered like teeth. There's a large blood stain on one wall, like a bullet went through one side of someone's skull and out the other. And I like it.

I graze my fingers along the wall. What used to feel like a prison now feels like a chapel of bones I've earned in blood. Like a god surveying the aftermath of a flood she sent. A cleansing.

The carnage in the dining room draws me in. I walk the length of the long table. A smear of blood stains the floor near the head chair. My father's seat. I crouch down and press my fingers to it. Cold. Satisfying.

This place was always rotten. Now, it finally looks that way.

We're back outside again, the air a contrast to the smoke still sitting heavy inside. It's cold and clean. My skin buzzes with leftover adrenaline, vengeance humming beneath it like a second pulse.

Then I see it. A white van idles in the dark. The kind kidnappers ride around in. No windows or markings. My voice cuts through the silence. "What's with the van?"

Blackwell's eyes are clouded. There's something he's hiding behind them. He exhales slowly, but doesn't look away. It's something I respect about him. When it comes to something serious, he will look me directly in the eye. Always.

"There's something else," he says. His voice flat and robotic. He's nervous about something. If he's nervous, then it's something real.

Before I can respond, he gives a single nod to Hawk. The back of the van opens up, and all the blood in my body ignites. Hot and cold. A firestorm in my veins.

One. Two. Three. Four.

My family.

Tied up.

Mouths taped shut.

Dirty.

Shaking.

And beautifully beaten.

They're dragged out like garbage and forced to their knees. Lined up between us and the house like a sacrificial offering. All four sets of eyes on me. None more burning than Blackwell's as he watches me with a disquieted unease radiating from him. He's unsure of how I will react.

He didn't tell me about this part, and with good reason. I'm not sure if I would have come if he had. The estate was already an internal battle, hard enough to survive.

I stare each of them down. To see them where they've always belonged. What I have always fantasized about. It's literally a dream come true.

I look to Blackwell. I can visibly see him questioning himself, unable to read me. Then there's movement out of the corner of my eye. A large duffle bag, then an even larger one, and a gas can all appear.

He doesn't need to say anything. Like the estate, these motherfuckers are mine. To break. To bleed. To burn.

Whatever I decide, I won't be merciful.

A smile curls at the corners of my mouth as I turn to Blackwell. His expression softens when he sees it. "Aw, babe. You shouldn't have," I murmur.

A half smirk cracks his face, but the tension in his shoulders never fades. I turn my focus back on my victims, almost foaming at the mouth with anticipation. My eyes lock with my father's. The patriarch of this monstrosity.

So many scenarios play out in my head. I've been imagining this day most of my life. But now that it's finally here, I can't decide how I want to do it. How exactly I want to make them suffer. All I know is that their end is on *my* terms.

I walk with deliberate steps towards my father. Stopping, I look down my nose at him like royalty addressing filth.

Where's your power now, daddy?

With not a shred of kindness, I peel the duct tape off unhurriedly. Never taking my eyes off his demonic gaze. He says nothing, and neither do I. Not yet. Moving down the line, I do the same to my mother, then Lincoln, then last and most definitely least, Royce.

All of them sneer at me as if they still hold any power. They have nothing while I walk tall, feeling like I have the whole world at my fingertips. And in a way, I do.

From birth to twenty-two years old, they were my world, because I was their prisoner. Their punching bag. Their entertainment. Their sin.

Until Blackwell whisked me away with force. Dragging me out by my hair. And despite everything we've gone through, he became my savior.

An idea sparks. "Hey, Deisel," I say to one of our men, the biggest one that I refer to as Deisel because of how massive the goon is. His eyes widen slightly, hesitant. "Let me borrow your piece, would ya?" I extend a hand out.

He looks to Blackwell, and I won't lie, it still stings when everyone still waits for Blackwell's approval on every single thing. His eyes flick back to me, and finally hands over his gun.

I can feel Blackwell trying to figure out what I'm up to. "I know he carries a Glock," I say without looking at him as I check the chamber and switch the safety off. "He prefers to use his hands. No need for a big gun." I've seen him in action. The man can crush a skull with his massive hands. His muscles aren't just for show.

"And you wanted a Glock because..."

I grin. "I don't want to kill them." I point the gun at Lincoln. "Yet."

Pop!

I pull the trigger, and it hits his thigh, right above his knee, careful not to nick an artery. I don't want him bleeding out on the first wound.

He goes down, growling and hissing through his teeth, writhing in pain. Hawk doesn't wait for instruction. He grabs Lincoln and pushes him back up to his knees. My cheeks hurt from smiling so hard. To see Lincoln bleed, red in the face with pain. *Weak.*

I am so happy right now.

Pop!

A bullet goes to the opposite hip. Down he goes, and Hawk pushes him back up. "You fucking whore," he snarls through his teeth. His greasy hair sticks to his face as he breaks a sweat.

Blackwell takes a step forward on instinct, and I stop him. "No." My voice cracks like a whip. His head snaps to mine, and I can see the fire in his eyes. He almost forgot this is *my* moment. *My* justice.

His jaw tenses as he holds his tongue and shuts down the urge to interfere. Reminding himself why we're even here.

My father chuckles, and it's the same nauseating, guttural sound that makes my skin crawl. "Look at you," he says to Blackwell. "All that power and you hand your balls over to the family disgrace, all because she spread her legs. Domesticated by the broken slut." He snorts. "Pussy must be magic," he mutters.

I have to ignore the heat rippling from Blackwell. The air between us is combustible. He's barely holding it together. I can feel him behind me, straining not to move, not to speak, not to tear everything apart. If I so much as glance his way, I know he'll implode. Splintering under the pressure he's bottling up just to let me have this moment.

I cluck my tongue and shake my head. "Patience, father. It's not your turn yet."

He starts in again, but as soon as I point the gun at his face, he snaps his mouth shut. My father is proud, but he's also a pussy. He doesn't want to die, and he'll beg for his life if it comes down to it.

I move the gun down the line, but not far. Right next to him. My mother. She's a blubbering mess. The opposite of the cold bitch she's always been. There was always a scowl on her plastic face. God, it feels so good to make her cry. I wish I could bottle every tear and line my shelf with them like trophies.

Pop!

Her scream echoes in the quiet of the night. I'm surprised a bunch of birds didn't just scatter from the thicket. That would make this moment perfect.

Hawk picks her up, and she tries going limp as she screams and cries. "Sit up or the next one goes in your head," I say, voice lethal.

Her bottom lip and chin quiver, but she complies as Hawk props her up again. I smile, then—*pop!*

She falls back, crying out when the next bullet hits her just below her belly button. Again, not fatal. If treated in a timely fashion.

Momentarily, I'm satisfied. But I didn't quite get what I wanted out of Lincoln, so I shift back to him. Aiming the gun at his abdomen, I pull the trigger.

Pop!

He finally howls out and keels over, his body hunched, and hits the ground headfirst. Unable to catch himself with his hands tied behind his back. He screams through his teeth as Hawk hauls him up. Spittle flying out like sparks. He looks at me with murder in his eyes, and I love it.

Now you see me.

I walk around the four of them, to their backs. Pressing the barrel of the gun to the peak of Royce's spine, he freezes. "You've been awfully quiet, brother." His breaths become more shallow, his heart rate picking up. "Anything you want to say? Huh?" Silence. But then Lincoln and my father start muttering nonsense. Suddenly finding their balls. It's just background noise to me. There's literally nothing in the world they could ever say that could ever hurt me again.

"If I shoot you here, full-body paralysis." I move the gun a couple inches down. "Here, you might be able to still use your arms, but the rest of you would be dead weight." Down a couple more inches towards the middle of his back, and he shivers. "But here, only your legs will be useless." I pause.

Pop!

His scream is earth-shattering. It fills me with something so much more than any high or gratification. His body slumps to the ground, and I watch with grim intrigue as everything thrashes in pain, except for his legs and feet.

Fascinating.

Knowing that it works as easily as I had hoped, I return to my father. Pressing the barrel to the center of his spine, I pull the trigger, and down he goes with a grunt and a whimper that he tries to hide. It has nothing to do with bravery and everything to do with his ego.

I instruct Hawk to bring my father and Royce into the house and leave them directly in the center of the grand foyer. Their bodies drag over broken glass and shards of marble. Howling and cursing the entire way.

When I tell Diesel to put my mother and Lincoln back-to-back to keep them upright, he doesn't hesitate this time. He does so without even a glance at Blackwell.

I climb the steps and walk into the foyer, the full gas can swinging at my side. Royce and my father are no longer bound with their hands behind their backs. Not necessary. They're sitting on their assess. Their legs stretch lifeless across the floor. They're not going anywhere.

They're seething, but they say nothing. That's okay. I'll do the talking.

"Please, don't get up, boys." I flash a grin. "Oh, wait...you can't." My father trembles with rage. "How poetic is this, huh?" I sweep my gaze over the wreckage. "You built this house on blood." I cut back to him. "Now, it'll burn with yours in it. Torched by the monster you cultivated." I crouch down, casual and amused. "The family disgrace." I dangle the gas can. "But here I am. Carrying the legacy and the fucking gas can."

My face stretches with a smile so big that my eyes squint. Starting just inside the threshold, I begin making a trail with the gasoline. Down the steps and stopping at the bottom.

I toss the empty gas can, and Blackwell appears at my side. He watches my face when he hands over a box of matches. We lock eyes, and I wish I could put into words what this means to me. For him to physically hand me closure. So, I do something better than any words of gratitude can do.

I let my mask crack. I let him see me. See exactly what I'm feeling in this very moment. His face glitches, the ghost of a soft smile flickering.

Curses are slung at me from inside, but it's effortless to tune them out. Taking a few matches out of the box, I strike them and they crackle to life. There's absolutely no reluctance when I toss the matches, then the whole box. The fire comes to life instantly.

I'm caught in a daze when a gentle touch goes to my hips to coax me backwards. Away from the heat and out of harm's way. I was so lost to the beautiful sight before me, I almost forgot about the other two.

Lincoln watches the house go up in flames without a word, and my mom's sobs begin to fade as she loses more blood. They'll die slowly and soon join the other two in eternal flames.

My eyes well up with tears. Not tears of sorrow, but tears of irrevocable happiness. I turn to Blackwell, and he's watching the show, so I take a moment to study his profile. I don't shy away when he catches me. I leave my vulnerability on display for him.

I press my palms to his chest, and one of his arms hooks around my waist. My hands slide up and clasp behind his neck as we stare at each other. My eyes flutter when he brushes some of my hair away from my face.

Taking a deep breath, I slowly release it, along with the nerves. "I love you," I say quietly.

He stills, then all the tension he's been holding in his body melts away. His smile is infectious, and when he leans in to kiss me, I meet him with everything I have.

And as my past burns to ashes, I finally feel free to find out who I am without it.